# Murder in Red

A *Murder, She Wrote* Mystery

# Murder in Red

## A *Murder, She Wrote* Mystery

### A NOVEL BY JESSICA FLETCHER & JON LAND

Based on the Universal television series created by
Peter S. Fischer, Richard Levinson & William Link

BERKLEY PRIME CRIME
New York

BERKLEY PRIME CRIME
Published by Berkley
An imprint of Penguin Random House LLC
1745 Broadway, New York, NY 10019

Library of Congress Cataloging-in-Publication Data

Names: Fletcher, Jessica, author. | Land, Jon, author. |
Fischer, Peter S., writer. | Levinson, Richard, writer. | Link, William, creator. |
Title: Murder in red : a Murder, she wrote mystery : a novel / by Jessica
Fletcher & Jon Land.
Other titles: Murder, she wrote (Television program)
Description: First Edition. | New York : Berkley Prime Crime, 2019. |
Series: Murder, She wrote | "Based on the Universal television series
created by Peter S. Fischer, Richard Levinson & William Link." |
Identifiers: LCCN 2018047869| ISBN 9780451489333 (hardcover) |
ISBN 9780451489340 (ebook)
Subjects: LCSH: Fletcher, Jessica--Fiction. | Women novelists--Fiction. |
GSAFD: Mystery fiction
Classification: LCC PS3552.A376 M86 2019 | DDC 813/.54--dc23
LC record available at https://lccn.loc.gov/2018047869

First Edition: May 2019

Printed in the United States of America
1   3   5   7   9   10   8   6   4   2

Jacket photographs: office building by Evening_T/Getty Images;
ambulance by Thomas Nord/Shutterstock Images
Jacket design by Katie Anderson

*For Bob Diforio, who made it happen*

A murderer is regarded by the conventional world as something almost monstrous, but a murderer to himself is only an ordinary man. . . . It is only if the murderer is a good man that he can be regarded as monstrous.

—GRAHAM GREENE

# Murder in Red

## A *Murder, She Wrote* Mystery

# Chapter One

"Well, Jessica, at least I wasn't murdered."

The quote read by the priest presiding over Jean O'Neil's funeral was received with a smidgen of laughter from those who'd packed the Cabot Cove Community Church. She'd been the town's librarian from the time I'd first moved to our town, fond of greeting me with lines such as "What will it be, Jessica—more books on poisons?" She retired a few years ago when her multiple sclerosis finally grew too bad for her to continue negotiating the stacks.

In lieu of a eulogy, Jean had penned brief snippets directed at any number of town staples. I thought mine would take the cake, until Sheriff Mort Metzger's—"Well, Mort, I guess I'm going to get away with not paying those parking tickets after all"—got a louder laugh.

Meanwhile, the snippet for Seth Hazlitt, Cabot Cove's resident family doctor, raised merely a collective giggle:

"I think you can cancel my next appointment, Seth." But then "Sorry, but I don't have a forwarding address to send my bill to" got a louder reception.

I hate funerals, but then again, I don't know anyone who likes them. Jean's was different in the sense that she'd beaten the odds at every turn: first by outlasting the dreaded disease's debilitating effects and then by drastically outliving her expected life span. She'd even enjoyed a final renaissance of sorts, thanks to an experimental new treatment provided by the Clifton Clinic, aka Clifton Care Partners, a state-of-the-art private hospital that had opened just outside town and was about to celebrate its first anniversary. Billed as a "rejuvenation" clinic as well as a hospital, the Clifton Clinic had drawn a steady flow of outsiders to our once bucolic town year-round, further roiling those of us who remembered what it had been like when we could greet everyone in Cabot Cove by name.

I learned a long time ago that you can't fight change; even the beloved home I'd shared with my late husband, Frank, was undergoing extensive renovations in the wake of a fire that had nearly claimed my life. Funerals always make me think of Frank, which, I suppose, is why I've come to detest them so much. Frank and I practically raised our nephew Grady, which meant he grew up witnessing my fits and starts of writing back in my days of substitute teaching high school English. It had been Grady who'd plucked my first manuscript, *The Corpse Danced at Midnight*, almost literally from the trash and given it to his girlfriend at the time, who happened to work for Coventry House, the imprint that would ultimately become my first publisher.

And if it weren't for him, I'd probably still be filling in for others instead of filling in the plot holes I inevitably found through my rewrite process.

Listening to the priest wax on with more of Jean O'Neil's testimonials left me feeling I should invite Grady and his family up for a visit soon. It had been too long since I'd seen them, especially young Frank, named after my husband, and more like a grandson to me, given that his namesake and I had raised his father through a great measure of Grady's youth. And Grady so enjoyed blaming some of the business scrapes he'd gotten himself into over the years pursuing this scheme or that one on having a fertile imagination to match mine.

Thinking of Grady and his family also made me realize it had been too long since I'd spoken with George Sutherland, the Scotland Yard inspector who was the only man I'd ever actually dated since Frank's death, though I'm not sure our get-togethers were dates so much as two friends enjoying some mutual interests and each other's company.

In other words, dates.


Since Jean had no family, the Friends of the Library had taken on the task of arranging her service and funeral arrangements, and passed on a wake or memorial in favor of a reception to follow her burial in Cabot Cove's local cemetery, which was part of the National Historic Register. As chair of the Friends, I had the official greeting responsibilities, which I was dutifully performing outside the church when I spotted Mimi Van Dorn approaching.

"Wonderful service, Jessica," she said, taking my hand affectionately. "I'm sure it would've made Jean proud."

"Thanks, Mimi. I sure do miss her."

Mimi looked around the front of our old church, shaking the platinum blond hair from her face. Once her natural color, it now came courtesy of a bottle. Mimi was several years older than I, but you wouldn't know that from her appearance. She joined the Friends of the Library as soon as she moved to Cabot Cove nearly a decade ago, and we quickly bonded over our mutual love of books. Not just reading, but the need to support the printed page and, especially, libraries. I recall a particularly contentious town council meeting in which we needed to beat back a proposal to relocate our beloved library to make room for yet another high-end housing development. Mimi had launched into an impassioned speech that left those council members flirting with voting for the proposal abruptly changing their minds.

"I leave you with this, ladies and gentlemen," Mimi had concluded, turning to face the standing-room-only crowd. "This isn't just a choice between books and buildings, wood and words; it's also a choice between dreams and development."

Mimi won me there and we'd been close ever since. She was one of my closest friends in town, having taught me how to play bridge, canasta, and pinochle, though gin rummy remained my favorite. She had come from old money and had settled in Cabot Cove long before it became fashionable to do so. We seldom, if ever, talked about our personal lives, but rather our favorite books over the years. We rarely agreed, which seemed to draw us even closer. I've bonded with people over many things, but never over anything as effectively as books.

"Well, I intend to make a sizable donation to the library in Jean's name," Mimi said. "Perhaps to name a new collection. What was her favorite genre?"

"Anything but mystery," I told her.

"I'm being serious here, Jessica."

"So am I. She was a fan of classical fiction and looked forward to the day, she used to say, when I finally wrote a real book."

"You're joking."

"Maybe, but only in part. She used to read my books only to offer me critiques of what she deemed the more relevant parts, all of three or four pages, normally. She did that for all forty-seven of my books, and I'll miss her doing it when number forty-eight comes out."

"A clever way of letting you know she'd read them." Mimi nodded, dabbing her eyes with a folded-over handkerchief, more to keep her makeup in place than out of grief.

Mimi hadn't seemed to have aged in the years I'd known her; if anything, she looked younger. I knew how vain she was about her appearance, just as I knew how averse she was to the surgical methods to which many women resorted. She'd become a health fiend in recent years and an obsessive follower of new diets meant to assure eternal youth. We'd first met when she caught me jogging along the sea and then again when I was riding my bicycle through town. She'd thought I'd eschewed driving to get more exercise until I confessed it was because I never learned how to drive.

*"But I heard you had your pilot's license,"* she'd remarked.

*"I do, thanks to my late husband, Frank, who taught me how to fly."*

*"But not drive? Really?"*

*"Not a lot of accidents up in the air, Ms. Van Dorn,"* I'd said.

*"So long as you don't run out of fuel,"* she'd quipped. *"And call me Mimi."*

"I'll see you at the reception, then," Mimi resumed today, angling away from me to cross the street toward her car, parked away from the funeral procession.

Most of the rest of the crowd had moved toward the parking lot that adjoined the church. I saw Mimi reach the street and noticed she'd dropped her handkerchief on the grassy strip we'd been standing on. I stooped to retrieve it, rising to see her pause in the middle of the road, speaking heatedly into her cell phone—as an SUV, an old Jeep Cherokee, suddenly wheeled around the corner, picking up speed, headed directly at Mimi.

I lurched into motion, charging into the street and practically leaping into Mimi just before the Jeep would have struck her, the two of us locked in an uneasy embrace as we spun to the other side of the road and squeezed between two parked cars.

"Jessica," a white-faced Mimi managed to utter, stiff and pale with shock.

"One funeral for the day is enough," I said, forcing a smile even though I was shaking like a leaf.

I walked off toward the car belonging to the Friends of the Library member who'd be driving me to the reception to get things prepared. Cocking my gaze backward to make sure

Mimi was okay, I spotted her back on her phone, yelling at whoever was on the other end of the line. Then I peered down the street, as if expecting the old Jeep Cherokee to come roaring back.

But it had disappeared.

# Chapter Two

The Cabot Cove Friends of the Library thought it fitting to host a reception at the library after Jean's funeral. Her replacement, the great Doris Ann, had missed the ceremony in order to supervise the catering team's setup and to make sure they didn't damage any of the books in the process. Doris Ann didn't greet me with the likes of "What will it be, Jessica—more books on poisons?" but she was always there to guide my research efforts, whether they be by traditional page or Internet site. Doris Ann had brought our little library into the twenty-first century, making it more popular, and relevant, than ever, and she'd jumped at the chance to organize the reception to honor her predecessor as Cabot Cove librarian.

Still shaken by Mimi's nearly being struck by that Jeep, I ducked away from the funeral cortege and skipped the gravesite portion in order to help Doris Ann and to act as official greeter for arriving guests on behalf of the Friends. I'd been going to more and more funerals as I grew older—expected for sure, but no easier to stomach. When the number reached as many real-life murders as I'd solved, maybe I should take that as a sign to move somewhere where nobody was older than thirty.

Our little library dated back to the time when Cabot Cove had been no more than a fishing village, offering entertaining respite to wives while their husbands were at sea for weeks at a time. I can picture any number of them devouring Hawthorne and Melville, though I suspect *Moby-Dick* never ranked among their favorites. Losing themselves in this book or that by candlelight would've made for the ideal distraction from the long nights spent alone fretting over the fate of their husbands, while their children slept soundly. I like to think that the many readers of J. B. Fletcher come to my mysteries for a similarly entertaining distraction, and I revel more than anything in those who profess to have lost themselves in my books, for a short time anyway.

In addition to the classics, Jean O'Neil's tastes in fiction seemed to run to more exotic, far-flung adventures, as she used her reading as a travelogue to visit places her deteriorating body prevented her from ever seeing in person. I recall she had a special fascination with Tahiti, but I never learned precisely why.

And now I never would. As Doris Ann and I supervised the efforts of Cabot Cove Catering in repurposing our local world of books, I tried not to fixate on the finality that came with funerals and the increasing number of them I'd been attending. I resolved again to reach out to Grady to schedule a visit.

The first guests started streaming in the very moment the

setup was complete. Most seemed to bypass the cold cuts and salads for the dessert table, accompanied by old-fashioned urns of the coffee that Cabot Cove Catering was known for. Dr. Seth Hazlitt was grousing in a corner with cup in hand, looking warm and uncomfortable in a dark tweed suit that made for a stark contrast with the white or khaki linen garb that had long been his trademark around town.

"Hiding, Seth?" I said, tossing a smile his way.

"If I wanted to hide in a library, Jess, I'd take up post in the science section, since nobody reads science anymore."

"There are far too many who don't read anything at all these days."

He toasted me with his cup. "Then it's a good thing for you that there are enough that still do, ayuh." Seth hesitated, his entire demeanor seeming to stiffen. "She fired me, you know."

"Who fired you?"

"Jean O'Neil. I'd been treating her MS for years, even consulted with experts down at the Brigham in Boston for the latest treatments and protocols. Then she fired me."

"I didn't know a patient could fire a doctor."

"Okay, replaced. With that clinic the zoning board approved for some ungodly reason."

"Technically, the Clifton Clinic is a private hospital, Seth, and they didn't need anyone's permission in Cabot Cove because they set up shop outside our boundaries."

"Still claim a Cabot Cove address, though, don't they, Jess?"

"Like I said—technically."

Seth took another sip of his coffee. "I think they killed her."

"Multiple sclerosis killed Jean. She credited them with buying her another year, thanks to that clinical trial."

Seth's expression was hovering somewhere between a snicker and a snarl. "A clinical trial Brigham and Women's Hospital knew nothing about."

"It's a big world out there."

"Not in medicine, it's not. I may be an old country doctor, but I've been working the Internet since I delivered the Mercer twins back in 1996, and I can't find anything about this experimental protocol anywhere."

"It bought Jean another nine decent months, Seth."

"Which I couldn't buy her."

"I didn't say that," I said, the loudening hum of voices in my ear telling me the lobby was starting to fill up.

"You didn't have to," Seth Hazlitt said, in a tone I'd never quite heard him use before. "Jean did when she fired me. Go on now, Jess. Leave an old man to his misery and continue with your hosting duties."

"Maybe I'd rather talk to you."

He drained the rest of his coffee. "I need a refill," he said, and walked off.

No sooner had Seth Hazlitt taken his leave than Mimi Van Dorn appeared in almost the very spot he'd occupied, looking none the worse for wear after nearly being struck by that Jeep Cherokee.

"You certainly know how to throw a bash, Jessica," she said, as the many residents of Cabot Cove continued to stream in to pay their respects.

"I think the credit for that belongs to Jean."

I reached out and brushed some stray crumbs from the jacket of Mimi's designer suit. "Don't want anything to make you less becoming, especially while wearing black."

Her eyes scorned me. "Such a keen eye for observation, and yet the suit is charcoal gray."

"So it is," I said, still not able to tell the difference.

"And if it hadn't been for you, it would be stained with red right now and plenty of it. And I'd be somewhere else entirely."

"When you write about murder for a living," I said, making light of the situation, "it's always nice to save a life from time to time. I was going to get a tea, but it's coffee for you, of course."

She smiled smugly. "Why, Jessica, you know I've given up caffeine."

"Since when?"

"Since she became my patient," I heard someone behind me say.

Turning, I saw a tall man with a silvery mane who looked vaguely familiar. "I don't think I've had the pleasure."

The man lifted his hand, about to introduce himself, when Mimi cut in between us, giving him a small plate bearing a cookie identical to the one she was holding.

"Jessica, this is Dr. Charles Clifton, director of—"

"The Clifton Clinic and Clifton Care Partners," I completed, extending my hand to meet his. "I recognized you from your pictures in the local paper, Dr. Clifton."

Clifton's expression tightened. "Oh yes, those. And, please, call me Charles."

He looked down at his cookie, as if to wonder where it had come from.

"Both gluten and sugar free, Doctor," Mimi said, lowering her voice. "I checked with the waitstaff."

"Well then, in that case, thank you," Clifton said, taking the plate and leaving his cookie untouched. "No cheating, remember?"

My eyes darted between the two of them. "Mimi, you never mentioned that you were—"

She touched a finger to her lips, lowering her voice to a whisper. "Prediabetic? Because I didn't want anyone to know about that or any other treatment I'm receiving."

I left it there, understanding now what was behind Mimi's more youthful appearance. Clearly, that "other treatment" referred to another of the Clifton Clinic's well-advertised wares, specifically something called regenerative medicine, aimed at restoring more than just the appearance of youth and actually turning back the clock. I'd long laughed off the possibility of it working, but now, looking at Mimi . . .

"Well, I'd better continue my rounds," I said, forcing a smile while hoping Seth Hazlitt hadn't spotted us in the company of Charles Clifton.

I waited for the line to go down a bit and made myself a cup of tea, joining Sheriff Mort Metzger in front of a display of pictures of Jean O'Neil, most of them with the Cabot Cove Library as a backdrop with a variety of its patrons filling out the shots.

"She really made a difference in this town, didn't she?" Mort said, without acknowledging me.

He'd come, appropriately enough, in uniform, leaving Deputy Andy to make the two of them a plate over at the serving tables.

"I'll say she did, Mort."

He finally turned my way. "Wish I'd known her better," he offered.

"She built this place into a real library. Used to employ a fleet of volunteer high school students to deliver books to those in town who had trouble getting out."

Mort frowned. "And now our biggest problem is keeping people out period," he said, his eyes narrowing on a pair of men who'd just entered the reception, one well below average height and the other well above it. "Thanks to Mutt and Jeff over there," he continued.

Known pretty much only by those monikers, they had been elected to the zoning board a few years back, helping to spur the building boom in our town, which had boasted only 3,500 residents when I'd first moved here and for many years after. Now that number had swelled to nearly three times that many year-round, and as much as ten times during the woefully crowded summer months that were upon us now. I half expected the crowd of relative blue bloods to greet the practically inseparable pair with a chorus of boos, given the antipathy with which true Cabot Covers had come to view any of those responsible for the traffic jams that dominated even the side streets this time of year. Mutt and Jeff's well-timed entry, though, had kept most from noticing their presence.

"They didn't create the tide, Mort. They just drove the boat."

"You use that language in your books, Jessica?"

"No."

"Good," he said, accepting a plate of snacks from Deputy Andy and going on his way.

Freeing me to approach Mutt and Jeff, who'd retreated into the same corner in which Jean O'Neil had stuffed unruly kids.

"Gentlemen," I greeted, smiling at the two men who'd spearheaded the movement to relocate this very building, "how good of you to come. I know how happy Jean would've been, given the board's acceptance of my proposal to deem this building part of the historic register."

They looked at each other, then back at me.

"Surely you recall our conversation and the petition I submitted, finishing Jean's work. All the t's crossed and i's dotted, you said."

Mutt and Jeff seemed to melt into the old wallpaper.

"You said you'd take the matter under advisement," I continued, "and when I didn't hear back from you, I took the liberty of informing the Friends of the Library of the zoning board's magnanimous gesture in Jean's honor, including that wonderful plaque proclaiming this as the Jean O'Neil House. Of course, if I've exceeded my bounds . . ."

"No," Mutt said.

"Of course not," Jeff added. "But we really should—"

"And I thought I'd make the announcement here, while we're honoring Jean. Unless you object, of course."

"No," said Jeff.

"We don't object," Mutt added.

"That's wonderful! Oh, and I've penciled you in to oversee the unveiling. I hope you don't mind."

"We're flattered," from Mutt.

"Just let us know when," from Jeff.

"I'll do that, gentlemen," I said, backing away. "And the Friends will be picking up the cost of the plaque to spare you the expense."

I swung away, not about to give them the chance to change their minds. I turned toward the post Doris Ann now manned behind the circulation desk and could picture Jean smiling at me in approval.

*There you go, Jessica,* I imagined her saying, behind that big smile she flashed even when she had little to smile about.

The plaque and the historical record made for a fitting testament to her legacy, to the point where I wasn't about to let politics intrude on the process.

I couldn't help but smile, too, as I returned to the role of unofficial host of the festivities.

And that's when I heard the scream.

# Chapter Three

I swung around in time to see Mimi Van Dorn dragging the tablecloth covering what was usually a display of recently released titles, taking all the baked goods with her to the floor.

"Help, somebody! We need some help over here!"

I wasn't sure if whoever had cried out was the same person I'd heard scream. Either way, I pushed myself through the clutter across the room, reaching a convulsing Mimi, in the throes of some kind of seizure. Charles Clifton followed a few steps behind me, starting to kneel over her with spoon in hand when Seth Hazlitt shoved him out of the way.

"Good idea, if you want her to swallow it. Let a real doctor do this."

He replaced Clifton alongside Mimi's frame and checked her pulse at the neck, turning her gently onto her side.

"That's in case she vomits, which is common during seizures," he advised Charles Clifton. "Watch and learn."

Clifton tried to roll with the punch. "If I didn't know better," he said, crouching by Seth's side, "I'd say it was an epileptic seizure."

Seth didn't so much as turn his head to regard him. "You don't know better because you're not her doctor—I am."

Across the library lobby, I spotted Mort with radio at his lips, calling for the paramedics, no doubt. Seth, meanwhile, checked Mimi's neck again. His finger moved up and down, then dropped to her wrist instead. The next instant found Mimi's seizure stop with a final jolt, her features pale white and lips turning blue.

Seth rolled her back faceup and began performing old-fashioned CPR, alternating between breathing air into Mimi's lungs and compressing her chest. I'd seen Seth in action before, but never like this, his face taut in grim determination and resolve, as if he were holding on to a rope he wasn't about to let go of. Mimi's body had stilled save for an occasional spasm. The color continued to bleed from her face, and her eyes seemed to be twitching beneath the closed lids.

Mort joined Seth on the other side of Mimi's body, waiting for instructions that never came. Seth kept up with CPR right until the moment the scream of sirens announced the arrival of the Cabot Cove Fire Department, led by our chief, Dick Mann. A pair of paramedics I recognized from my own brush with death a few months back rushed past him, taking over the resuscitation efforts seamlessly, as two firemen wheeled a gurney across the lobby between the guests, who'd separated to create a route down the middle.

"I'm going with her!" Seth insisted as the paramedics eased Mimi atop the gurney and then raised it.

His comment drew no response from Charles Clifton, who remained stoic and still as she was wheeled right past him.

Mort and I were waiting when Seth emerged from behind the curtain where Mimi was being treated in the emergency room of Cabot Cove Hospital. We both rose from our seats as he approached.

"An allergic reaction of some kind is what I'm thinking, or maybe an adverse reaction to some medication that quack prescribed her," he said, his tone sharp and biting. "She's critical but stable. Comatose at the moment."

"Oh no," I heard myself say. "I was just speaking with her and she seemed fine."

"Nobody knows better than you, Jess," Seth told me, "that these things come on fast without any warning. Treated it a bunch of times myself, almost always with children."

"Could Clifton have been right about an epileptic seizure?"

Seth stared at me instead of answering. "Mimi had become a patient of his, too, hadn't she?"

"Seth—"

"That answers my question. Man's poaching all my patients. I ought to . . ."

"Careful there," Mort said, smiling thinly as he squeezed Seth's shoulder. "I don't want to be looking at you from the other side of my jail cell."

"It's Clifton you should be arresting."

"On what charge?"

"Quackery!"

"I don't think that's a crime, Seth," I noted.

"How about practicing medicine without a license?"

Mort scratched his scalp through his still-full head of hair. "Think I read in the *Gazette* that he graduated from Harvard Medical School."

"Sure, where he specialized in salesmanship." Seth swung abruptly toward me. "What was Clifton treating her for, Jess?"

"Mimi didn't say exactly."

"How about not exactly, then?"

"Well," I said, not wanting to get Seth any more riled up than he already was, "I think she may have been diagnosed with type two diabetes."

"Of course, she was—by me. I've been pushing her to do something about that for years, but her A1c just kept climbing like a fireman up a ladder."

"Well," I started, instantly regretting it.

"Well *what*?"

"I think Mimi may have also been a patient at Clifton's Regenerative Medicine Department."

Seth shook his head, scowling. "Regenerative medicine . . . It's a fake, a folly, a sham, a joke. And if Mimi had bothered telling me what she was up to, I'd have told her as much."

"It was her decision," I said to him, my hand replacing Mort's on his shoulder, remaining in place this time. "And she does look wonderful for her age."

"She looked just as wonderful when I was treating her."

"Well," I followed, trying to lighten his mood, "you never have to worry about losing me as a patient to regenerative medicine."

"Pardon my ignorance," Mort said, "but what exactly is regenerative medicine?"

"Which one?" Seth asked him. "Because there are actually two. One based entirely on science and the other quackery."

"Let's start with the science."

Seth continued to grouse. "In a perfect world, the goal is to find a way to replace tissue or organs that have been damaged by disease, trauma, or genetics, as opposed to merely focusing on treating the symptoms."

"What about in a not-so-perfect world?" I asked him.

"It's just a fancy phrase used by the rejuvenation clinics that have sprung up around the country, almost strictly cosmetic," Seth explained, his tone clearly disparaging. "Patients seek out the likes of Charles Clifton and his Clifton Care Partners to make them feel and *look* younger. Doctors like Clifton will claim they're using never-before-tried methods when all they're really doing is packaging promises aimed at wrinkle reduction, cosmetic cell treatment, body sculpting, and the like in a fancy new box. Lots of Botox, new approaches to face-lifts, the use of lasers, dermabrasions, face peels, et cetera, et cetera, et cetera," Seth finished, sounding like he had tired of reciting the list himself.

"In other words," I picked up, "antiaging, which fits Mimi Van Dorn to a T."

"And now she's in a coma. Do the math."

"Hold on there, Seth," Mort chimed in. "All we know now is that Mimi had a seizure. There's no indication whatsoever at this point that it had anything to do with whatever treatments she was receiving at the Clifton Clinic."

"Use your imagination."

"I prefer to deal in facts."

I cleared my throat, forming the words I needed to break the tension between two of the best friends I'd ever had.

"If you've got something to say, Jess," Seth started, but let the sentence dangle there.

"You were treating Mimi for diabetes, right?"

"Type two." Seth nodded. "If you want to call it treating her, since everything I said went in one ear and out the other. But I had her on meds and doing reasonably well, so don't you go telling me she started some newfangled treatment at that charlatan's clinic."

"Not at all. I was merely pointing to a possible cause of her seizure."

"So now you're a doctor, too, Mrs. Fletcher?"

"You want to tell us what's really bothering you here, Jessica?" Mort chimed in.

"Isn't it enough my friend's in a coma?"

"It would be normally, but I'm guessing you've got other thoughts on the matter."

I shrugged. "Did I ever tell you how much I miss Amos Tupper?" I asked him, referring to his predecessor as Cabot Cove sheriff.

"Every time I point something out you don't like."

"There's nothing like that this time, Mort."

But that wasn't true, at least not entirely. Something was plaguing me about the moments before Mimi had collapsed. It was there, then it wasn't, and I just couldn't put my finger on what my memory was toying with. Something out of place, something that didn't quite fit, like a missing piece of a puzzle.

"Nothing," I repeated, but I could tell Mort wasn't buying it.

\*     \*     \*

We went to the cafeteria, while Seth pursued an update on Mimi's condition and worked to arrange a spot for her in the hospital's intensive care unit.

Mort had his usual black coffee, while I stuck to tea.

"I saw Charles Clifton walk into the waiting room when we were leaving, Mort."

"Uh-oh . . ."

"What's the 'uh-oh' for?"

"Because whenever you mention seeing somebody, Mrs. Fletcher, there's always something that follows, usually beginning with 'Maybe I should have—'"

"A talk with him," I completed.

"See, you've proven my point."

"What do you know about the Clifton Clinic?" I asked him.

"Pretty much the same thing everybody in town does. Private hospital that caters to a different crowd."

"What kind of crowd would that be?"

"Only those who have full-service health plans or don't mind paying out of pocket for services. They specialize in treating serious diseases with serious drugs, and they've got patients flying in from all over the country. I've seen Clifton Care Partners compared to the Mayo Clinic in one respect and to those shady European hospitals in another."

"Runs quite the gamut, then."

"With the actual truth likely to reside somewhere in the middle."

"That multiple sclerosis trial drug bought Jean O'Neil nine extra months, Mort."

"I wouldn't mention that in front of Seth. He's been the doctor of choice in Cabot Cove for so long, he tends to take such things personally. But nobody's perfect and neither is medicine itself. I don't have to remind you of that."

I knew he was referring to the death of my husband, Frank, from heart disease and an autoimmune disorder that had left him especially susceptible to the kind of infection that ultimately killed him. Cabot Cove Hospital hadn't been able to save him all those years ago, and neither had any of the elite places in Boston. His one chance, we were told, was an experimental procedure not yet available in the United States. We'd have had to go all the way to Sweden, and neither my private insurance nor the care provided by the Veterans Administration would cover that. Strange, ironic even, how I became a published writer only in the wake of Frank's death and only now had the means to perhaps have prevented his passing.

"I need to be getting back to the office," Mort said, his coffee just about drained.

"And I think I'll see if Charles Clifton is still about somewhere."

Mort's gaze narrowed on me. "Jessica . . ."

"What?"

"Never mind. You wouldn't listen anyway."

I found Clifton in the hospital's reception area in the main lobby. I'd caught up first with Seth, who was still in the process of working out the next phase of Mimi's treatment. Her condition hadn't changed, something I took as a positive, because not getting worse provided reason for hope. Seth had canceled his afternoon appointments so he could attend Jean O'Neil's funeral and all that came after, leaving him free to devote all of his attention to Mimi.

"Dr. Clifton," I said, rousing him from the magazine he was reading.

He rose from his seat in a rare gesture of chivalry. "Mrs. Fletcher, I didn't notice you there."

He had a stately demeanor about him that would've looked even more dignified if the skin didn't look stretched across his face to mask age's wrinkles and lines. He had the tanned coloring of a weekend golfer, though I suspected it was from cosmetics instead of the sun. His white hair, sprinkled with flecks of gray, papered his scalp without a single strand out of place, adding to my sense that his appearance had been chiseled over the aging skeletal structure beneath. He looked even thinner than I'd noticed back at the library, bordering on gaunt, which I supposed passed for healthy-looking in the minds of some these days.

"I thought I saw you entering the emergency room, Doctor."

"Yes, to check on Ms. Van Dorn. I'm sure you've received the same update."

He sat back down in his chair and I took the one next to it. "I was wondering if you had any idea what caused her seizure."

"Most obvious would be something related to her diabetes."

"Even though she'd sworn off gluten and sugar?" I said, recalling Mimi's comment to that effect back at the library.

"Only recently. Her type two was dangerously close to type one, according to some standards, and I didn't expect the changes in her diet to work overnight."

"What do you know about endocarditis, Doctor?"

"You mean, besides the fact that your husband died of it?"

His comment threw me for a moment, the surprise obviously clear on my features.

"Ms. Van Dorn told me the whole story. She told me quite a lot of things, Mrs. Fletcher. You should know she holds you in great esteem."

"That means a lot to me, Dr. Clifton. We've grown very close over the years."

"She envies your penchant for physical activity. All that biking around town. And Ms. Van Dorn also told me you were once a runner."

"A jogger, actually. And I've taken it up again, thanks to the treadmill in the Hill House hotel's fitness center."

Clifton nodded, a slight grimace stretched over his expression. "Ms. Van Dorn also told me about the fire that claimed your house and almost claimed you."

"It's being rebuilt as we speak. Tell me, have you ever dealt with contractors?"

"As little as possible. I hear they're even harder to talk to than doctors. As much as I'd like to believe otherwise, we can't save everyone, Mrs. Fletcher, just like your late husband's doctors couldn't save him. Our success rate at treating cases of endocarditis as advanced as his is quite low."

I studied his features, trying to get a better sense of him, but it was like trying to get a fix on a reflection in a cracked mirror. "Did Ms. Van Dorn tell you that, too?"

He shifted, the magazine sliding from his lap to the floor. "She must have."

"Strange, since I don't recall ever being that specific with her. Makes me wonder how exactly you came by the information, without a detailed study of my husband Frank's medical records, of course."

Clifton didn't flinch. "I'm quite sure it was Ms. Van Dorn who told me."

"Very kind of you to take the time out of your busy day to come check in on her."

"Actually, I'm here to meet a new patient who's arriving from out of town."

I watched Clifton's eyes drift across the hospital lobby toward the main entrance, narrowing as he rose from his chair again.

"And here he is, an old friend of yours, I believe."

I turned to follow his gaze and saw George Sutherland striding toward us.

# Chapter Four

We hadn't seen each other in . . . I couldn't even calculate how many years it had been, but at least one since we'd last even spoken.

"Jessica!" He beamed, smiling broadly. "What a wonderful surprise!"

I put aside for the moment the fact that Clifton had referred to him as a patient, and strode across the polished floor, meeting George halfway from the door, hugging him as tightly as I could recall ever hugging anyone. I didn't want the embrace to end, but it had to, as all things do.

He held me by the shoulders at arm's length. "Look at you, lovely lady, not a single day older," he said in the accent that made the words feel like silk.

"We're both older, George, and by plenty more than a single day. Welcome back to Cabot Cove."

He swept his gaze about the hospital lobby, as if seeing the entire town beyond it. "Yes, well," he started, features sinking.

Still, I didn't want to press him on what had brought him here as another of Charles Clifton's patients, not if it meant spoiling this moment. Sometimes you ignore things; other times you put them off. I honestly wasn't sure which category my willful avoidance fell into.

"We'll have plenty of time to talk, Jessica," George said, as if reading my mind.

*I hope so,* I thought.

I'd met George Sutherland for the first time in his hometown in England while visiting the manor house that belonged to a fellow mystery writer. Unfortunately, Marjorie Ainsworth, her generation's version of Agatha Christie, fell victim to the very subject she'd become famous for writing about:

Murder.

Normally, the case would have gone to the local constable. Given Marjorie Ainsworth's fame, though, Chief Inspector George Sutherland of Scotland Yard was dispatched to take charge of the investigation. Amos Tupper was sheriff of Cabot Cove back then, and I imagine if George had called him, he'd have known to expect my involvement. As it was, we solved the case together from among the varied guests present for that weekend at Marjorie's manor house, after nearly killing each other several times, as I recall.

Nothing bonds better than murder, especially solving one, and George Sutherland became the first man I'd found myself romantically attracted to since my husband Frank's passing. I respected his investigative skills and we'd found our common ground in discussions of our various experiences with murder.

To make up for imposing myself on his investigation, George returned the favor while visiting me in Cabot Cove over Thanksgiving. Mort Metzger hadn't seemed to like him at all, unable to stomach interference from yet another civilian, given that the chief inspector was well out of his Scotland Yard jurisdiction. But we'd managed to solve that case, too, the experience tightening our bond even more, and I worried whether we'd have anything in common outside of murder.


"Don't tell me you're here on a case, Jessica," George picked up, breaking the silence that had settled between us.

"If I was, I'd enlist your help immediately. But I'm just here because a good friend was rushed in after suffering a seizure." I realized Charles Clifton was approaching us as I resumed. "A patient of Dr. Clifton's as well."

"Then it's good to see the two of you acquainted."

"We met formally only today," I said as Clifton drew even.

"I'm sorry to break up this reunion," he said, already steering George. "But we're running late as it is."

I didn't ask why he'd instructed George Sutherland to meet him here instead of the Clifton Clinic. Perhaps because Cabot Cove Hospital boasted state-of-the-art scanning devices that a smaller private hospital would never have gotten enough use out of to justify the expense. I didn't want to raise that, though, because it would open a dark door I was desperately afraid to peer through. A man like George Sutherland wouldn't traverse the Atlantic for something as simple as a second opinion. No, it could only be something more in the treatment area that had drawn him here.

Treatment for what, though?

"I'll call you later, Jessica Beatrice Fletcher. Same number?"

"You always ask me that, George, every time you call."

He flashed the smile that had attracted me to him from the first time we'd met in Crumpsworth, England. "I'll take that as a yes."

"Use my cell, though. I've been staying at Hill House while my house is undergoing some rather extensive renovations."

"Someone try to blow you up?"

"Burned it down with me inside."

He held his ground, resisting Clifton's efforts to tug him away. "You're not joking at all, are you?"

"What do you think?"

"That I'm glad I'm staying at Hill House as well. We can chat later, as soon as I'm done here."

But George never called later that day or evening. I tried calling his room, but the receptionist informed me that he hadn't checked in yet. At ten o'clock at night.

Only one thing is worse than waiting anxiously, expectantly, for a phone call, and that's waiting for a call from someone whose health is at issue. Being a writer, a creature of my own imagination, left me conjuring up various worst-case scenarios, of both what had brought George Sutherland to Cabot Cove and what the tests he must have undergone had revealed.

"Actually, I'm here to meet a new patient who's arriving from out of town. . . . An old friend of yours, I believe."

How exactly had Charles Clifton learned that? I suspected he could have only from George himself.

Unable to distract myself with anything on the television, I fired up my computer and enlisted my favorite research partner, Google, in a search for the Clifton Clinic. I'd typed my early books on an old Royal manual typewriter and done all my research in the Cabot Cove Library with Jean O'Neil's help. The Internet was speeding along by the time Doris Ann had succeeded her, but I still did the bulk of my research on the library's computers instead of my own, because of the sense of familiarity. I was comfortable with the sights, smells, and sounds, the way the light streamed through the nineteenth-century window settings. I also found it healthy to write in a different setting from where I researched, though I couldn't say why exactly.

Tonight was an exception in two ways, then, the second being that I had no idea what I was looking for. The Clifton Clinic, for starters, was chartered as the first of what was envisioned as a chain of private hospitals from coast to coast under the umbrella of Clifton Care Partners. Already ground had been broken at a half dozen other sites, with many more soon to follow. All the locations were chosen for their reasonable proximity to first-class medical institutions, like Johns Hopkins in Baltimore, Anderson in Houston, or Cedars-Sinai in Los Angeles. With its proximity to Boston, of course, Cabot Cove boasted numerous facilities of that level.

The Clifton Clinic's specialty, from what I could glean, was cutting-edge treatments . . .

And here's where I choked up a bit.

. . . of diseases ranging from difficult to terminal, through a variety of experimental procedures often culled from clinical trials. I suspected some of these might be European in nature, that Charles Clifton may have found a way to game the system a bit by offering what larger hospitals couldn't or wouldn't. I wondered if he'd found a road map to bypass the difficult route imposed by the Food and Drug Administration. By all appearances, though, the FDA seemed to have granted the Clifton Clinic a rare exemption from their traditional procedures, a fact that pushed a shudder through me, since I'd never heard of such a thing before. I couldn't be sure of this, but it's what the anecdotal data suggested. Difficult to confirm, since the inaugural facility of Clifton Care Partners based here hadn't been open long enough to leave much of a trail behind it.

I nearly jumped out of my chair when my cell phone rang just past midnight. I fumbled for it, expecting George Sutherland to be on the other end until I saw SETH light up in the caller ID.

"Just wanted to give you an update," he said, his voice hoarse and weary with fatigue. "Mimi is still critical but stable. Her vitals are strong and she's responsive to stimulus."

"Has she woken up yet?"

"No, and it's probably best that she hasn't at this point. Easier for the body to heal itself this way, at least for a time."

"What about the cause?"

"The tox screen didn't reveal anything out of whack other than a spike in her A1c and her glucose level," Seth explained, referring to the primary markers for diabetes. "So I suspect in this case the simplest explanation of all might account for her seizure."

"But you're not sure."

"Maybe tomorrow, Jess. Right now, I'm going home."

"You've been there through the night?"

"Where else would I be? Regardless of what that snake oil salesman Clifton thinks, I'm still Mimi's doctor."

"And she's lucky to have you."

I was about to say good night when he spoke up again.

"What's wrong, Jess?"

"Nothing. I'm just tired, too."

"I don't think that's it at all."

"Am I that easy to read, Seth?"

"Your voice is. Want to meet at Mara's Luncheonette?"

"It's after midnight."

"Oh, that's right. Want me to come over so you can tell me all about it in person?"

"That's not necessary."

"Yes, it is," Seth said, as firmly as his tired voice could manage. "I am still your doctor, unless I've lost you to Charles Clifton, too."

"You haven't lost me to Clifton," I assured him.

"Is he the source of what's plaguing you?"

"Partially."

"And to what do I owe the remainder of my concern?"

"Something else for tomorrow, Seth."

"Breakfast at Mara's?"

I thought of George Sutherland finally checking in and rousing me early for a breakfast downstairs. "How about lunch?"

"I have patients to see, remember?"

"I know. I'm one of them, remember?"

\*　　\*　　\*

I slept fitfully, my slumber marred by unsettling dreams better described as nightmares. Everyone has that one recurring nightmare that remains terrifying no matter how much you experience it. For me, that's being up in the air piloting a plane. First, my husband, Frank, is manning the controls; then it's me and I'm alone in the cockpit. I look at the fuel gauge and it's reading empty, lights flashing and warning buzzers sounding even though the engine's still cranking. Then, in the next beat, the plane is going down, screaming through the air, me frozen behind the controls.

I always wake up with a jolt, left to wonder what it would feel like in the dream if I did crash. I've heard it said that never happens, but have no idea where such folklore originated. On this night, I woke up with something still plaguing me from yesterday about Mimi Van Dorn. So much had happened with regard to her in the past twenty-four hours: from meeting her outside the church and yanking her from the path of an on-rushing Jeep Cherokee, to the heated phone call that had distracted her, to . . . *what*?

That was the missing piece, something I couldn't quite put my finger on. But in those early postdawn hours, I remembered something else that I couldn't make sense of:

The old Cherokee that had nearly run Mimi down had no front license plate.

I knew some Massachusetts drivers, as many as a million, had older plates that required only a rear one to be displayed. The odds here certainly didn't suggest that, given that the other states most likely to send visitors to Cabot Cove all required both plates. It probably meant nothing, but now I couldn't chase the sudden realization from my mind, especially when coupled with the argument Mimi was clearly having with whoever was on the other end of the phone line. Not to mention that third observation I couldn't pin down yet.

I was still trying when the phone rang with an early morning call from Seth, perhaps giving me another choice to meet him for breakfast.

"What time?" I greeted.

"Now, but not at Mara's—the hospital. Mimi Van Dorn died an hour ago."

"Oh no . . . How?"

"I don't know. That's why I need you and Mort down here, Jess. I think she may have been—"

"Don't say it, Seth."

"Do I really have to?"

# Chapter Five

Mort had just arrived at the hospital by the time I got there, both of us approaching Seth, who was waiting for us in the lobby.

"Why doesn't anybody in this town ever seem to die of natural causes?" Mort asked, as we walked through the glass doors together.

"Seth may have been exaggerating."

"Seth never exaggerates."

"Good point."

Seth stood in the center of the lobby, looking harried and flustered. It was hardly like Seth to look ruffled, but this morning his white hair was uncombed and he'd either thrown on or never taken off yesterday's dark suit.

"Nurses found her unresponsive after her room alarm button sounded. She died of respiratory arrest."

"But you said—"

"I know what I said," Seth interrupted, "because the ventilator machine was partially unplugged."

"Partially?" Mort asked, before I could.

"It's possible Mimi caused it herself with another spasm. That's been known to happen."

"How often?" I asked.

"Not very, ayuh."

Mort loosened his tie a bit. "How good are the hospital's security cameras?"

"Also not very."

"I'll want to have a look at their footage anyway. Right now, we don't know what we don't know, and there just might be something there that can help us."

"Wouldn't the alarm have been triggered by the machine switching off?" I asked Seth.

"It should've been."

"Meaning," Mort picked up, "it wasn't."

"The hospital's investigating."

"Not anymore," Mort said. "I want to see the room."


Cabot Cove was one of those hospitals with a dedicated floor of single rooms for intensive care unit patients, a practice that became common once it produced a significantly smaller rate of infection. The rooms were small, some without windows or even individual bathrooms. Mimi Van Dorn's boasted both, something I'm sure she would have appreciated had she been in any condition to notice.

She was still lying in bed, covered up to the head and looking serene. Other than the doctors and nurses who'd rushed in to try to revive her once the Code Blue had been called, no one had disturbed the room. If I didn't know better, I would think Mimi was sleeping peacefully in the early-morning light.

I'd seen dead bodies before, of course, more than I wish to count. You never get used to it, and there's something about seeing the body of a person you know that feels almost surreal. It felt almost as though I were trapped in the clutches of the kind of nightmare that had rattled my sleep the night before.

"Is that the way they found the cord to the ventilator?" Mort asked Seth, pointing toward the plug that looked about two-thirds detached from the wall socket into which it had been inserted.

"I told them to make sure of that much when they paged me."

I looked at Seth closer, understanding why he looked so rumpled. "You were here at the time?"

"I went home for a time and then came back when I couldn't sleep. I was in the lobby when the page came over the PA."

Maybe it was something in the cookies Cabot Cove Catering had served for Jean O'Neil's funeral reception. I hated considering the fact there'd soon be one for yet another Cabot Cove resident I was close to.

I studied the position of the ventilator machine near the bed, picturing the tube running from it attached to the intubating device wedged down Mimi's throat.

"Was the tube in place when you got here, Seth?" I asked, drawing a frown from Mort, since I'd posed the very question he'd been about to.

He shook his head. "Removed to allow for CPR to be properly administered."

"What about when the crash team entered the room?"

This time, Seth nodded. "In place. I made sure to ask."

Again, I considered the logistics. "So, given the distance of the machine from the bed, how could another of Mimi's spasms have yanked the plug from the wall socket? Maybe jostled or loosened it if the spasm produced a firm enough tug on the tube. I guess it's possible, but not very likely." I glanced toward Mort. "We need to have a look at that security camera footage."

"We?" he asked.

The camera offered a pretty decent view of the hallway beyond Mimi's room, decent enough to see no one about who didn't belong and no one entering the room, besides the duty nurse on her routine pass. According to the time stamp, that visit had occurred just short of an hour before Mimi died. And since checks were every hour, that meant if someone had murdered her, he or she had the timing down to a T.

Another angle from the same time period featured the nurses' station. Even in the quiet of the predawn, the desk was manned by two nurses at any time, no surprise given this was the intensive care unit. Mort fast-forwarded the recording through the period where someone may have entered Mimi's room, to find nothing amiss until the moment the alarm must've begun to screech, drawing both nurses away from the desk. We glimpsed doctors rushing onto the scene just behind a crash cart, the image including a wall-mounted digital LED clock; the red numbers mirrored the time stamp exactly.

"Well," Mort said, rubbing his eyes as he turned away from the screen, "ICU's on the first floor, which means somebody could have gotten in through the window."

"I thought of that. But the ICU hall is perched on the hospital's higher side, meaning you'd still need a ladder, at least a stepladder, or a hearty boost to reach the sill."

"I need to check to see if the window's locked."

His eyes followed me to the door of the security monitoring center, where the video feeds were directed.

"Where you going?"

"Outside. Care to join me?"

Once we were outside, it took us several minutes to pinpoint Mimi's room in relation to the building. I remembered it was the third door of eight or nine on the south-facing side of the hall, but it could really have been any of them, since the dry grass, kept alive through the parched summer only thanks to sprinklers, yielded no footprints or impressions anywhere. Mimi's room featured no smudge marks on the window glass or any other evidence indicating some form of entry and exit had been made through the single window taking up half the wall in her tiny intensive care room.

"Notice any security cameras about?" Mort asked me.

"Nope."

"Me either. Not that they'd have anything to show us, given there's no evidence to suggest Mimi's window was used as an entry point."

"What about the windows on either side of her room?"

"What's it matter?"

41

"I was thinking the killer, if there really is one, could have used an adjoining room's window to gain entry to disguise any evidence. Maybe even a room on the other side of the hall."

"You forgetting that the security camera showed nobody coming or going from any direction around the time the cord must've been tampered with and the machine's alarm mechanism deactivated, Mrs. Fletcher?"

"No, just trying to keep each piece of potential evidence an island unto itself."

"Sounds like something Sherlock Holmes might say."

I forced a smile. "And I'm sure Holmes would've felt right at home here in Cabot Cove."

Back inside, we heard arguing as soon as we rounded the corner of the ICU, spotting Seth Hazlitt engaged in a heated discussion with none other than Charles Clifton.

"The hell you will!" I heard Seth say, just short of a yell.

"Mr. Hazlitt—"

"It's *Dr.* Hazlitt, you dunderpuss!"

When was the last time I'd ever heard anyone use the term "dunderpuss"? I couldn't even tell you the word's meaning.

"Ah, Sheriff," Seth said in a softer voice upon recognizing Mort's return, "I was just explaining to Dr. Chilton here that he requires law enforcement permission to examine the body."

"It's *Clifton*, and you're forgetting the woman was my patient."

"No, I'm forgetting you're a doctor, since you don't seem to act like one."

Clifton decided to try ignoring Seth and turned to Mort instead. "Sheriff, I'm only trying to be of help here."

*"Ayuh,"* Seth snapped. "As in help yourself avoid a malpractice suit. Jean O'Neil and now Mimi Van Dorn. Suppose it's not a good week to be a patient in that clinic of yours."

"Seth," Mort said, his gaze remaining fixed on Clifton, "I see no harm in Dr. Clifton here taking a look at the body— under your supervision, of course, and with both myself and Mrs. Fletcher present to keep the peace."

Clifton shot me a condescending glance. "I'm not sure I understand a mystery writer's place in an actual investigation."

"Oh," I started, "I assure you, Dr. Clifton, I've assisted or consulted on any number of actual investigations, both in Cabot Cove and elsewhere."

He knew that, of course, given George Sutherland was his patient.

*George . . .*

I hadn't thought of him since leaving Hill House, and the fresh thought of George stirred renewed concern over the fact that he'd never checked in the night before or even this morning. Mort had tugged Seth Hazlitt aside, either calming him down or filling him in on what we'd been up to—maybe both— leaving me alone with Clifton.

I noticed both sides of his pants were torn slightly at the knees, as if his tussle with Seth had turned physical, before addressing him. "You knew I was acquainted with George Sutherland, of course."

"It came up in our preliminary discussions about his coming to the clinic," Clifton said, without nodding. "You understand why I couldn't bring it up with you, including Mr. Sutherland's pending arrival in Cabot Cove."

"It's Chief Inspector Sutherland, and yes, I understand doctor-patient confidentiality."

"Then you're also aware I can't answer any of your questions regarding his condition."

"It's why I haven't posed any, Doctor, and I'd be disappointed if you did."

"Including about why he hasn't made it over to the local hotel yet, Mrs. Fletcher?"

Clifton's tone was more baiting than biting. A man who liked not just holding the upper hand but also waving it.

In my experience, many accomplished people hide their egos behind a facade of charm and charisma that makes them palatable, even pleasant, to be around. A snake in the grass, yes, but a friendly one. There was no such pretense with Charles Clifton, no effort made to appear to be anything but a snarky egoist who thrived on control and manipulation. I imagine that's what made him both a master salesman and spokesman for the clinic that claimed a Cabot Cove mailing address and was envisioned to be the first in a chain of for-profit private hospitals under the auspices of Clifton Care Partners. Concierge medicine taken to the next level.

"I am curious about one thing, though, Doctor," I heard myself say, my words stretching ahead of my thoughts.

"I told you I can't speak about—"

"This has nothing to do with George Sutherland. I'm curious as to how a small private hospital like yours has managed to participate in clinical trials normally reserved for much larger and established institutions."

"The key word is *participate*, Mrs. Fletcher. Clinical trials come with a considerable cost associated with them, derived from a combination of patient care and research. Smaller facilities like my clinic are able to handle all the heavy lifting at significantly less expense due to the streamlined costs only the private sector can provide."

"Clinics plural before much longer, from what I've heard."

"That's the hope," he said with a smile as sharp as his words. "All of them private and, thus, not bearing the same excessive costs springing from the burden of bureaucracy."

"Isn't it just that bureaucracy that's supposed to oversee the safety of patients enrolled in clinical trials, Dr. Clifton?"

His response was to glare at me, suddenly seeming even taller. At five feet eight, I'm used to looking most men in the eye. I had to look up, though, to meet Clifton's, and he seemed to relish that fact, as if he was transposing his looking down on me onto other facets of superiority. His gaze felt vaguely like an unspoken threat, given that he had the air of a man not prone to bothering anymore with the pretense of insincere charm he'd been fast to display when I'd met him for the first time yesterday, after Mimi had introduced us.

*Mimi . . .*

That memory flashed through my mind, along with something else—that out-of-place image I'd been missing from the funeral reception at the library, which had tried to break through from my subconscious to conscious mind only after Mimi lapsed into the coma from which she'd never awakened.

"Mimi was quite proud of the progress you encouraged her to make with her diet, Doctor. Giving up sugar and gluten."

"A key to her avoiding developing type one diabetes and becoming insulin dependent."

"And yet, after she suffered that seizure, her blood levels were found to be consistent with that of a full diabetic."

Clifton's gaze turned disparaging. "Dr. Hazlitt tell you that?"

"I'm curious about something," I said, instead of answering him. "You're confident in Mimi Van Dorn's strict adherence to the diet you placed her on."

"I would consider her dedicated to that diet, yes."

"Strange," I said, getting to the point, "because when I first saw her at the reception, I brushed some crumbs and white flakes off her dress. Cabot Cove Catering is well-known for the cookies they bake in-house, including the sugar cookies Mimi must've eaten several of when no one was watching."

"Stressful occasions, like funerals, can lead to cheating. Surely you aren't blaming me for your friend's indiscretions."

"No, I'm blaming you for your *patient's* indiscretions. Because if she were truly following your protocols, how is it her diabetes got worse?"

Clifton made himself chuckle and flash a smile that vanished as quickly as it had appeared. "I don't need to explain myself or my methods to a mystery writer who fancies herself a detective."

"No, but you may need to explain them to Sheriff Metzger. Cabot Cove Catering's sugar cookies may be as good as it gets, but they shouldn't be to die for, Dr. Clifton."

He turned in a huff and strode off, leaving me thinking about George Sutherland again. But those thoughts quickly turned to another memory of the phone call Mimi Van Dorn had made or received while crossing the road in front of the church yesterday, the call that had nearly ended her life when she never saw the old Jeep Cherokee barreling down on her. Not something I had been likely to pay further attention to, even with Mimi's passing. The disconnected cord to her ventilator and the lack of an alarm being triggered at the nurses' station had changed all that, suggesting at least the possibility of murder and opening up fresh consideration of everything that might've appeared otherwise mundane.

I heard footsteps and realized Mort Metzger had drawn even with me. "Seth and I are going to grab some breakfast in the cafeteria, Jessica. Care to join us?"

I wonder if he noticed me gazing over his shoulder toward Mimi Van Dorn's room. "Something I have to do first. I'll be right along."

## Chapter Six

Mort's mention of breakfast reminded me I hadn't eaten yet, but I wasn't all that hungry. I waited for him to take his leave before slipping back into Mimi's room.

In keeping with traditional practices, her personal items would've been gathered up and stowed in a plastic bag that would follow her to whatever room she was assigned to following her admittance to the hospital. I wasn't sure if that practice extended to the intensive care unit, but sure enough, I found the plastic bag in question on the ledge inside the small closet built into one of the room's walls. I reached inside, fished around a bit, and felt my hand close on Mimi's cell phone, which was a slightly larger version of my own.

My shoulders stiffened with the thought of her lying in the bed behind me, looking as if she were sleeping peacefully. I felt myself act as not to disturb her, guilty somehow over invading her privacy. Going through a person's phone these days is akin to the way people used to think about going through someone else's wallet. So many secrets, so much material contained on the SIM card with only a thin firewall separating the world from its content.

*I'm sorry, Mimi.*

I almost said that aloud but kept the words to my mind in the end. I switched on Mimi's phone in the dimness of the room, broken only by the morning light making its presence felt through the window Mort and I had checked just minutes before. Once the phone was activated, I jogged it to CALLS.

The one I was looking for had begun at 1:37 the previous day, the last one Mimi had received prior to suffering her seizure. As I'd suspected, the lack of shadowy phone icon next to the call indicated it was incoming instead of outgoing and read BLOCKED. While my redialing would yield nothing, then, it could certainly be traced by even the likes of the Cabot Cove Sheriff's Department.

Which begged another question.

Might the Jeep Cherokee speeding toward Mimi's position in the middle of the street have been connected to the call? Could the caller and the driver have been the same person, the call timed as a distraction and making her a sitting target waiting to be plowed over?

Something the murders I write about in my books have in common with real-life ones: I can feel the revelations coming, can feel when things start to come together.

That's what I felt now, as I walked along the halls, still sparsely traveled this early in the morning, to meet Mort and Seth in the cafeteria. I needed to come clean about that call

Mimi had received as she was crossing the street, so Mort could trace the blocked number. Because whoever was behind that number might also be behind Mimi's potential murder.

I reached the entrance to the cafeteria to see Mort and Seth seated with a third man. I cringed, hoping it wasn't Charles Clifton. Then Mort spotted me and the third man turned around in his chair:

George Sutherland.

"I'm sorry I left you in the lurch," he apologized, after Mort and Seth had left us alone at the table. "But the tests took much longer than expected, and Dr. Clifton wasn't around to check me out once they were completed."

"It figures," I said under my breath, leaving it there so as not to burden George with my feelings toward Charles Clifton, the last thing he needed now.

I'd forgotten all about Mimi's phone, now held in my bag for safekeeping, and would have to speak with Mort later about what I'd uncovered. I felt my heart hammering in my chest. George's arms rested atop the cafeteria table. I reached out and took one of his hands in mine.

"It's an adrenal disorder," he explained, not needing to be prompted further. "My endocrinologist back in London arranged for me to see Dr. Clifton."

"Is he a specialist?"

"No, but his clinic is currently sponsoring the only clinical trial available for something called pheochromocytoma."

"Pheochromo—" I started to repeat, when George interrupted me.

"Pheochromocytomas are tumors of the central portion of the adrenal gland and can play havoc with the body's ability to regularize heart rate and blood pressure. They're almost always benign, and even when they're malignant, it's normally a mere matter of treating the symptoms."

"But not in your case."

He squeezed my hand back. "No, because in my case those nasty tumors have metastasized."

"You're telling me there are no more traditional treatments available."

"None that have shown much promise, Jessica."

"And this clinical trial?"

"It's only just become available, so there's no data yet either way. Anecdotally, the manufacturer would've needed to clear some hurdles just to make it this far."

"So this disease, once it spreads, is it . . ."

"Life-threatening?" George completed for me. "It is indeed. I could go at any time, right here maybe in the middle of my tea. But, then again, can't we all?"

"Don't make light of this," I scolded.

"Back home, they treated me for Addison's disease for months. I wasn't responding, because it's not what I had. Would it shock you to hear the diagnosis was actually a relief?"

"Yes, George, it would. Actually."

"It shouldn't." He cupped my hand with both of his. "The two of us, me in my investigations and you in your books as well as your investigations, are enraptured with finding closure, about *knowing*. I hated not knowing, Jessica. It made me feel like a prisoner even more than these tumors do."

"What did Clifton say about your prognosis?"

"Nothing. He needs his endocrinology staff to review the test results to establish benchmarks for the protocol and to see if I'm even eligible."

"You mean, you're not even sure of that yet?"

He shook his head. "That's what all the testing yesterday was about. I've been poked and prodded just about everywhere. I'll be black-and-blue for months, but that can be another symptom of the disease."

"George—"

"Don't say it, dear lady," he said before I could finish, squeezing my hand tighter.

"You don't know what I was going to say."

"It doesn't matter, because there's nothing you can say. You have any idea how happy I was to learn I'd be coming to Cabot Cove?"

"Not happy enough to give me some notice. You know, like a phone call or an e-mail. People use those things a lot these days."

He grinned at the sharpness of my voice. "I'd tell you I was coming and you'd ask why. If I told you the truth, you'd start worrying immediately. I thought this was news better delivered in person."

"They must have some idea of your prognosis back home, George."

"They do."

"And?"

He smiled warmly and patted the back of the hand he'd been holding. "I'm here, aren't I?"

George Sutherland leaned back, studying me. He looked as eager to change the subject as I felt.

"You've got that look, Jessica."

"You mean the one when I receive news of a dear friend's troubles?"

"More like, when you've come to believe a dear friend, or somebody else, has been murdered."

"Well, now that you mention it . . ."

I told him everything, a perfect distraction and subject changer, the two of us instantly back in our element, thrown back together just as we had been in our first meeting while investigating the murder of Marjorie Ainsworth at her Crumpsworth manor house.

*"You're my prime suspect,"* he told me, before we'd gotten to know each other.

*"And why's that?"*

*"With no more books coming from the reigning queen of mystery writers, I imagine it will tick up your sales a notch or two."*

*"A worthy motive, Chief Inspector."*

*"George. And the truth is you're the only one here I've ruled out as a suspect."*

*"Why's that?"*

*"Because I know the work of J. B. Fletcher well enough to be sure you would've come up with a much better means of dispatch."* He'd lowered his voice at that point. *"By the way, I enjoy your books much more than hers."*

*"A fan of mysteries, are you?"*

*"Reading Sherlock Holmes made me want to become a detective. Reading the likes of you has made me a better one."*

All these years later, George remained silent through the

whole of my tale, absorbing it all in silence as was his custom, nodding occasionally. I imagine if he'd happened to have the steno pad he was fond of scribbling in with him, he'd be jotting down notes.

"So?" I prodded him once I finished.

"I'm still waiting for the motive."

"Haven't gotten that far in my thinking yet."

"Which hasn't dampened your suspicions about Charles Clifton," he noted, clearly skeptical about that part.

"Something's off about him, that's all. Off about all this."

"All what?"

I left it there, partially because I didn't want him to think less of the man to whom he was entrusting his life, and partially because I couldn't elaborate on my feelings much beyond that.

My thinking veered in another direction, remembering the cell phone belonging to Mimi Van Dorn, which was currently stuffed in my bag.

"George," I started.

"Uh-oh," he interrupted, a glint flashing in his eye.

"What's that mean?"

"Nothing, just uh-oh."

"Remember that case we worked that time in Chelmsford?"

"I remember all the investigations that brought us together, dear lady."

"I'm talking about the one where you were able to get the actual number of a blocked call. You said there was a trick to it."

"There's a trick to everything."

"Stop."

George Sutherland pretended not to know what I was talking about. "Stop what?"

"Teasing me."

"Was I teasing you? Terrible manners on my part. You must forgive me. Maybe it's a symptom of my condition."

"You were teasing me a long time before you had this condition."

"Was I good at it?"

"Very."

"I don't remember. Memory loss—maybe another symptom."

George could see my frustration with him starting to build, as always knowing just the moment to pull back. "Might you have the phone with you, dear lady?"

I extracted Mimi's from inside my bag, jogged the screen to that particular incoming call, and handed it across the cafeteria table.

"Don't tell me," he said before he regarded the screen, "this belonged to your late and potentially murdered friend."

"Your deductive powers are strong as ever, Chief Inspector."

"So when a friend of yours died in this very hospital, and you have reason to believe murder might have been to blame, what am I to think of a cell phone suddenly thrust into my grasp?"

"It wasn't thrust," I said. "More like handed."

George took the phone in hand, already jogged to that blocked number of the call she'd answered yesterday while crossing the street outside Jean O'Neil's funeral. I watched him copy it and then plug it into some kind of app on his own phone.

"Might take a few moments. Gives us more time to get acquainted, dear lady."

"We're already quite well acquainted."

"*Re*acquainted, then." He laid his phone down on its face as the app worked its magic.

"How's this app work exactly?"

"You call that getting reacquainted?"

"Since our acquaintances seem to always center around murder, absolutely."

George lifted the phone briefly to check on the progress. He seemed to have relaxed, his smile genuine and not forced. Back in his element, as they say—*our* element, actually. Amazing how something as unsavory as murder never failed to bring us closer, our lives as occasional companions seemingly centered on the deaths of others.

"It's a relatively simple process that's recently reached the masses and is used mostly to flesh out those annoying robocalls. The number may come blocked, but the phone where it originated must have a number. The app I'm using, available strictly to law enforcement—"

"And anyone who knows how to work the Internet," I interrupted.

"—traces the call back to that originating phone and pulls the actual number from its internal call log. Call it a form of reverse engineering."

I looked down at Mimi's phone, lying facedown on the cafeteria table. "I thought it would be more complicated than that."

"It used to be. Technology changes everything."

"Including allowing numbers to be blocked in the first place."

"Well, there is that," George conceded.

A beep sounded from his phone and he snatched it up from the table, as eager as I was, it seemed, to see the number revealed. Without his reading glasses, George squinted to better regard the results the app had come up with.

"Look familiar?" he asked me, holding the phone close enough for me to see clearly.

I looked at the number. "Well, six-one-seven is the area code for Massachusetts."

"Lots of people, potential suspects, in Massachusetts."

"Only one that I'm interested in," I said, retrieving Mimi's phone and plugging the number revealed by George's efforts into the keypad.

"You can't be serious," George said.

But he knew I was. "Why not? I've got a few minutes to kill."

"Potentially, so might the person on the other end of the line, dear lady."

"Well, I do have you to protect me."

"In my weakened state, I'm afraid I might not do all that good a job of that."

"No matter," I said, touching the green phone icon to place the call.

# Chapter Seven

"What do you want?" a craggy male voice greeted me.

Well, not me, I had to remind myself. Since I'd placed the call with Mimi Van Dorn's phone, the man on the other end of the line assumed it was her.

"I'm calling for Mimi Van Dorn," I said, after clearing my throat.

"She's not here. And why are you calling on her phone?"

"I meant on behalf of."

"What's that mean?"

"That I'm calling in her place because she's, well, indisposed."

I put the phone on speaker so Chief Inspector George Sutherland could listen in as well. "Can't you just speak English? Did she put you up to this?"

"No," I said, electing to play out the string a bit longer without informing the man on the other end of the line—who'd triggered a heated discussion with Mimi little more than an hour before her seizure—that she was dead. "Not at all."

"What, then? What does she want? Why can't she just call me herself? And what are you doing with her phone?"

"You spoke with her yesterday, just after one thirty in the afternoon, I believe."

Silence filled the line, broken only by the man on the other end's loud breathing.

"Who is this?" the male voice demanded finally.

"A friend of Mimi's."

"I don't think that's what I asked. Answer me or I'm hanging up."

"I don't think you will."

"Interesting conclusion, given that you don't even know who I am."

"I should think you'd rather speak with me than the police."

More silence.

"What's this about?"

"You called her just after one thirty yesterday, yes?"

"Why would that be interesting to the police?"

I knew I couldn't keep up the ruse any longer without the man almost surely hanging up. "Because she died early this morning."

The man's noisy breathing grew labored. Something in his voice had me picturing him as young, probably around thirty. I tried to discern the other sounds coming from him, but the speaker blurred them.

"Police in Cabot Cove in the habit of investigating all deaths?"

*If only he knew,* I mused to myself before responding. "Only when murder is a possibility."

"Wait, you're saying Mimi Van Dorn was *murdered*?"

"I said it was a possibility."

"And since I was one of the last people to speak to her . . ." the man started, letting his thought dangle.

"Speak to her rather heatedly, I might add."

"Who told you that?"

"No one. I witnessed it for myself. She ended up frozen in the middle of the street when a Jeep came bearing down on her."

"She was hit by a car? That's how she died?"

"No," I said, again couching my meaning in as few words as possible.

"Then how—how did she die that suggests murder?"

"I need to know who you are first."

"How'd you get my number?"

"I had help."

"Police help?"

I looked toward George Sutherland. "I guess you could say that."

"You're a friend of Mimi's, right?"

"Yes." Something made me continue, changing the tone. "My name is Jessica Fletcher and she was one of my closest friends. She suffered what appeared to be a diabetic seizure of some kind and died early this morning under suspicious circumstances."

"Are you calling for my alibi, Mrs. Fletcher?"

"Your name will do for now."

"Wait, Fletcher . . . J. B. Fletcher? The mystery writer?"

"One and the same."

"I should have guessed, should have known."

"And why's that?"

"Because I've heard so much about you. From Mimi."

"I trust I'm not what you were arguing with her about yesterday."

"No, that was something else. More of the same, actually."

"You still haven't told me your name, sir," I reminded him.

"Then I suspect the lovely Mimi Van Dorn didn't speak to you about me in the same manner she spoke to me about you."

"I can't be sure of that without knowing your name."

"Yes, you can. There were times when I thought she didn't know mine; at least, that's the way she acted."

"It sounds like you knew her quite well."

"As anybody could, I suppose. You see, Mrs. Fletcher, I'm her son."

I nearly slipped out of my chair, watched George Sutherland do a double take. Just contemplating a potential investigation had flushed the color back into his cheeks, chased the fatigue and whatever else was plaguing him from his eyes. Strange how it was death, a possible murder in particular, that had brought him back to life.

My reaction was genuine, because how could I not know Mimi had a son? She had told me about all three of her failed marriages, but she'd never mentioned a child springing from any of them. Another puzzle piece that didn't seem to fit.

"My name is Tripp," the man who claimed to be Mimi Van Dorn's son resumed, before I could. "And that's my real name.

You'll find it printed on my birth certificate. Tripp Van Dorn Jessup. My mother dropped the Jessup a long time ago."

"Your father would've been her . . ."

"First husband. She learned enough from the experience with me not to have another child. I'm not sure which of us was worse: me as the son or her as the mother."

"What were you arguing about yesterday, Tripp?"

He laughed loudly. "You're just like she told me you were."

"What's that?"

"Fact and fiction. How you write what you live."

"Some would say it's the other way around."

"Whatever, Mrs. Fletcher."

"I'm sorry to be the one to break the news to you."

"I'm lucky you did," he said, sounding genuine. "I doubt very much I'm listed anywhere that would be convenient. On the will maybe, but that's it."

I didn't press him on the oddity of that statement, waited for him to resume on his own.

"How did she die?"

"The seizure left her comatose. She died this morning after her ventilator tube was dislodged."

"Hence, a possible murder."

"There's some evidence to suggest that, but all of it's vague."

"But that's what you do for a living, isn't it? Speculate."

"I guess, though I never looked at it that way."

"Maybe because you have trouble telling your fiction from the cases you investigate in fact. I started reading your books after my mother told me the two of you were friends. Started right at the beginning with *The Corpse Danced at Midnight*. I'm about a third of the way through your list, fifteen and counting."

"In that case, I imagine you can anticipate what I'm going to say next."

"You want to know where I was earlier this morning, as in, do I have an alibi?"

"Actually, I was going to tell you that I'm sorry for your loss. But now that you've opened that door . . ."

"Where was I when my mother was murdered? Pretty much where I always am."

"I'm afraid you've lost me, Tripp."

"Of course, how could you know when my mother never even told you I existed?"

"Know what?" I asked my late friend's son.

"That I'm a quadriplegic."

I could feel my mouth drop open and saw George's do the same, the two of us left looking at each other, spared a response when Tripp Van Dorn continued.

"Car accident. Totally my fault, mine and alcohol's. I crashed the sports car my mother gave me for my twenty-first birthday. Both of us totaled, you might say."

"And this would've been when?" I found enough of my voice to ask him.

"Nine years, eight months, twenty-six days. Would you like the minutes and seconds, too?"

"I'm so sorry to hear about all this, Tripp," I said, the genuine compassion I was feeling clear in my voice. "As sorry as I am about your mother and to be the one delivering you the news."

"You shouldn't be. The fact of the matter is, her death might well prove to be a blessing, thanks to some issues you're not aware of."

"Having something to do with that phone call yesterday afternoon, perhaps?"

"Everything," Tripp Van Dorn corrected, leaving it there.

"I know how difficult this must be, Tripp, but could you share some of that call's content?"

"Sure, but not over the phone. Such conversations are better held in person, don't you think? I'm in a long-term care center a few hours away from Cabot Cove. But take your time," the son of Mimi Van Dorn advised us. "Visiting hours don't start until noon."

"Mind if I tag along?" George Sutherland asked me as soon as the call ended.

"As George or Chief Inspector Sutherland?"

"How about your driver, unless you think you can find a more suitable chauffeur?"

I had to admit I liked the prospect, more for George's company. "An offer I'd normally jump at, except . . ."

"It'll take Charles Clifton and his staff until well into the afternoon to review all my test results," George said when I let my thought dangle. "Gives us plenty of time."

He could tell I was hedging.

"Come on, Jessica, it'll be good for me. Unless you're afraid of my showing you up, of course."

"Have at it, my good gentleman," I said, rising.

# Chapter Eight

The Good Shepherd Manor for Rehabilitation was a misnomer in Tripp Van Dorn's case, given that he was a long-term care patient for whom rehabilitation had produced only minimal effects typical for someone with a severed spinal cord. It was a stately redbrick building that looked vaguely like an old mansion, which I suspected had been its origins. A single parking lot with only a modest number of spaces sat before it, the primary congestion of which I took to belong to the staff, since visiting hours were still thirty minutes off when George and I arrived.

"You don't think the young man killed his mother, do you?" he asked me.

"Not for a minute, but I think he might have an idea why somebody may have."

"Lots of qualifiers there, Jessica."

"As is the case with all murder investigations, something I don't have to remind you about."

"Unless my brain is going soft," George tried to quip. "Perhaps mental incapacity is an advanced symptom of that bloody disease I'm suffering from."

His comment made me regret letting him accompany me to meet Tripp Van Dorn. The last thing George needed right now was to see the lifestyle of those he might soon be joining. Better to be left with hope of successful treatment than resign himself to a future spent in a place like this.

The Good Shepherd Manor was located in Newburyport, Massachusetts, near the New Hampshire border. In all, the drive took almost three hours, because we stopped for a real breakfast on the way. As predicted, George's mood seemed to have brightened over having something to distract him from the concerns and worries related to the disease that had brought him across the ocean. I fought to detach myself from my personal feelings about Charles Clifton, hoping that beneath that stodgy and arrogant demeanor might lie a doctor who put his patients first.

The front desk had been alerted to expect us, and a friendly attendant whose name tag identified her as Molly offered to take us up to Tripp Van Dorn's room. The facility maintained the charm and many of the furnishings of a true manor, not unlike the one in England where George and I had first met and worked on our first case together.

*Might this be our last?*

I dreaded forming that thought, but reality could be a true beast better confronted than ignored. I busied myself with surveying the modifications designed to make the building hospitable for its ambulatory residents. These included handrails across the walls, stained to match the laminate-tile floors that looked like real wood but wouldn't chip or scratch. Whoever was behind Good Shepherd Manor had spared little expense in making sure such necessary upgrades didn't detract from the overall decor and ambience. I imagined its residents appreciated this for the homelike atmosphere it provided, making them feel as if they were someplace other than a long-term care facility.

Molly knocked on the closed door just a few down from the elevator on the third floor.

"Come in," a voice I recognized as Tripp Van Dorn's called.

She opened it and with a smile bade us to enter. We passed before her to find Mimi's son seated by the window in the kind of wheelchair reserved for those with only minimal physical capabilities. At the very least, Tripp wasn't on a ventilator or breathing device of any kind, and I watched his fingers move nimbly about the controls to turn his chair around toward us.

"I like looking out the window," he greeted. "Imagining what might be behind all the comings and goings."

"I'm Jessica Fletcher, Tripp, and this is George Sutherland."

We approached the young man, but stopped short of extending our hands. Tripp bore only a vague resemblance to Mimi at best, his features not as angular and ice-blue eyes significantly lighter than her deep shade of blue, and he boasted thick, dark hair in contrast to her fairer shade. He was attractive in a way I imagined must've made him quite the hit with young women at one time. This despite the fact that his cheeks were sunken now and his color sallow from too little time spent outside. It reminded me of the way recently released prison inmates look, the sickly look as difficult to shed as a bad smell. Thinking of Tripp that way made his current plight seem even sadder.

"Another writer?" Tripp said, eyeing George.

"A chief inspector with Scotland Yard, actually," George said by way of introduction.

"I hope you're not here to arrest me."

"Not unless you committed a crime in my jurisdiction."

"I don't get out much," Tripp said, trying to sound light.

"We're both terribly sorry about your mother," I said, drawing even with George in front of him.

"Why don't you sit down?" Tripp offered. "I'd say 'we,' but as you can see, I'm already sitting."

George and I took seats on a couch that rested against the wall opposite Tripp's hospital bed. His room was done up with as many furnishings from his former life as could be squeezed in. The built-in bookshelf was crammed with books, magazines, and personal memorabilia, everything but photographs, which wasn't at all unusual for someone whose life had changed so dramatically. Only a single family photo hung on the wall next to the window, but I was too far away to get a good look at any of those pictured.

"You wanted to know what we were arguing about yesterday," Tripp started. "It was the same thing we always argued about, only more heated and for good reason."

"Money," George said when he stopped.

"Man, they teach you well at Scotland Yard, don't they? Tell me, are you of the opinion that my mother was murdered, too?"

"That's my theory," I interjected, sparing George a response.

"Tell me, Mrs. Fletcher, does anyone around you ever die who *wasn't* murdered?"

"Not when someone pulls the cord from the wall, disconnecting the victim's breathing machine."

"You think that's what happened to my mother."

"I feel it's a genuine possibility, yes."

"And you were hoping I might be able to enlighten you on the subject of potential other suspects."

"Interesting choice of words, Tripp, as was your comment about your mother's death potentially turning out to be a blessing. You were speaking of that phone call, the argument from yesterday."

"And we're still speaking of it."

He turned his head about as best he could to better survey his surroundings. "Look around you, Mrs. Fletcher. These surroundings don't come cheap, far from it. Insurance picks up only a portion, not quite half. The rest is out of pocket to the tune of ten thousand dollars a month—that's out of pocket, not in total. Pay to play, right? And when I can't pay anymore, they'll toss me out like last week's linens."

"When," I echoed. "Then yesterday's phone call . . ."

"My mother's finances have taken a turn for the worse. Partially because of any number of bad investments, but mostly because she's always had a habit of spending beyond her means."

"Which in this case," George Sutherland piped in from alongside me, "affects your means."

"She placed the money required for my long-term care into a trust that pays Good Shepherd directly and, theoretically, in perpetuity."

"In my experience perpetuity inevitably costs more than anyone was expecting."

"Not relevant in my case, because my mother decided to break the trust."

George and I exchanged a glance.

"She shouldn't have been able to do so, of course, but I wasn't exactly in a position to stop her. Yesterday's argument concerned the second payment missed to Good Shepherd. Another thirty days without some accommodation and I'm out. Not on the street per se, but in a state facility, which isn't much different or better."

"Do you have any idea where the money went?"

"Oh, my mother was forthcoming about that after the second monthly payment never came in. Admitted she needed the money to support her own health issues. I asked her why all her various health plans weren't paying. Her answer was to say the state facilities weren't so bad. I told her, no, they weren't all that bad; they were awful."

"Did she elaborate on the health issue in question?"

"Well, she's been diabetic in some form since around the time of the accident, but that wouldn't account for the million dollars that went missing from the trust."

I tried hard not to look as shocked as I was by that number and felt George Sutherland do the same.

"It wasn't even her money. It was money from her second husband that was supposed to go to me on my twenty-first birthday. I'd just picked up the car I crashed a couple of days before the accident. When the diagnosis became clear, my mother transferred the money into that trust to provide for my care, with her as the sole administrator. She had it structured like some kind of annuity to ensure it would take years well beyond my life expectancy to run out."

Making herself administrator, I reasoned, was how Mimi had been able to break the trust in the first place. I tried not to consider what would make someone I considered a close and trusted friend do something so monstrous and indefensible. And how could Mimi have gone through so much money so quickly? Had she made a bad investment in the stock market or real estate? Had her love of card playing extended into the gambling variety?

"I threatened her with a lawsuit yesterday," Tripp went on, "that she'd left me no choice. A lawyer came down here to see me—from Cabot Cove, just like you. I figured that was the best way to go."

"What was his name?" I asked the young man, thinking I might know him.

"Fred something. He left his card somewhere. If you give me a moment . . ."

Tripp Van Dorn started to turn his wheelchair around, then stopped and spun it back around. "Cooper, that's it, Fred Cooper."

The name didn't ring any bells. "Did he take the case?"

"At first."

"At first?" George Sutherland questioned, before I had a chance to.

"He said he'd look into things. Then he e-mailed to say he wouldn't be taking the case."

"Did he say why?" I asked, beating George to the punch this time.

"No, that was it. I asked him repeatedly, via both e-mail and phone, but that was the last I ever heard from him."

That stuck in my mind, an anomaly I needed to resolve.

"The money's gone, anyway," Tripp lamented. "No lawyer can change that, get blood from a stone, as they say. And whatever's left, whatever comes my way in the will, won't be enough to keep me here very long. That ought to get me off the hook in one respect, right, Mrs. Fletcher?"

"What's that?"

"I didn't really have a motive for killing my mother, did I?"

# Chapter Nine

George Sutherland and I sat in his rental car with the air-conditioning pumping, just taking in what Tripp Van Dorn had told us without commenting further.

"I'm sorry, Jessica," he said finally. "I know she was your friend."

"I had no idea about any of this, George, not even a hint. I didn't even know she had a son."

"My deductive reasoning tells me you didn't become acquainted with her until after the accident."

"Your deductive reasoning would be correct. I've known her for about nine years, so she must have moved to Cabot Cove just after the accident."

"And she never mentioned it to you, nothing at all about her son?"

"No. Maybe she said something that I'm just not recalling."

"Since when do you forget anything?"

"It was a lot of small talk between two friends over cards and tea, so it's possible it didn't even register. I can say for certain, though, that she never mentioned anything about Tripp's condition. That's something I'd never forget."

"A lot of gentlemanly, or gentlewomanly, types don't like burdening their friends with such things. Suffer in silence, as they say."

"There's another possibility, of course: that Mimi had written her son off after the accident to the point where, to all intents and purposes, he didn't exist."

"Strange way of dealing with grief."

"I never got the impression she was grieving about anything. But what kind of mother does something like this to her child?"

"I might pose the same question to you, dear lady, given your closeness to this woman."

I chose not to try to answer, hating the fact that I found myself thinking so much less of a woman I'd considered to be a close friend. I guess I hadn't known her as well as I'd thought I had. Had we ever discussed my husband, Frank, how we'd raised our nephew Grady after an accident claimed the lives of his parents? So I guess maybe Mimi knew as little about my personal life as I did about hers. Maybe that's what made us friends.

"I won't be able to join you, Jessica," George said from behind the wheel.

We were several miles down the road, and for the life of me, I couldn't remember us getting there. "Join me where?"

"Visiting Fred Cooper, Tripp Van Dorn's lawyer."

"Not for very long, though, was he?"

\*   \*   \*

George dropped me off at the office of Fred S. Cooper, Esq., apologizing again for abandoning me.

"You have more important things to do than follow along on one of my crusades."

"From my experience, your crusades prove almost inevitably fruitful. And I don't just 'follow along.'"

"This is different, George. Who am I helping? Certainly not Mimi, certainly not her son. No friend or acquaintance of mine has been wrongly jailed, and my relationship with the victim herself was superficial at best. I can't think of a single serious conversation we ever engaged in. We talked about the changing nature of our town, all the places we'd both visited, and other exotic places Mimi had gone but I only wrote about."

"You enjoyed her company."

"Very much."

"Then, Jessica, just leave things there."

I opened the door to his rental and started to climb out. "I can't. That's why I need to see this lawyer."


"*The* Jessica Fletcher?" Fred Cooper asked after I'd introduced myself. "As in J. B. Fletcher?"

"Yes, Mr. Cooper." I smiled, pulling my hand from his determined grip.

"Well, it's truly a pleasure to meet Cabot Cove's most celebrated resident."

"You must not be keeping up with our rising population, all

those famous people and celebrities relocating here from the Hamptons, Nantucket, or Martha's Vineyard."

Cooper frowned. "Well, my landlord sure is."

Cooper's practice was a solo one, though he shared the office and a receptionist with another lawyer, whose name didn't appear on the plaque outside. I suspected he was in his early thirties but looked older, thanks to hair that had gone prematurely gray and a paunch that suggested the long hours it must've taken him to make a Main Street rent; even a third-floor office in a building that housed a boutique nail salon, a hairstylist, and our local bookstore on its ground-floor storefront level would be fetching an outrageous rent these days. I'd sat in a stiff chair alongside a matching couch in the reception area while waiting to see him, fiddling with a piece of tape I finally pried from the arm.

"To what do I owe the pleasure?" Cooper asked, retaking the chair behind his desk only after I claimed the one before it.

"You've heard the news about Mimi Van Dorn?"

Cooper tried to look nonchalant. "I've heard the name around town, but I don't believe I have."

"She passed away this morning."

"How?" he asked matter-of-factly.

"Technically, respiratory failure after she lapsed into a coma."

"Why 'technically'?"

"Because the cord to her ventilator was unplugged."

"I don't practice criminal law, Mrs. Fletcher, if you're the one who pulled it."

I nodded, letting the levity settle between us to ease the tension of an initial meeting. "I visited Tripp Van Dorn earlier today, Mr. Cooper."

"That would be Mrs. Van Dorn's son?"

"You know he is, because he tried to hire you to file a lawsuit against his mother."

Cooper stiffened inside his jacket, which was wrinkled in more places than it wasn't. "You know I can't discuss such matters."

"I said *tried* to hire you. You never took the case, so there can be no attorney-client privilege."

"That might be true in your books, Mrs. Fletcher, but in my code of conduct, I prefer to keep anything discussed with even a potential client confidential. As a courtesy, you understand."

"Why didn't you take the case, Mr. Cooper? I imagine you can tell me that much."

"I can: because there was no case to take."

"A mother breaking the trust her son desperately needed for his long-term care? There would seem to be a case there to me."

Cooper leaned back, nodding. He ran his hands through his prematurely gray hair, and they came off shiny from whatever product he'd used to slick it back.

"Is that what Mr. Van Dorn told you?" he asked me.

"It's not true?"

"The truth is, Mrs. Fletcher, that Tripp Van Dorn willingly executed papers that allowed his mother to do exactly what she ended up doing. We might have prevailed eventually, but I'm a one-man shop here and couldn't afford the time and expense involved, not with the rent I'm paying for the privilege of having an office on Main Street in Cabot Cove."

"Then I'm a bit confused, Mr. Cooper."

"About what?"

"All of those facts you just recited would have been plain

when you gave Tripp Van Dorn the impression you were going to take his case. What changed?"

"Nothing, because Mr. Van Dorn got the wrong impression."

"So you didn't provide any false hope for a young man about to be kicked out of his long-term care facility because he can no longer pay the bills."

"I may have laid out some options for him, Mrs. Fletcher, but I'm afraid none of those options panned out."

"But you pursued them."

"Well . . ."

"Yes or no, Mr. Cooper."

"I performed some due diligence, nothing beyond that." I watched his expression change, from grudging placation to barely restrained obstinance. "Your reputation appears to be well earned."

"What reputation would that be?"

"As someone who revels in inserting herself in other people's business."

"True enough, I suppose," I conceded, "but only when that business involves murder."

"My business doesn't involve murder, Mrs. Fletcher."

"Of course, with you not being a criminal lawyer and all. Could you describe this due diligence you performed, what it yielded, or failed to yield, that made you change your mind about representing Tripp Van Dorn?"

"I told you—"

"I know what you said, but performing such due diligence suggests the case originally intrigued you."

"The contingency fee, a third of a million dollars, intrigued me."

"I appreciate your honesty, Mr. Cooper," I told him, leaning forward so I was closer to his desk. "But that's all the more reason for not abandoning the case so quickly. I'm sure you can see my point."

"Actually," he said, "I don't."

"Then let me put it a different way. Did the due diligence you performed on Mr. Van Dorn's case involve the Clifton Clinic in any way?"

"I'm not at liberty to say."

"Well then, are you at liberty to discuss the new office furniture you recently purchased?"

"Excuse me?"

"I peeled some tape off the chair in the waiting area that must've held the price tag until recently. And the dark blue color hasn't faded at all, even though that area gets direct sunlight for most of the day. Oh, and that Oriental rug that matches the color scheme? It's still showing folds in the nap, meaning you couldn't have rolled it out more than a few days ago."

"Are you implying something, Mrs. Fletcher?"

"No, just commenting."

"You would've made a good lawyer."

"I prefer writing about them at times, Mr. Cooper."

"But you're not just a writer, are you? You also fancy yourself a detective of sorts."

"I don't fancy myself that at all."

Cooper didn't seem even remotely convinced by that. His amicable tone and demeanor had vanished behind a mask like that donned by a kid caught sneaking a peek at an exam paper atop someone else's desk.

"I'm still curious as to why you didn't take Tripp Van Dorn's case."

"I explained that to you already."

"I thought you may have left something out. Mr. Van Dorn said you never got back to him, save for a single terse e-mail."

"There was no point in rehashing the matter beyond that."

"Did your due diligence turn up what Mimi Van Dorn did with the money she took from her son's trust?"

"I'm not at liberty to say."

"Attorney-client privilege again?"

"I'm not at liberty to comment on that either."

Cooper rose from behind his desk, blocking out a measure of the sunlight that had yet to fade the upholstery on his brand-new furniture, and checked his watch dramatically.

"I have another client coming in."

I stood up, too, and ran a finger along the sill of his desk. "Another office upgrade?"

Cooper grinned, nodding. "The real estate boon in Cabot Cove has been good for business." He extended a hand across his dark wood desk, mahogany or cherry, I surmised. "It was a pleasure finally meeting you, Mrs. Fletcher. You're exactly as advertised."

I took his hand, managing a smile. "So glad I didn't disappoint you, Mr. Cooper."

# Chapter Ten

I could have Ubered home, but it was a beautiful day for a walk, the summer heat tempered by the luscious breeze coming off the ocean. I needed the exercise and I always did my best thinking when walking or riding a bicycle.

I was worried about George Sutherland, looked forward to getting back to my Hill House suite to research everything I could about this adrenal disease afflicting him. Age is the one thing even the cleverest mind can't solve. It catches up to everyone, despite the determined attempts of those like Mimi Van Dorn to defeat or deny it. There is no doing either, and learning of a good friend's battle with mortality inevitably conjures thoughts of our own. Maybe that was why I couldn't resist investigating murder as much as writing about it: because it took my mind off such things, including the fact that I was alone. But I never felt alone when I was losing myself in the pages of my latest book, inevitably surprised at what came next, as if I wasn't really in control. First on the old Royal typewriters I'd used to write my early books, including *The Corpse Danced at Midnight*, then later on an old Windows computer before settling on Macs. I took to writing because I could control in fiction what I couldn't in fact.

Like the sudden illness that claimed my husband, Frank's, life. When we met I was interning at the old Appleton Theater and substitute teaching as a way to pass the time before my career as a journalist took off, which it never did. I happened to be volunteering at the theater on a show that Frank designed sets for—a hobby of his, I'd later learn. I'd never been a romantic, never believed in anything as sentimental as love at first sight, but that's what it was like for us. Today I can't even tell you the name of the play; my memories are so consumed by those first days spent with Frank.

I believe to this day that losing him was so painful that I avoided anything close to romance afterward. As close as I was to George Sutherland, and as pleasant as our occasional relationship was, we were separated by an ocean, and both of us were wise enough to know we'd never be able to recapture whatever it was our younger days had granted us. We enjoyed each other's company enough to want to maintain it without the weight of a traditional relationship holding us down, because Marjorie Ainsworth had forged a bond between us based on something we could share with no one else:

Murder.

Death had brought us close and now, I feared, might be about to drive us apart forever.

Strolling past Mara's Luncheonette, I caught a glimpse of

Seth Hazlitt sipping an iced tea at his usual table and decided to join him, needing to see a friendly face after such difficult ruminations in the wake of my meeting with Fred Cooper.

"You're just in time, Jess," he greeted, his hooded eyes looking up from the condensation that had formed over his glass from the humidity that had trailed me through the door. "I'm waiting for Mort to review the latest findings about Mimi Van Dorn's passing."

"Passing or murder?"

"I leave such questions to the professionals."

"Since when, Seth?"

"Since your friend became the latest patient to leave me for the Clifton Clinic."

I checked my watch. "Which explains what you're doing here in the middle of the afternoon."

"Ayuh, I could use a hobby all right. Maybe I'll try my hand at writing."

"Writing's not a hobby."

"Was for you when you first got started."

Seth Hazlitt was right, of course. Following Frank's death, I'd written my first mystery just to take my mind off things. I'd done other writing before, short stories mostly, but had never had an inkling I'd ever publish a book.

"Maybe I'll take up golf," Seth groused.

"You hate golf. You always say it's only for people who can't find anything better to do with their time."

"Which kind of describes me these days, doesn't it?" Seth said disconsolately.

"Seth—"

"Couldn't afford the new dues at the country club, anyway. If I retire, promise me you won't take your business to the Clifton Clinic."

"I'm not sure I could afford it," I said, thinking again of Mimi Van Dorn breaking her son's trust to put the money to her own use. "Can I ask you a question?"

"Since when did you need to ask, Jess?"

"You spoke with George Sutherland."

Seth nodded. "I did."

"And did he mention anything about . . ."

I started to choke up, spared the need to continue when Seth completed the thought for me.

"His illness? Matter of fact, he did."

"And?" I managed.

"Well, I'm hardly an expert on the subject."

"The subject of pheochromocytomas."

"First time I've heard anybody pronounce that properly. Tumors of the nervous system, specifically the adrenal gland. Almost always benign."

"That's what George told me. He wasn't specific about the prognosis."

"What did I just say?" Seth asked me, using his sterner voice.

"That you're no expert."

"That's the problem, Jess—nobody is. You know the term 'orphan drug'?"

I nodded. "Drugs used to treat rare diseases, often so rare it's not worth it for a pharmaceutical company to manufacture them."

"Pheochromocytomic tumors are one of those rare diseases,

a cancer for which no established protocol has proven effective and no dedicated protocol exists, since the clinical study required to produce one would hardly be worth the expense."

"Tell that to somebody suffering from the disease."

"You mean George," Seth said, sounding again like the old country doctor he'd probably been since graduating medical school. "He says he came to the Clifton Clinic because they're running a trial of a drug that so far has shown great promise in treating tumors much like pheochromocytomas."

"But not exactly like them."

"Chief Inspector Sutherland didn't tell you this himself?"

"I didn't ask."

Seth reached across the table and squeezed my hand. "My feelings about Charles Clifton aside, the chief inspector is in the best hands possible."

"He's not a former patient," I reminded him, "like Mimi was."

That thought, thankfully, veered me back on course.

"In a word, Dr. Hazlitt, how would you describe Mimi Van Dorn?"

He pulled his hand from mine and settled back in his chair. "So it's Dr. Hazlitt now. . . ."

"It's your professional opinion I'm after."

"Then my answer, in a word, is 'vain.' I don't think I'm violating any doctor-patient privilege by saying that much."

"Nor do I. But I think it went beyond that, Seth. Isn't there a condition where people become obsessed with their appearance?"

"Well, there's body dysmorphic disorder, or BDD. Just about everybody has something they don't particularly like about the way they look, some minor flaw or imperfection. But people suffering from BDD are obsessed with those flaws and imperfections to the point where they become hostage to them. And the symptoms are normally worsened by age since their perceived flaws become harder to disguise and tend to be exacerbated by the normal aging process. They can't control their negative thoughts and don't believe it when people tell them they look fine. Their thoughts can result in severe emotional distress and interfere with their daily functioning. They might miss school or work, try to avoid as many social situations as possible, and isolate themselves, even from family and friends, because they are worried other people will notice their flaws."

"So someone suffering from BDD might go to extreme lengths to do whatever it takes not to grow older, or at least not appear older."

Seth flashed me that look of his. "Are we still talking about Mimi Van Dorn?"

"Just in general."

"I'd say they'd go to lengths comparable to someone addicted to drugs."

"Desperate measures, in other words, that become more desperate with age."

"No one's found the fountain of youth yet, and I doubt anyone will soon." Seth's expression flirted with a smile. "I'm starting to wonder if we're talking about you, Jess. Get a look at one of your old jacket photos?"

"I've been using the same one for twenty years."

"Maybe you're jealous of J. B. Fletcher, then, since she never ages. Good thing, because the answer to your question is yes. Aging can either trigger body dysmorphic disorder or exacerbate it."

"Ever notice any of the symptoms with Mimi?"

"You mean, before she fired me? Never thought about it much, but now that you mention it, she'd started asking me what I thought about some of those new antiaging concoctions and treatments. Hmmmmm . . ."

I watched him start to stroke his chin, seeming to scratch at his small cleft.

"What is it, Seth?"

"Something I was going to tell Mort, about Mimi Van Dorn's tox screen. There was something in her blood that routine analysis couldn't identify. I've forwarded the sample on for a more detailed study."

"No idea what it might be?"

"None." He checked his watch, suddenly looking impatient with Mort's failure to arrive. "What time do you have, Jess?"

I checked my phone, even though a glance at my watch would've been faster. "Three twenty-two," I told him, eyeing the big white numbers displaying the day and date beneath them.

Seth adjusted his watch. "Five minutes slow. Think I'll set it five minutes ahead to compensate."

And that's when I realized something, something I'd missed before.

"What's wrong?" Seth asked me.

I realized I'd risen from my chair, my mind somewhere else entirely. I was picturing my visit with Mort to watch the security tapes for the hour preceding Mimi Van Dorn's death, from the point the night nurse last made her rounds to the time the alarm went off when she stopped breathing.

"We need to go, Seth," I heard myself say, as if it were someone else's voice.

"We?"

"Cabot Cove Hospital. You're driving. And we need to find Mort."

"Well," I heard his voice chime behind me, "here he is."

"Just in time," I said, swinging toward him.

"In time for what?" he asked, eyeing Mara's pastry racks forlornly, since he'd already figured out he wouldn't be sampling today's special.

"To see what we missed this morning," I told him.

# Chapter Eleven

"There it is!" I said. "Freeze it right there!"

The uniformed guard familiar with the workings of the Cabot Cove Hospital security system froze the screen on the same shot of the nurses' station Mort and I had glimpsed that morning.

Mort moved closer to the screen, squinting. "What am I missing here, Mrs. Fletcher?"

"I remember when you used to call me that all the time."

"Like you used to call me Sheriff. That would be, what, maybe a hundred murders ago? You might say it was homicide that brought us to a first-name basis."

"Look at the screen, Mort."

He squinted again. "I'm still not seeing whatever it is I'm supposed to be, *Jessica*."

"The digital clock over the nurses' station."

"What about it?"

"Notice the time?"

"Four fifty-five. Forty minutes before Mimi Van Dorn coded."

"And the date?"

"Monday—" That was as far as he got. "But today . . ."

"Is Tuesday," I completed for him.

"Well, I'll be . . ." Mort was squinting toward the screen again, as if to confirm what he already knew to be the truth. "How did I miss this?"

"You mean, how did *we* miss this? The way all clues are missed: We weren't looking. And because if you keep watching, the date goes back to today's sometime before the code was called."

"But after whoever killed Mimi Van Dorn snuck into her room."

"Wait a minute," interjected the security guard. "Are the two of you saying what I think you're saying?"

"The tapes," I started.

"Somebody switched them," Mort picked up.

"Made Tuesday look like Monday," I followed. "Which kept us from seeing whoever murdered Mimi Van Dorn."


"How hard would that be?" Mort asked the guard, whose name was Frank, an easy one for me to remember.

"Pretty easy for anyone who knows their way around a system like this," Frank told him. "Simple matter of copying the loop in the same time period from yesterday and subbing it in on today's."

"Almost like cutting and pasting into a document," I said.

"I suppose."

"Is the original still there?" Mort wondered. "Any way we can retrieve it?"

Frank shook his head, expression stretched into a grim frown. "Like the lady said, cutting and pasting. Once you do that, it's gone."

"And who could have done it?" I chimed in. "Who could have accessed this room and made the switch?"

"Pretty much anyone with a hospital key card, ma'am. Even this early in the morning, that's a whole lot of folks."

"Even more when you consider whoever did it wasn't necessarily on duty at the time," I noted, which meant the work logs might go only so far in helping us.

"What about the password required to log in to the system?" Mort said. "It had to be somebody who knew the password. That might serve our cause, right?"

Frank frowned again as he lifted up the desk blotter on which the computer rested. Beneath it was a strip of tape on which a sequence of letters had been scrawled in big, bold print: *CCHSECURITY.*

"Well, I'll be," Mort said, back in the hallway.

"You said that already."

"I did?"

"I'm glad I'm not the only one around here whose memory isn't what it used to be."

"Well, Mrs. Fletcher, we know one thing almost for sure now, don't we?"

I nodded. "Mimi Van Dorn was, in fact, murdered."

"Which reminds me," Mort said sternly, holding out his hand, "I think there's something you forgot to give me."

I remembered I still had Mimi's phone in my bag, fished it out, and handed it over.

"Then I think I'll put this where it belongs," Mort said, dropping Mimi Van Dorn's cell phone into an evidence bag. "You know the penalty for tampering with evidence?"

"I wasn't tampering."

"No? What would you call it, then?"

"Following up on a lead."

"You conveniently forget to mention that?"

"I didn't know it would go anywhere."

"Then, Mrs. Fletcher, why don't you tell me where it ended up going?"

"Mrs. Fletcher again? Really, Mort?"

"Takes me back to the time years ago when you used to respect the law."

"Your memory must be even worse than mine. I've always respected the law."

"Is that what you call removing potential evidence from a crime scene?"

"We didn't know it was a crime scene at the time, Sheriff."

"You did, just like you always do. Otherwise, you wouldn't have come back for the phone. Now, where did whatever was on it take you?"

I told Mort about Mimi's heated phone call the day before as she was crossing the street. How she'd received a call from a blocked number. George Sutherland's fancy Scotland Yard app revealed the actual number for me, which turned out to belong to Mimi's son, Tripp.

"It's not so fancy, Jessica," Mort chided, waving his phone at me. "I've got one, too. And what did you learn from Tripp Van Dorn?"

I told him about our meeting earlier in the day at Good Shepherd Manor, where the young man was on the verge of getting kicked out for nonpayment, and the grudge he bore for his mother after she broke the trust responsible for providing his long-term care. How he'd attempted to hire Cabot Cove lawyer Fred Cooper, only to be rebuffed.

"I've met Fred a couple times," Mort noted. "Didn't impress me very much."

"To afford a Main Street rent, he must be impressing someone."

"Real estate closings in all probability, just like he told you. A lawyer can make a killing with all these new homes and condos in the area."

I cleared my throat. "No pun intended, of course."

Only two nurses had staffed the intensive care unit desk the night before. The chief ICU nurse, Amy Billings, was working a split schedule and had fortuitously just returned to her station when Mort and I approached.

"Nurse Billings," Mort said, his uniform providing any introduction that was necessary, "I was hoping I could steal another moment of your time."

"Of course, Sheriff," Billings responded, seeming not at all put off by Mort's request. "Have you made any progress looking into Ms. Van Dorn's death, poor woman?"

"Some, including the fact that the security tapes from around the time of her death were altered."

"Altered?"

"The footage from this morning was actually from yesterday, according to the time stamp."

"How odd."

"That was our thought, too, ma'am."

Hearing the word "our" led Nurse Billings to acknowledge me. "Oh, Mrs. Fletcher, forgive me. I didn't notice you standing there. So nice to finally meet you. Are you here in an official capacity?" she asked.

"Unofficially," I said, returning her slight smile. "Ms. Van Dorn and I were friends."

"I recall that from this morning."

I nodded, aware now how little I truly knew about Mimi. Can you really be friends, at least close friends, with anyone it turns out you know so little about? Mimi knew no more about me than I knew about her. We had shared moments, not memories or the minutiae of our pasts, with each other. That might have made for a different type of friend, but a friend all the same. The world has a way of changing things up on you.

"I'd like to go over the same period in time in a bit more detail, if you don't mind," Mort said to Nurse Billings.

"Not at all, Sheriff."

Billings moved to a quieter section of the counter, away from the comings and goings of three other ICU nurses who were currently on duty.

"But," she continued, "you should know that old security system isn't the most reliable. We encountered a similar problem when we were looking into some missing inventory from the hospital supply closets, and in that case entire blocks of time, even whole days, were missing when we tried to review the footage."

Mort nodded, accepting her disclaimer. "Getting back to the approximate time we believe Ms. Van Dorn died, you and another nurse were on duty. Is that correct?"

"Yes, a third, Wilma Lodge, had called in sick, but we didn't bother fielding a replacement because we only had six patients to tend to."

"Checks every hour, I believe. Would that be correct?"

"At minimum."

Mort jotted down a note in that magical memo pad of his that never seemed to run out of pages. "And the last time you checked on Ms. Van Dorn would have been . . ."

Nurse Billings sidestepped to check the actual logs. "Four forty-five a.m."

"And she coded at . . ."

Another check of the log. "Five thirty-five."

"So Ms. Van Dorn was unattended for fifty minutes."

"Well, Sheriff, I wouldn't go so far as to say unattended."

"Figure of speech, ma'am."

"Then the answer's yes."

I slid a bit closer to the counter. "Nurse Billings, you said the alarm in Ms. Van Dorn's room went off at five thirty-five, signaling she had coded. How long would it take that to happen from the time her ventilator was unplugged?"

"Certainly no more than two minutes."

Mort squeezed me out of the way a bit. "Do you remember anything, anything at all, that stands out from right around that time?"

Nurse Billings shook her head slowly. "Like I told you this morning, Sheriff, no, nothing. I'm sorry."

"Nothing to be sorry for. Were you alone at this counter when the alarm sounded?"

"Yes, I remember that distinctly, because Nurse Willow was making her rounds at the time. She joined me in Ms. Van Dorn's room just after the crash cart arrived."

"And you recall nothing that indicated the presence of someone else about on this hall in that same period?"

Billings shook her head. "No one at all. Just Nurse Willow."

"We'll be wanting to speak to her as well," Mort noted.

"She's due in for a shift in about an hour. I could give her a call and ask her to come in a bit early to talk to you."

"That would be much appreciated, ma'am."

We were waiting in the lobby for Jane Willow when she arrived thirty minutes later, toting a thermos still riding the smell of hot coffee. We claimed a small nesting of chairs around a solid rectangular table littered with old magazines.

"Thank you for seeing us," Mort said to her. "We'll keep this as short as possible."

"Yes, well, I'm just glad to be coming back in. After what happened this morning, the last place I wanted to be was home alone."

"I can understand that," I interjected.

"Nurse Willow," Mort resumed, "according to Nurse Billings's recollection, you were performing your rounds when Ms. Van Dorn coded. Is that correct?"

"Precisely."

"And during those rounds, did you see or hear anything that stands out, perhaps indicating someone else was on the ward?"

"Did you check the security camera footage?"

"Unfortunately, it was malfunctioning at the time."

"It seems to act up on those occasions we actually need to refer to it."

"Getting back to this morning," Mort prompted.

"I can't recall anything out of the ordinary. I was in another patient's room when I heard the code and came running." She stopped, seeming to think for a moment. "There was one thing, but it happened earlier, at least an hour prior to the code, while Amy was on her break."

"Amy?" Mort asked.

"I'm sorry, Nurse Billings. I was at the desk when the doctor from that clinic appeared."

I jumped in before Mort could. "Charles Clifton?"

"Yes. He demanded to see Ms. Van Dorn and was quite insistent. I told him since he wasn't on staff, I couldn't allow it unless he'd been cleared, relented only when he insisted he was Ms. Van Dorn's doctor."

"Did you accompany him to her room, Nurse Willow?"

"No, Ms. Fletcher. I couldn't leave the desk unattended. But I made sure to check on her as soon as he left."

I leaned a bit closer. "And this would have been after Dr. Clifton departed."

"Oh, definitely."

"Nurse Willow," I started, "you said you checked on Ms. Van Dorn after Dr. Clifton had been in to see her and that she was fine, undisturbed, nothing awry."

"Yes. I'm certain of that."

"What about her room?"

"Her room?"

"Anything strike you as strange or out of place, different from when you'd last been inside it?"

"Well, I closed the closet door because someone had left it open, but that doesn't mean it was Dr. Clifton."

I looked toward Mort. "I suppose we'll have to ask him, won't we?"

# Chapter Twelve

I t had been a whirlwind day, one of those that felt more like a week. Given my lack of sleep and all that had transpired since I'd gotten word of Mimi's death, I knew I was running on fumes but wasn't about to put off a visit to Charles Clifton at the clinic that bore his name.

"Is that really who you want to see there?" Mort asked, after we'd set out from the hospital in his sheriff's department SUV.

"I'm worried about George," I confessed.

"You ask Seth about his condition?"

"He gave it to me straight."

"That's Seth. His bedside manner always could use some work."

It should've been no more than a ten-minute drive from Cabot Cove Hospital to the Clifton Clinic, but every route Mort tried, even the ones usually less traveled, was clogged with summer traffic. I'd lived in Cabot Cove longer than he, but both of us remembered when the town had boasted only 3,500 hearty souls, for whom summer was a time to celebrate instead of dread. Nowadays our beaches filled up by midmorning even on weekdays, those residents with cherished parking passes unable to take advantage of them because the lots were always full. Sure, business was booming, but so were the rents, and the town council had hatched many a plan to keep outside speculators from coming in and swallowing our town up entirely in a series of gulps. Court fights abounded, and so far, the council hadn't fared too well. Now that I thought about it, Fred Cooper had likely been the beneficiary of some of that legal work.

"Well, Mrs. Fletcher," Mort said as his SUV inched its way around the jam-packed streets, "I've finally found something more difficult to deal with than your interference in my cases. If I wanted traffic, I could have stayed in New York."

"Amos Tupper used to say the same thing," I noted. "But for him a real jam was five cars in front of him at a traffic light. We drove to Boston once, and I thought he was going to have a heart attack on the Southeast Expressway. I almost took the wheel."

"You don't even know how to drive."

"We weren't going anywhere at the time anyway."

The Clifton Clinic had been open for nearly a year, and I'd passed by it innumerable times without ever going in. It was a modern four-story building constructed on the bluffs that rimmed the Cabot Cove coast in a location that had been

inaccessible for centuries. The area had been considered pro-
tected wetlands, but the clinic had inherited an easement from
the previous developer, allowing construction to proceed as
long as the developer adhered to very strict environmental parameters, which were subsequently loosened. Because the land
in question technically resided between Cabot Cove and our
neighboring townships, the property fell under the domain of
the state of Maine. So neither I nor anyone else in Cabot Cove
really had a clear notion of why such an exception had been
granted by a state that was normally unyielding in the protec-
tion of its natural resources.

The clinic had been constructed to conform to the contours of the bluffs, set along a narrow peninsula that stuck out
like a finger into the bay that had defined Cabot Cove as a typical New England fishing village long before the rest of the
world had discovered it. The building was wider at the front
and narrowed as it stretched outward toward the sea. And at its
narrowest point there was little more than a ledge of black
rocks separating the structure from the waves crashing on
the stone-laden shore at least two hundred feet below. I've lived
in Maine plenty long enough to consider Ogunquit's Mar-
ginal Way to be among the Northeast's greatest architectural
wonders, and this sliver of land extending out high over the
ocean reminded me of the most impressive, and imposing,
parts of that.

The parking lot was located on the far side, at the thickest
point of the bluffs, so as not to harm a casual view of the sur-
rounding scenery with a clutter of vehicles. I had to admit the
whole structure blended aesthetically into the scene as much as

any building could, but I still detested the notion that it had been allowed here in the first place.

Though it claimed our village's zip code, thanks to some clever zoning manipulations, the clinic actually rested on the outskirts of the far less hospitable village of Rockland, which had been named for the terrain that had come to define it. According to old legend, Rockland had been the unlucky recipient of all the rocks somehow steered away from our sandy cutout of the coastline, which featured white sand beaches and crystal blue waters. I didn't know the name of Rockland's sheriff, but was quite certain he didn't have to deal with the murder rate of Cabot Cove.

I remember a town council meeting in which I was speaking on behalf of the Friends of the Library when someone suggested we begin advertising our rather excessive murder rate to discourage additional expansion. My burly fisherman friend, Ethan Cragg, had turned with a wink toward me before rising.

"I make a formal motion we stop listing our out-of-date population on that 'Welcome to Cabot Cove' sign, and replace it with a running tally of murder victims."

The motion, of course, didn't pass.

The clinic featured sandy-colored shingle siding to better blend in with the world nestled around it. The construction had been environmentally friendly to a fault, Charles Clifton able to save considerable time and expense since another business looking to develop the land had already completed the voluminous stack of environmental-impact studies required to win approval from the Maine Department of Environmental Management and Coast Resources Commission. That fact had always stuck in my mind, rekindled when I'd met Clifton for the first time at the reception following Jean O'Neil's funeral. He definitely impressed me as the kind of man who'd pay off the previous developers to take control of their land, or even find a more malicious way to make such a move, like bribing a state official or two.

Mort and I had appeared unannounced in the hope Clifton would see us anyway. Normally, the police showing up produced just that effect, even in Cabot Cove. And sure enough, we were escorted by a security guard from the reception desk up to Clifton's third-floor office in the three-story stately building.

In contrast to the rustic exterior, the interior had all the hallmarks of a high-end medical institution, with bright lights and halls swimming with lab coat–wearing doctors. The clinic had the structural equivalent of a new-car smell. Everything about it—from the walls, to the furnishings, to the accents, to the name tags we'd been provided with—was new and unsullied by the harsh ocean elements as well as wear. We didn't see much in evidence from a medical standpoint, other than a few doctors and other personnel in lab coats, and the elevator spilled us out on what must've been the hall dedicated to offices.

Clifton himself was waiting outside the elevator when it slid open. "Sheriff, Mrs. Fletcher," he greeted.

"Thank you for seeing us, Doctor. Mrs. Fletcher and I wanted to give you an update on our investigation in person."

"I appreciate that," he said. "Come right this way."

He closed his office door behind us. The clinic might be ultramodern, but Clifton's office looked like an ad for the traditional. Wood paneling covered walls dominated by a library of medical books bound in leather. Leather-upholstered English pub–style chesterfield furniture formed a sitting area atop a dark Oriental rug, set before a beautiful hardwood desk that looked too big to even get through the door. A gas fireplace was built into the far wall, and it was easy for me to imagine Clifton keeping a fire going through much of the winter that would be upon us before we knew it.

He led us to the sitting area and took one of the stiff leather chairs, leaving Mort and me to take seats side by side on the matching couch. I noticed he was wearing a fresh suit, having likely sent out the one he'd been wearing that morning to have the tears in the knees repaired.

"Now, Sheriff, to this update," Clifton started.

Mort leaned forward. "This isn't easy to say, Doctor. It's never easy for me to tell a person someone they knew was murdered."

Surprise flashed across Clifton's stately features, stopping short of ruffling his shock of white hair. "Are we talking about Mimi Van Dorn here?"

"We are indeed, sir. I'd like to say it was just an assumption, but from what we've been able to learn today, it's more than that. A virtual certainty, in fact."

Clifton stole a glance my way, as if expecting me to chime in, but I remained silent.

"These clues you're speaking of, Sheriff . . ."

"I can't go into the specifics—us cops have a certain code we live by, too. But everything we've learned suggests that Ms.

Van Dorn was murdered early this morning, right around five thirty-five, just before the code alarm went off in her room."

"How terrible," Clifton reacted, shaking his head.

"I hope you don't mind me accompanying Sheriff Metzger here, Doctor," I chimed in finally, "or assisting his efforts in general."

"Not at all, Mrs. Fletcher. Given how close you were to Mimi, I'd expect nothing less. In fact, I'm grateful for it, since you enjoy a unique level of expertise in such matters."

"Well, I have written a lot of books."

"And solved a lot of crimes."

"*Helped* solve, Doctor," I corrected politely.

"And what does your keen sense tell you about Ms. Van Dorn's passing?" he asked me, as if Mort weren't in the room at all.

"The sheriff already made it clear we didn't come here to mention specifics."

"Then why did you come?"

"A duty nurse mentioned you showed up in the ICU shortly before Ms. Van Dorn's passing," Mort said before I had the chance to.

Clifton's eyes darted between Mort and me, as if he was trying to gauge our intentions. "Just checking in on her, that's all. She is a patient of mine, after all."

"I didn't mean for my comment to sound threatening in any way," Mort told him. "I was just wondering if it's your practice to visit patients in the wee hours of the morning."

"I couldn't sleep and felt utterly helpless. I thought checking in on Ms. Van Dorn might help me feel better."

"And did it?"

"Not at all, actually. It made me feel worse, in fact, since her prognosis wasn't positive. I think I went there hoping for otherwise, but that's not what I got."

"Well," I interjected, "that certainly explains one thing, Doctor."

"What's that, Mrs. Fletcher?"

I glanced at Mort before answering him. "Well, it would seem you left Mimi less than an hour before the code was called. The call I got from Dr. Hazlitt came about a half hour after she was declared dead, and Mort picked me up just minutes after that."

"I'm not sure if I see your point."

"You were in the ICU when we arrived. Given the driving distance to the home you're renting in Kennebunkport, I have to assume you never left the hospital after you stopped into Ms. Van Dorn's room."

"The ICU had my cell phone number. What if I told you they reached me while I was driving back home?"

"I'd tell you they only informed Ms. Van Dorn's physician of record, who was still Seth Hazlitt. He called us, Dr. Clifton. No one called you, but they didn't need to, did they? Because you were still in the hospital."

Clifton nodded, meeting my eyes the way a caged predator does sometimes through the bars of a zoo. "I was," he admitted, "again, because—"

"You felt helpless. Yes, you mentioned that already. I find myself curious as to exactly what you were treating Mimi Van Dorn for."

"I thought I had mentioned the escalating prediabetes she was suffering from."

"You did. I was wondering if there was something else you might've been treating her for, perhaps as part of another of these trials your clinic seems so adept at landing."

Clifton turned toward Mort, trying very hard to pretend I wasn't there. "Any further questions, Sheriff?"

"If you don't mind, I'd like to hear your answer to the one Mrs. Fletcher just posed."

"Doctor-patient privilege prohibits me from sharing that with you."

"Doctor-patient privilege doesn't extend beyond death," Mort reminded him.

"That's a legal issue, not a medical one. The Clifton Clinic prides itself on both its discretion and maintaining the confidentiality of our patients, living or dead."

"In other words, you want me to get a court order."

"I would prefer not, but whether to go through the considerable expense and legal headaches is totally up to you."

"Thanks for acknowledging that, Doctor."

"And if you have questions you'd like answered in a more expeditious fashion, I'd suggest contacting Ms. Van Dorn's lawyer. Much of the business side of our relationship was conducted through him," Clifton continued. "You may save yourself time and trouble, Sheriff, if you reach out to him instead. I have his name and number here somewhere."

He moved to his desk and fished a hand about until he came to a small slip of paper wedged into a side of his old-fashioned desk blotter.

"Here you are," Clifton said, returning to the sitting area and handing the paper to Mort.

Mort looked at me for a long moment before handing it over. I never regarded the number, my focus locking on the name:

Fred Cooper.

"Would you like to see Mr. Sutherland while you're here, Mrs. Fletcher?" I heard Charles Clifton offer, breaking my trance.


George was seated in a lavish reception area reserved for patients; it resembled one of those high-end membership-only airline lounges I've frequented from time to time. He looked up from reading a book at my approach, and drawing closer, I saw it was a paperback reprint of one of my books from a couple years ago.

He smiled and made a show of trying to tuck it under the seat. "Bollocks! Caught in the act!"

"Since when did you need to hide a book at my appearance?"

"Since I fell several titles behind and didn't want you to know. If nothing else, this treatment will help me catch up on my reading."

I took the chair next to his. "Did you sit down with Clifton about all the test results?"

He snatched the paperback back out from beneath the chair. "Yes."

"And?"

"He's in the process of determining if I'm a candidate for a clinical trial not actually associated with my specific disease at all."

"Is that good or bad?"

"It could turn out to be miraculous if the fates are with me, Jessica. Besides, I don't have a lot of treatment options to choose from."

"What can I do to help, George?"

He smiled. "Just what you're doing now. And make sure they don't give away my room at Hill House."

"Consider it done."

Something was plaguing me about the Clifton Clinic, a combination of things actually, from Mimi Van Dorn's extraction of money from her son's trust, to Seth Hazlitt's musings on how a facility this small could attract so many clinical trials.

"George, I need to ask you a question."

He held that recent paperback in his lap. "I'm listening."

"How did you learn of the clinical trial you're hoping to be admitted to?"

"Why, from my oncologist back in London, of course."

"And how did he learn about it?"

"Research, I suppose."

"Because it occurs to me that—"

Before I could finish, a well-dressed woman approached casually, smiling. "Chief Inspector Sutherland, Dr. Clifton is ready for you now."

He rose a step ahead of me. "As they say, dear lady, to be continued."

"Let's hope so," I said, looking toward the woman.

I didn't tell Mort anything about my exchange with George Sutherland. As we headed toward his SUV in the parking lot, though, I thought back to one of the last things Charles Clifton had said to us:

*And if you have questions you'd like answered in a more expeditious fashion, I'd suggest contacting Ms. Van Dorn's lawyer.*

According to his records, that lawyer was Fred Cooper, which explained why Cooper had rejected Tripp Van Dorn's overtures to take him on as a client. If that were the case, though, such a conflict of interest would have been obvious from the start, in which case Cooper would've had no reason to lead him on for the days it had taken to ultimately turn Tripp down.

"You still have Mimi's phone, don't you?" I asked Mort as we approached his department-issue SUV.

"In an evidence bag, where it belongs."

"Want me to put on evidence gloves before handling it?"

"Given how much you've handled it already, that's hardly necessary." I watched Mort remove the plastic pouch containing Mimi's phone from a small safe he kept in the spare tire well of the SUV's rear compartment. "Have at it," he said, handing it over.

I immediately brought up the recent calls Mimi had made or received. One number flashed repeatedly, over and over again, lit up in both red and black to denote incoming and outgoing calls.

I pointed it out to Mort. "That's Fred Cooper's office number. Looks like Charles Clifton was telling the truth."

"Anything else I should be seeing here?"

I pointed out one of the calls. "Mimi made this one to Cooper just before the reception for Jean O'Neil at the library put on by the Friends. Not long after she had that argument with her son."

"Care to tell me what I'm missing?"

"What was it about that call with Tripp she needed to share with her lawyer so fast?"

# Chapter Thirteen

We caught Fred Cooper just as he was locking his office door behind him.

"Back so soon, Mrs. Fletcher?" he said, spotting me before he noted Mort's presence.

"I thought I could save some time by bringing the sheriff around with me, Mr. Cooper."

Cooper nodded in what looked like defeat and threaded the key back into his lock, opening the door for us.

The receptionist had left for the day, and the office belonging to the other lawyer was open and dark. He closed the door behind us and moved toward the sitting area, but all of us remained standing.

"Did you forget to mention you were representing Mimi Van Dorn during my first visit?"

"I don't recall you asking me if I was or not."

"You might have made note of it when we were discussing your decision not to represent her son."

"I seem to recall saying how much I value attorney-client privilege during that same discussion, Mrs. Fletcher."

"As Mrs. Fletcher, I'm sure, told you," Mort interjected in a firm and unyielding voice, "attorney-client privilege does not extend beyond death when the commission of a crime is suspected."

"And what crime would that be, Sheriff? Mrs. Fletcher intimated several things about my client's passing. Since she wasn't acting in any professional capacity capable of confirming a criminal act, I saw no reason to share any information, proprietary or otherwise, with her about my dealings with Ms. Van Dorn. And I suggest if you have any problems with my behavior, you take it up with the Maine Bar Association."

"Why not just say that to Tripp Van Dorn when he first asked you to represent him?"

Cooper didn't answer right away, long enough for me to resume before he had the chance.

"Did you report back to his mother on what you discussed? Did you share any information, proprietary or otherwise, with her that he shared with you in confidence?"

"There was no expectation of such confidence, Mrs. Fletcher, because he wasn't my client and I wasn't acting as his attorney."

Mort's face creased into a frown. "I suspect that's something the bar association might find interesting, Mr. Cooper."

Cooper bristled at that. If steam really could pour from a person's ears, I thought it would be pumping out of his right now. "Was I party to, or did my actions precipitate, a crime, Sheriff?"

"Not that I know of, Mr. Cooper."

"Then I suggest we end this conversation now for the good of all concerned." He looked from Mort to me. "Have you ever been sued, Mrs. Fletcher?"

"Have you, Mr. Cooper?" I let my retort settle for a moment before continuing. "I believe a workman once sued me for payment on a fence repair to my house he never completed. Mort, you remember that, don't you?"

"Amos Tupper was sheriff at the time."

"Oh, yes, he was, wasn't he?" I turned my attention back to Fred Cooper. "Anyway, the workman claimed that I—"

"I'll take that as a no, Mrs. Fletcher. So believe me when I tell you it's not a pleasant experience, especially when the complainant is an attorney bearing none of the requisite expenses you'll have to bear."

"Well, I believe I featured a courtroom scene in *The Corpse Swam by Moonlight*, or maybe it was in *The Dead Must Sing*. Any idea which, Sheriff?"

Mort was fighting back a smile, maybe a laugh. "Not off the top of my head, Mrs. Fletcher."

"Anyway," I continued to Cooper, "I seem to recall an especially nasty lawyer's attempts to impeach the integrity of a police officer who'd caught him red-handed stealing from a client."

"What are you accusing me of exactly?"

"Not being terribly forthcoming with me. Beyond that—"

"Nothing, in other words. Now, if you'll excuse me . . ."

"You didn't let me finish, Mr. Cooper. I'd like to know why you strung along a disabled young man for several days, when you could have simply cited a conflict of interest or confessed the truth. I find the fact that you did that odd at the very least and suspicious at most, potentially even criminal."

"Criminal?" Cooper challenged, as if he'd never heard the word before.

"Mort, would you define criminal conspiracy for this young man? Simply stated, of course."

"Simply stated, an agreement between two or more people to defraud another party."

I swung back toward Fred Cooper. "So my question would be, did you conspire with Mimi Van Dorn to steal the money set aside in her son's trust for his care?"

"You should get your facts straight before you go around accusing people of a crime, Mrs. Fletcher. Tripp Van Dorn's trust was established with his mother as sole administrator, free to act as she saw fit at her own discretion, including the breaking of the trust should she elect to do so. I represented her in that effort and nothing more."

"For a handsome fee, no doubt. So at least we know how you paid for all this new furniture."

"Is that a crime, Mrs. Fletcher?"

"You could use a new interior decorator, Mr. Cooper. Beyond that, no."


"A new interior decorator?" Mort repeated when we were back in his SUV. "Is that the best you could do?"

"Can we run the sirens and lights on the way back to Hill House?"

"That's your answer?"

"For now. Fred Cooper's guilty of something, Mort. I just haven't figured out what yet."

He started the engine and squeezed the steering wheel tighter, not ready to go anywhere yet. "What's the latest on Chief Inspector Sutherland?"

"I don't think it's good," I responded frankly. "He wouldn't be here if it wasn't bad."

"Why don't you just say 'we'll see about that' again?"

I gave him a longer look. "I'm sorry. I really do appreciate you asking, Mort."

"I've never had the chance to get to know him that well. This morning marked our longest conversation ever. He seems like a fine man."

"He is. In all the right ways. And he's a brilliant detective, true to the heritage of Scotland Yard."

"You sure can pick them, Jessica."

"Men or investigators?"

Mort angled the car into summer traffic and began inching his way along toward the snarl at the traffic light. He looked back at me when we came to a stop again.

"You weren't very precise in your answer to my question about George Sutherland."

"Something's wrong, Mort."

"Well, Mrs. Fletcher, that's why he's here, isn't it?"

"There's something he's not telling me. Why not let me know he was coming? A phone call, an e-mail, anything. If I didn't know better . . ."

Mort's expression softened. "Let it go, Jessica."

"Let what go?"

"Sometimes the reason you can't see what's there is because

there's nothing beyond the obvious, as strange as that may seem."

"You think I don't want to admit that George is sick. You think I'm groping for another explanation for his coming to Cabot Cove."

"Aren't you?"

I was spared a response when a horn honking behind us got Mort moving again through the intersection.

I do my best thinking alone. Call it the stuff of a writer. Assembling the pieces of a real puzzle for me requires the same solitary process as assembling the pieces of my fictional ones. I often wonder where Jessica Fletcher ends and J. B. Fletcher begins. Someone once asked me if I ever confuse my fictional crimes with the very real ones in which I often find myself embroiled.

The true answer is both yes and no. No, because it's never hard to separate reality from fantasy. Yes, because the approach to how I solve a real crime is much the same as how J. B. Fletcher solves a fictional one. I don't know any more when I start a book than I do when an actual case presents itself and demands my attention. Indeed, J. B. Fletcher is very real to me, to the point where I ask myself, what would she do now?

I couldn't chase the lawyer Fred Cooper's part in this puzzle from my mind, the sudden windfall all that new office furniture suggested. So I decided to follow up on Mort's suggestion that his good fortune might have somehow involved real estate, and dialed up Eve Simpson, who was Cabot Cove's number one agent.

"Jessica, I haven't seen you in forever!" she greeted enthusiastically.

"Well, summer is your busiest season."

"Writers don't have a busiest season."

"Except whenever we have a deadline looming. I was wondering if I could ask you a question about a lawyer in town, Fred Cooper."

"What about him?"

"Has he handled any of your real estate transactions?"

"No."

I was starting to feel vindicated in my suspicions until Eve resumed.

"He handles *all* of them."

"All?" I repeated, feeling deflated.

"He's a stickler for detail and terrific with the paperwork. I believe he's overseen nearly twenty closings for me in the past few months alone. Was there anything else, Jessica?"

"No, that's it."

"Tit for tat, then."

"Tit for tat?"

"The whole town's talking about Mimi Van Dorn's murder. Might your interest in Fred Cooper be connected to that?"

"Thank you very much for your help, Eve," I said, and ended the call.

I guess maybe I wasn't as smart as J. B. Fletcher, after all. We saw the same things, but she often proved to be a step ahead of me. Now, as I sat at the Victorian desk that was part of the furnishings in my suite at Hill House, I asked myself what I would do if I were writing this mystery, instead of living it.

*Look in another direction.*

I thought I heard J. B. Fletcher's voice in my head, which was strange, because it didn't sound like mine at all.

*If the answer's not in front of you, ask a different question.*

I never experienced writer's block, writing at a feverish pace and never letting my characters stay still. No respites. If one door led only to a wall, they found another door. If the door didn't open, they used a window.

I needed a door now, at least a window.

*Stick to what's bothering you.*

J. B. Fletcher's voice again.

Lots of things were bothering me here, not the least of which was George Sutherland's condition. But there was nothing I could do about that, any more than I could bring Mimi Van Dorn back to life or fully explain what had led her to take the money that assured her son a decent life. Thinking of George again brought me back to Jean O'Neil's funeral, just one day ago, which felt like a month. Jean O'Neil had been a patient of Charles Clifton.

So had Mimi.

So was George.

The common denominator between them was clinical trials at the Clifton Clinic, the first Clifton Care Partners facility in what was envisioned as a chain across the entire country, with ground having been broken on several more already.

Clinical trials . . .

I had my phone at my ear the next moment, having dialed one of the numbers listed among my few Favorites.

"No," the voice of Harry McGraw greeted.

"I haven't even asked you a question yet, Harry."

"Whatever it is, the answer's no. Haven't you heard? I'm retired."

"Since when?"

"Oh, maybe fifteen seconds ago. I swore on the Bible that the next time you called, it would be time to take down my shingle."

"You don't have a shingle, and when was the last time you went to church?"

"Either my third marriage or my oldest daughter's second."

"Long time ago, Harry."

"I do have a Bible."

"Really?"

"Swiped it from the desk drawer of a hotel. A faster read than whatever you're working on."

"How do you know if you haven't read it?"

"Educated guess."

"I need your help," I told the best private investigator I'd ever known.

"Of course you do. And I need a new place to live."

"What happened?"

"My building got bought up and with that went my rent control."

"Do you neglect to send bills to all your clients or am I the only one?"

"I don't have clients. I have friends who I occasionally do favors for."

"You mean like Travis McGee?"

"Who's that, your new boyfriend?"

"A kind of detective created by John D. MacDonald."

"Is that your new boyfriend?"

"He's dead, Harry."

"Sorry to hear that, Jess. I never even got to meet him."

"Can I ask the question now?"

"Go ahead, but my answer's not changing."

"Do you still have that contact at the Food and Drug Administration?"

"Yes. Oops, does that make me a liar?"

"No, Harry, a friend. I need you to call him for me."

# Chapter Fourteen

Harry was waiting for me early the following afternoon when I stepped off the escalator into the cavernous waiting area of Union Station in Washington, DC.

"Look at this—what a coincidence," he said, his trademark scowl plastered over a face that looked like it was cut from clay that had never quite hardened.

"Really, Harry, really?"

"You didn't think I was going to leave you alone down here. By the way, I'm expensing my train ticket. Don't worry—I took the Regional, not the Acela like you."

"How'd you know what train I'd be on?"

"Simple: This was the first one that could've gotten you here if you rode the late-night train out from Portland to Boston."

"Am I that predictable?"

"Maybe I'm just a much better detective than you give me credit for."

"I give you plenty of credit."

"An occasional tip would go a longer way."

"I can't tip you if you never send me a bill to pay."

"Maybe I'm independently wealthy."

"Are you?"

"Closer to homeless. I'd move in with you in Cabot Cove, except I'd feel much safer living on the streets of New York."

I started walking across the sprawling waiting area, and Harry quickly joined me in step.

"Did you arrange for my appointment at the FDA?"

"You mean *our* appointment, Jessica?"

"Do I?"

The scowl flashed again. "Only way my guy will see you."

"You tell him what this was about?"

Harry nodded. "Turns out clinical trials are right up his alley."

"Really?"

"No. But he's a big shot there at the FDA. I think maybe they dedicated one of the letters to him."

"*F, D,* or *A*?"

"*H* for here we go again."

We rode the Metro not into Washington proper but to the station in Silver Spring, Maryland, home of the Food and Drug Administration's White Oak campus, where many of its departments were housed. The FDA had so many employees, it had branched out from its main-headquarters facilities in Montgomery and Prince George's counties, also in Maryland. The overflow of workers staffed a warren of office buildings in

Greater Washington, making the FDA truly labyrinthine in more ways than one.

The White Oak campus, as luck would have it, handled oversight of the vast number of clinical trials ongoing at any given time through the FDA's Center for Drug Evaluation and Research. I'd really never given much thought to the nature of clinical trials before the Clifton Clinic moved into Cabot Cove, and I was determined to do a deeper dive as to how a relatively new and little-known facility could have landed so many studies aimed at determining the fitness of therapeutic medications to be made available to the masses.

Located on New Hampshire Avenue in Silver Spring, the White Oak facility resembled the Pentagon in its sprawl and design, the interconnected swath of buildings uniformly beige in color and fitted with blackened windows that looked like the kind that never opened. It wasn't like this was the Centers for Disease Control, in Atlanta, where this or that microbe might launch a determined escape at any time. No, these were strictly administrative offices where analysis ruled the day, as opposed to actual experimentation, which took place under the auspices of the pharmaceutical companies hoping to bring the next miracle drug to fruition.

"You haven't told me your friend's name," I said to Harry, after we checked in at the security station in the lobby.

We hadn't been given our building passes yet, and a uniformed security guard's gaze never seemed to leave us, perhaps because we were the only people seated in the waiting area.

"Arthur Noble," Harry answered. "Way back when I actually had a career, he was a trusted source, working out of the FDA's field office in Jamaica."

"The country?"

"No, Jess, the New York City neighborhood. I got him out of a scrap once."

"Did he pay you?"

"He's still paying me. That's what today's visit is all about."

No sooner had Harry said that than a tall, wiry man emerged from an elevator.

"And here he is now."

I'm not sure I'd ever seen Harry hug anyone, and Arthur Noble was no exception. They barely shook hands, while I hung back, waiting for my cue to approach, when Harry nodded my way.

"And this is Jessica Fletcher. Be nice to her, Art, or she might write something bad about you in one of her books."

"Is that why you're here, Mrs. Fletcher? Research?"

"I am indeed, Mr. Noble," I said, not bothering to add that it wasn't for a book.

We shook hands, Noble's long-fingered grasp swallowing my hand while barely squeezing at all.

"How about we talk in the cafeteria?" Noble suggested, and lowered his voice. "The less people that see us, the better."

Harry's expression bent into his trademark scowl. "Nobody seems to like having me in their company. I'm starting to take it personal. Such things take their toll, you know."

"I'm buying," Noble offered.

"Not so personal anymore, then."

The lunchtime rush had ended, the tables cleared off and wiped down. I grabbed some tea and a muffin, just coffee for Harry and Arthur Noble, poured from big urns running along a half wall.

"My favorite brand," Harry said, setting his cup on a Formica table set far back in the rear of the room.

"What's that?" I asked him.

"Anything that comes with free refills."

Arthur Noble finally joined us after paying. "So what can a simple bureaucrat do for America's favorite mystery writer?"

"You're much too kind, Mr. Noble."

"That's not what I heard."

"He means from me," Harry interjected.

"No wonder it's an exaggeration."

"Harry tells me you had some questions about clinical trials. What would you like to know?"

"Could we start with everything?" I asked him.

"That would take some time, Mrs. Fletcher."

"Ching-ching," intoned Harry. "That was my cash register jangling."

"How about the general parameters of how a trial happens and progresses?" I suggested. "Just the broad strokes."

"Then you're talking about the clinical-research stage."

I looked at Harry, who was no help at all. "I suppose so."

"Well then," Noble said, extracting a set of trifolded, stapled pages from his suit jacket, "I brought you a document that summarizes the four stages of a typical clinical trial."

I opened the pages and gave them a cursory glance. "This looks like something you'd use to hand out in schools."

Noble grinned. "Precisely what I normally use them for. Just the broad strokes, of course, but something you can refer back to when you're writing."

"What if I wanted to probe a bit deeper than those broad strokes?" I asked him.

"As in . . ."

"As in, how are specific hospitals or treatment centers chosen to participate in such trials?"

"Oh, any number of factors, most notably size and experience to ensure a wide-ranging staff capable of overseeing the testing and appropriately analyzing the results. It's normally based on the existing relationships the drug company in question maintains with the participating institutions."

"Then drug companies choose their own test site?"

"More or less. That's not what you assumed, obviously."

"I assumed the FDA supervises all the studies."

"We do, but more from afar than up close and personal. Essentially, we serve as a data-collection and analytics clearinghouse. Based on the results provided by the testing facility, we make the determination whether to advance the study or stop it, approve the drug or suspend it."

"Quite a responsibility, Mr. Noble."

"At every level, and one we take very seriously, since lives are at stake: both those that can be saved if the drug reaches market and those who might be harmed in the research process leading up to that."

Now I leaned forward. "Can I cut to the chase now?"

"Absolutely."

"Can the system be corrupted?"

"I'm not sure if I understand your question, Mrs. Fletcher."

"Can the system be gamed?"

"As in," he said again.

"How might a clinic or hospital that's just starting up become eligible to hold clinical trials?"

"By proving themselves over time."

"How long?"

"Years, decades even. It should come as no surprise that the bulk of most groundbreaking clinical trials have been held at the likes of the Mayo Clinic, Boston's Brigham and Women's Hospital, Cedars-Sinai out in Los Angeles, the Cleveland Clinic, the Lahey. . . . The list goes on from there, and, especially for the latter phases of the trial, such institutions are the only ones with the kind of resources to conduct them."

"So a relatively small, private hospital that's been open barely a year . . ."

"Would stand little or no chance of landing such a trial until it had been open far longer than that. It takes time to build up relationships of trust with the drug companies that make the ultimate decisions as to placement. But, even then, the participating clinic or hospital would have to be cleared by us, and, absent a track record, it would be extremely problematic to grant such approval."

I glanced at Harry before responding. "So, Mr. Noble, theoretically this office would have a record of every single ongoing clinical trial in the country."

"More than theoretically, Mrs. Fletcher. Our oversight is exacting and never compromised under any circumstances. There's just too much at stake. We may not be able to achieve one hundred percent certainty with any given drug, but we strive to come as close to that as we can."

"So, also theoretically, if I gave you the name of this upstart clinic, you'd be able to tell me which clinical trials they're conducting and currently have ongoing."

Noble hedged. "Well, I'd be able to confirm or deny the fact of their involvement, but I couldn't share with you the nature of the specific trials."

"Good enough," I told him. "Does the Clifton Clinic ring any bells?"

# Chapter Fifteen

"Not off the top of my head," Noble told me, "but I wouldn't expect it to. There are currently nearly three hundred thousand clinical trials progressing through various stages in fifty states and more than two hundred countries."

"Did you say *three hundred thousand*?"

No wonder the Clifton Clinic didn't register immediately for Arthur Noble, given that the FDA was involved in every one of those at some level. But he promised to check his records and get back to Harry with his findings.

We headed back to the Metro and then Union Station, so I could catch the next train back to Boston and then Cabot Cove. I wouldn't be getting home until almost midnight, meaning I'd be covering sixteen hours of travel for a single twenty-minute meeting. It hadn't produced much, besides educating me on the minutiae of the clinical-trial process, but I'd also opened a door that could prove crucial to figuring out how the pieces of the mysterious puzzle that was forming back home all fit together.

We were entering Union Station when I got a call from Seth Hazlitt.

"How's Washington?" he greeted.

"Hot as blazes."

"Not the usual sea breeze you're accustomed to up in these parts?"

"No breeze at all. The air just hangs there getting hotter and hotter."

"Next time an investigation takes you down there, better hope it's wintertime. I'll be at the station to pick you up when you get in."

"I didn't ask you to do that."

"Didn't have to, Jess. What are friends for? Mort and I flipped a coin for the honor."

"Who called it?"

"He did. Heads."

"I'd check that coin to make sure it's not heads on both sides. At least you don't call me Mrs. Fletcher."

"Mort start in on that again?"

"I thought I'd broken him of the habit. Maybe he makes an exception whenever we're investigating a murder."

"Which is pretty much all the time, isn't it?"

I moved to the ticket window, checking the schedule to find the next Boston-bound train left in only ten minutes.

"Was there something else you called me about, Seth?"

"Oh, yes, of course. I just got the autopsy report on Mimi Van Dorn."

"And?"

"Well, we've now identified the substance the tox screen couldn't, as if we needed another complication."

"What's that mean?"

"Ever heard of a drug called Benzipan?"

"No. Should I have?"

"Can't think of a reason why you would. Benzipan is the trade name for BEZ741. It acts on a crucial cellular pathway of the immune system, preventing cancerous tumors from reproducing themselves."

I froze and let the next person in line move before me to the ticket window that had just opened up. "Are you saying Mimi was being treated for cancer?"

"She didn't have cancer, as also confirmed by the autopsy, but she had a very high clinical level of Benzipan in her system, indicating she'd been taking it for some time."

"So if she didn't have cancer . . ."

"Right. If that doesn't beat all."

"This makes no sense, Seth."

"Neither did Mimi dying in the first place," he said, the bitterness lacing his voice telling me he was still grieving the loss of Mimi.

"Are you saying Charles Clifton was treating her for a disease she didn't have?"

"Now, Jess, no investigator worth his or her salt would make that claim without proof, but somebody was giving her Benzipan, and it wasn't me. That sure does make Clifton suspect number one."

"You tell Mort?"

"I did, and he reacted about the same as you did, 'cept I believe he put in a call to the force down in New York to see if he could get his old job back."

"He retired ten years ago."

"Sure did. Took him long enough, didn't it? I'll see you at the train station when you get in."

"It'll be too late, Seth."

"I'll take a nap. One thing good about having less patients these days is less phone calls once I get home."

"I'll call you more often."

"Don't bother. I've come to like the quiet. Gives me an idea what retirement will be like . . . or death."

"Which?"

"Same thing from my perspective."


"Benzipan," I said to Harry McGraw, as he walked me to the track after I'd finally gotten back in line and snared my ticket home.

"Benzi-*what*?"

"Some kind of newfangled cancer drug. Can you ask Arthur Noble about it when he calls you?"

"What makes you think he's going to call me at all? Be easier for him if he just forgot that meeting ever happened, the way you laid things out."

"You mean the truth?"

"Not everybody has the same regard for it that you do, Jess."

"Well, they don't know what they're missing. You'll mention Benzipan to Noble?"

"Sure. I'll just add it to your bill."

"Means a bigger tip."

"Right, what's twenty percent of nothing?" Harry asked, flashing that scowl.


Harry called me about the time the Amtrak train rumbled into Penn Station en route to Boston.

"I've got news, Jessica."

"Good or bad?"

"Well, Arthur Noble wouldn't give me the names of the drugs the Clifton Clinic is running trials on."

"Bad," I noted.

"Not exactly. He wouldn't give me the names because there aren't any."

I tried to make sense of what I was hearing. "Could you repeat that?"

"Sure, to pad my bill. According to the Food and Drug Administration, the Clifton Clinic isn't conducting a single clinical trial."

"You ask Noble about Benzipan?"

"He said it rang a bell somehow, but wasn't sure why. Said he'd check and get back to me."

"He say when?"

"The whole world doesn't move at the speed of Jessica."

"Maybe it should."

"You want to tell me what you've got yourself involved in this time?"

"Right now, Harry, I have no idea."

So I called Seth.

"You in the station already?" he greeted. "What'd you do, teleport from Washington?"

"Can you look up the side effects of Benzipan?" I asked him.

"Way ahead of you, Jess. I was saving it for a surprise."

"What?"

"Why don't we wait until later when I pick you up?"

"What's wrong with now?"

"Suit yourself," Seth sighed. "According to its manufacturer's warnings, among the side effects are seizures. And among those advised not to take the drug are those suffering spikes in their glucose levels."

"Diabetics, in other words. Even at Mimi's level?"

"She was type two, Jess, rapidly ascending to the promised land of insulin diabetes, regardless of her diet."

"She was cheating anyway," I said, recalling those sugar cookies I'd caught evidence of her eating.

"I suspected as much. I wonder if it was one of the reasons she left me for Clifton, since I was very firm in my insistence she needed to make radical changes to her diet and lifestyle to avoid pricking her finger and injecting insulin every day."

"What troubled you about her lifestyle, Seth?"

"Nothing you're not aware of already, and I prefer not to speak ill of the dead. But she was driven by shortcuts, and the more I think about it, the concerns you expressed over how she viewed her appearance are very well-founded. I'm worried she may have gone to extreme measures to fight back the effects of aging."

"Like what?" I asked him.

"Cosmetic surgery stretching well beyond the few minor dermatological procedures she'd had done. She started asking me a lot of questions about the side effects in her last office visits before she fired me."

"She didn't fire you, Seth."

"No? What would you call it, then?"

"Replaced."

"Same thing."

"A patient can't fire her doctor."

"No, she can betray him for another practice. Again, same thing."

"I have another question for you," I told him.

"To change the subject?"

"We've exhausted the subject. My question for you now, Dr. Hazlitt, is this: Benzipan is an approved drug, right?"

"It is indeed. Prescribed for the immunological treatment of certain cancers."

"So it couldn't be part of an ongoing clinical trial."

"Where are you going with this?" Seth asked.

"I'm not sure yet. It's just an oddity, an inconsistency I can't get out of my mind. Why would Mimi be taking a cancer drug if she didn't have cancer?"

"I only know one man who might be able to answer that question. Goes by the name of Charles Clifton, and I've asked Mort to arrest him."

"On what charge?"

"Stealing—my patients, specifically."

"You still going to pick me up at the station, Seth?"

"Of course, Jess, so we can continue this lovely conversation."

I started to nod off, fighting against the sleep I felt descending upon me, in order to continue trying to fit together the pieces of what I knew to be the truth before me.

That Mimi Van Dorn had suffered a seizure . . .

That the seizure had likely been brought on by her having taken a cancer drug even though she didn't have cancer . . .

That the beginning of her treatments at the Clifton Clinic closely coincided with her liquidating the trust paying for her son's desperately needed care . . .

That she was using an attorney who had rebuffed her son's request for representation after a still unexplained delay . . .

That she displayed all the symptoms of body dysmorphic disorder . . .

That she'd been murdered two nights ago in Cabot Cove Hospital's intensive care unit . . .

And the last person to see her had been Charles Clifton. . . .

With all those facts floating in thought bubbles over my head, the one I kept coming back to was the liquidation of that trust at the dire expense of Tripp Van Dorn's well-being. What kind of mother does that? I thought I knew Mimi well enough to believe her incapable of such a heinous act. And if that was the case, might I be missing something here, something that had forced Mimi to take such a desperate action? If she had been suffering from cancer and needed to pay out of pocket for a drug like Benzipan, everything would make some degree of sense. But she did not, in fact, have cancer, in which case it made no sense that the drug had shown up in her blood at all.

I felt myself falling asleep, unable to resist slumber's overtures any longer. Next thing I knew, I was being jarred awake in my train seat by the ringing of the phone still tucked in my bag, resting on the free seat next to me. I noticed it was from a blocked number but answered anyway.

"Hello?"

"Mrs. Fletcher, it's Tripp Van Dorn."

I cleared my throat. "Tripp, it's so nice to hear from you. I hope I didn't offend you too much with all my questions in our initial meeting."

"No, no, not at all."

There was something . . . off about his voice. He didn't sound drunk, wasn't slurring his speech or anything. I thought it might have something to do with his condition, or perhaps some of the medication he was on. But I couldn't put my finger on exactly what I was hearing.

"Anything but, in fact," Tripp continued. "You see, Mrs. Fletcher, I wasn't totally forthcoming in our meeting."

"No?"

"I'm surprised it slipped past you."

I was still fighting to chase the sleep from my mind. "Surprised what slipped past me, Tripp?"

He continued to ramble. I pictured him seated in his wheelchair by the window, even though it was night, speaking through the Bluetooth device clipped to his ear, perhaps eyeing the family photo hanging on the wall, which must have pictured his late mother.

"I've been reading your books for two solid days. Well, not really reading—listening to them. I'm already on my third, thanks to one of the aides here helping me download the MP3s on my phone. I'm surprised you missed the same thing everybody else has for so many years."

"What's that?"

"Not on the phone. We need to do this in person. That British guy who came with you, the chief inspector or something . . ."

"George Sutherland."

"He doesn't have any authority over here, does he?"

"No, only back home."

"Then you need to bring someone who does. I don't want to have to tell this story twice, Mrs. Fletcher."

The fog had finally cleared from my head. I wanted to ask more, but not too much for fear of scaring the young man off. "Does it have something to do with your mother?"

He laughed, the gesture lacking any semblance of true amusement. "Only everything."

The sharpness of his tone was hardly a surprise. Again, I forced myself not to push.

"When do you want me to come down, Tripp?"

"Would the morning be too soon?"

"Not for me, but I'll have to check with our Sheriff Metzger, the man in authority you requested. I don't think it'll be a problem."

"Good, because I can't wait any longer. I've waited too long already. I've been a fool for too long, Mrs. Fletcher. It's about time I smartened up."

"I think we can be at Good Shepherd by eleven o'clock, maybe even a bit earlier."

"I hate that name. Always makes me think of the dog."

"Eleven o'clock tomorrow morning, Tripp. I'll call you when we're on our way," I said, but he'd already hung up.

I clutched the phone in my hand for several moments after the call had ended, having finally identified what I was hearing in Tripp Van Dorn's voice:

Fear.

# Chapter Sixteen

Seth and I didn't talk much on the ride from the train station in Portland back to Cabot Cove. Exhaustion had finally gotten the better of me, and we'd pretty much said everything in our phone call earlier in the evening.

"How's Harry?" he did ask at one point, just making conversation, since he didn't know Harry McGraw that well.

"Harry's Harry. But his contact at the FDA revealed that, according to their records, the Clifton Clinic isn't currently holding any clinical trials."

"Did I just hear you right?"

"You did indeed, and I know—it makes no sense."

He glanced at me across the passenger seat. "George Sutherland came a long way thanks to a clinical trial they're offering."

"Not according to the FDA, Seth."

"No sense I can see in that. Clinical trials don't happen off the books, Jess. They're expensive and that's even before you get to the potential legal costs if something goes wrong. No reputable pharmaceutical outfit would even consider such a thing."

"I never thought much about the nuts and bolts of such trials."

"Just consider the number of staff you'd need to keep the paper trail intact and tabs on each and every study participant. Then there's the geographic logistics to these studies. For diversity and a wide choice of subjects, big metropolitan hospitals are almost always selected as hosts for clinical trials. Cabot Cove, obviously, doesn't fit that bill at all."

"You were stark in your criticism that the Clifton Clinic doesn't even reside in the town proper."

"Which puts it even farther from a reasonable center of population. You know what I'd do if I were you, Jess? I'd get a list of everyone enrolled in their clinical trials. Maybe many came from afar like George Sutherland."

"Hill House doesn't have near enough rooms to host that many patients."

"Makes you think, doesn't it?"

"Everything makes me think, Seth. Maybe I write as much as I do to distract myself from all those thoughts."

"And what are those thoughts telling you now?"

"That something's wrong here. That there are some things we're looking straight at but can't see yet. That everything we're dealing with is connected, but I can't see how."

Seth looked across the seat at me again, this time long enough for me to detect his smirk through the darkness, broken only by the lights dotting the freeway. "You mean 'yet,' don't you? Because you always end up seeing what you need to, so long as you remain patient."

"That's the thing this time," I told him. "I'm not sure George Sutherland has enough time left for me to be patient."

Loss affects everyone differently. Each one you suffer leaves you more determined not to take anything, and especially anyone, for granted. You start making more calls, fretting and worrying more, e-mailing just to check in, or getting together for lunch or dinner because you don't want to feel the regret, even guilt, you just experienced with the loss of someone else. I think we do such things out of the godlike belief that as long as we care and we're around, nothing bad can happen to a loved one or friend, as though death claims only those we've forgotten or neglected.

I think instinct steers us in that direction because it provides the impression that we're in control of our environment. The problem is the resolve wears off, sometimes in direct alignment with our grief. As it subsides, as we grow used to the loved one or friend being gone, those visits and calls to other friends and loved ones slowly diminish until we're back where we started, ready to repeat the process all over again the next time a call comes with the kind of news no one wants to hear.

I felt so comfortable when I was with George, the most comfortable I'd ever felt with any man outside of my husband, Frank. I'd lost Frank and, subconsciously, was afraid of losing George. So I hadn't stayed in touch nearly as much as I should have, because it was easier to forget what made me uneasy than remember what made me happy.

As luck would have it, George Sutherland was seated in the

Hill House lobby, reading a newspaper, when I entered after waving good-bye to Seth.

"Waiting up for me?" I asked lightly, taking the chair next to him.

"How'd you guess, dear lady?"

"So, how'd your day go?"

"Well, it turns out my test results indicate I'm an excellent candidate for the particular protocol the Clifton Clinic is testing."

"That's wonderful news," I said, even though my suspicions kept me from fully believing it.

"Too bad I couldn't enjoy it. You gave me an awful fright, my dear lady, disappearing for such a stretch, no doubt looking into the murder of your friend."

"Mimi's son, the young man we visited yesterday, called me this evening, by the way."

George's eyes scorned me. "Don't go changing the subject."

"I wasn't. You just reminded me that Mimi's son called and I wanted you to know about it."

"And what did the poor lad have to say?"

"I'm not sure. He asked to see me, so I thought I'd drive down with Mort in the morning."

"Replacing me on the case so fast, are you?"

"I think you have more important matters on your mind, George."

He smiled. "More important perhaps, but not nearly as much fun. Have I ever told you how much I enjoy our little adventures?"

"If you call solving murder little."

"You know what I mean."

"I think I do. I'm sorry for always showing you up."

"Hmmmmmm . . . From my recollection, I'm always holding back to give you a chance to catch up."

"That's because I've already lapped you and am closing in again."

He gave me a closer look, approvingly, I think, as he folded the newspaper and tucked it in his lap. "Well, you are in remarkable shape. All that bicycling and walking have done their wonders, and the sea air clearly agrees with you."

"It agrees with anyone, even more so when there aren't so many about to share it with."

"Me included?"

"Cabot Cove was nothing like this the last time you visited."

"That was over Thanksgiving, I believe. Far from your busy summer season. Must mean it's your turn next."

I managed a smile. "I was thinking of making a trip to Ireland, pay my respects to whatever's left of the MacGills," I said, speaking my maiden name for the first time in longer than I could remember.

"I could meet you there."

I reached out and took his hand. I half expected George to pull away for some reason, but he didn't. "If attitude is as important as most say it is, I give you a great prognosis."

"Nothing wrong with defying the odds."

I felt my stomach sink. "Why here, George, why the Clifton Clinic?"

"Because it's the only place in the world where this new drug is being tested. It's actually an enhanced version of a more well-known drug called Torimlisib, which is used to fight breast cancer. Turns out those nasty tumors of mine grow through the secretion of estrogen, of all things. This offshoot of Torimlisib blocks that secretion and starves the tumors in the process."

"Making them far less nasty."

"Thanks to the clever researchers at LGX Pharmaceuticals."

I hated the thought of what I knew I needed to say. His hand felt so good in mine I was tempted to leave things as they were and my hand where it was. But I couldn't, of course.

I pulled my hand from his, the gesture enough to tell him I had something on my mind before he got a look at my taut expression. "I need to share something with you, George."

"Uh-oh . . . Pertaining to the investigation, I suspect?"

"Pertaining to the Clifton Clinic. I was in Washington earlier today."

"I know. Sheriff Metzger told me."

"He probably didn't tell you I was visiting the Food and Drug Administration to educate myself on clinical trials."

George forced a smile. "You could have just asked me. I've become quite the expert on them myself."

"I'm sure you have. I was curious as to the general process and, specifically, how an institution as small and new as the Clifton Clinic could have landed trials for at least two drugs and maybe three."

"Well, there's me, of course, and you mentioned that dear librarian who recently passed. Who's the third?"

"Mimi, perhaps. The autopsy turned up a drug in her system normally used to fight cancer. Only Mimi didn't have cancer."

"Interesting."

"I was thinking suspicious," I couldn't stop myself from

saying. "You see, according to the FDA, none of these trials are actually being conducted at the Clifton Clinic, because no trials are."

George swallowed hard, his expression giving up nothing of what he might be thinking. "Any chance they might be wrong, Jessica?"

"This is the Food and Drug Administration, the government."

"I know. That's why I asked. Wouldn't that be the simplest solution, the one our fictional counterpart Mr. Sherlock Holmes would find himself considering?"

"Simplest doesn't make it the most accurate, George."

"What, then, my dear lady?"

"Did you discuss any of this with Charles Clifton?"

George laid the newspaper on the floor by his feet. "You mean, did he admit I was enrolled in an unregistered clinical trial?"

"Did you ask him how many other subjects are included in this particular trial or how those from earlier in the study have fared?"

"I don't believe he's allowed to share such proprietary information with me."

"Even though it would seem more proprietary to you than anyone else?"

He rose stiffly from his chair. "I think I better turn in. Long day tomorrow. I start treatment."

I joined him on my feet, looking up into his eyes, although he seemed a bit shorter than his six feet two inches. "I thought you should know, George. I had an obligation to tell you."

He took my shoulders in his hands. "And now you've done your duty, my dear lady, and can sleep easier because of it."

"Then Clifton made no mention, provided no inkling, that this trial was unregistered and thus, well, illegal. That he's treating you like a lab rat."

"Why, Jessica, all those chosen for clinical trials are lab rats. It's the nature of the beast."

"What about the illegal part?"

George looked deeply into my eyes. I expected any number of reactions from him in that moment, though not the one I got.

He took me in his arms and hugged me tight, his smile genuinely warm and inviting after we finally separated.

"That's what I love about you, Jessica. You have my back—you have everyone's back. Always looking out for someone else, even if it means sometimes looking in the wrong direction."

"And this is the wrong direction?"

"Would you mind doing an ill man a favor?"

"George," I started to protest.

"I apologize for playing that card, my dear lady. But I simply need you to let me answer your question and be done with it. Can you do that?"

"I'll try."

He nodded. "Yes, I knew I came here, to the Clifton Clinic, to take part in an unregistered clinical trial."

"But how could—"

George silenced me with two fingers against my lips. "You promised."

"No, I said I'd try."

He smiled again. "You need to try harder this time, Jessica, and leave me to my business."

Nothing's worse than lying restless and awake in bed, despite being exhausted. I blamed the bed, the noises coming through the open window, even the unfamiliar surroundings I'd been living in for months now, when the truth was I should have blamed myself. I had ruined a wonderful moment with a man I cared deeply about, taken his privacy from him and involved myself in a part of his life George Sutherland had every reason to want me excluded from. I'd forced him to share something he much preferred keeping to himself, and the price I paid for that was a restless night when I desperately needed a long, deep sleep.

I always have the most trouble falling asleep when I know I have to awaken early, in this case to call Mort with the news that Tripp Van Dorn wanted to see me and, thus, us. I had no idea what he had to tell us. . . . Needing to probe deeper, I replayed parts of our conversation in my mind, through my fitful night's rest, in search of something he'd said that might give me some notion as to the source of the fear I'd detected in his voice.

*I'm surprised it slipped past you.*

What had slipped past me? What was it Tripp Van Dorn knew that he was surprised I didn't know as well? Something about Mimi, perhaps, as suggested by an exchange from our last phone call:

*"Does it have something to do with your mother?"*

*"Only everything."*

He'd laughed as he said it, with no trace of amusement whatsoever.

There must've been more to what was going on here, more to the story, than even I'd anticipated. Clearly this indicated, not surprisingly, the level to which their relationship had deteriorated. I can only imagine what Tripp must've felt upon learning that the trust fund ensuring his care, the one truly stable element of his tragic life, was gone. Certainly it would be cause for considerable angst that could end the relationship between mother and son forever. Something was starting to occur to me on that front, something connected to my strained conversation with George Sutherland the night before. It was just starting to form, and I didn't push for fear of losing the tighter focus I so needed right now.

Which brought me to the last part of my conversation with Tripp Van Dorn, which came at me like an itch I couldn't reach.

*I can't wait any longer. I've waited too long already. I've been a fool for too long, Mrs. Fletcher. It's about time I smartened up.*

I tried to recall his precise tone as he'd said that. *Determined* was the first word that came to mind, as if there was something he should've dealt with long before but had not. Because he had "smartened up," as Tripp had put it. And what exactly made him feel like he'd been a fool?

There must be some secret, something shared only by mother and son, that might answer those questions.

When it reached eight o'clock, with the summer sun streaming through my Hill House window, I figured it was finally time to give Mort a call and alert him to the day's plans.

"Mrs. Fletcher," he greeted, "I was just going to call you."

"'Mrs. Fletcher' again? Really, Mort?"

"Just trying to recapture simpler times."

"We'll have plenty of time to do that in the car. Hope you're up for a road trip, because we're meeting with Tripp Van Dorn, who sounds like he's got quite a story to tell."

"Well, Jessica, you can consider the meeting canceled," Mort said in his official voice. "I just learned Tripp Van Dorn was found dead this morning."

# Chapter Seventeen

The police cars were still rimming the stately Good Shepherd Manor in force when Mort and I arrived, equally mixed between the Newburyport town police and the Massachusetts State Police, a few with their lights still churning.

A state trooper, who looked big enough to be a pro football player, manning the entrance denied us entry at first, fortunately not asking for my name or reason for being there. He radioed a superior who was overseeing the potential crime scene and, after reciting the explanation behind Sheriff Metzger's presence, received permission for Mort to come upstairs. I followed along sheepishly, waiting for the officer to call out something like "Just a moment there," or "Where do you think you're going?" but he never did.

A state police captain whose name tag identified him as Barnes met us in the hallway a bit down from Tripp's room, where all the activity was centered, discomfiting me with a harsh stare focused my way.

"Sheriff Metzger, please tell me this isn't who I think it is."

"In the flesh, Captain, and well acquainted enough with the victim to potentially be of substantial assistance to the case."

"At this point, Sheriff," Barnes said, his gaze continuing to focus on me, "there is no case and Tripp Van Dorn is only the deceased, not a victim. Our preliminary assessment is that his death was due to suicide."

"Would you mind if we took a look, Captain?" I asked quietly. "You see, I was very close with the young man's mother, who also recently passed. If nothing else, I can formally identify the body in her absence."

Barnes looked at Mort, then nodded to both of us, a single nod. "Just to ID the body, so we're clear on that."

"We are," I said.

"She is," Mort followed.

Inside the room, Tripp Van Dorn had maneuvered his wheelchair so that his face was pressed flush against the sheer curtain inside the open drapes. The television was still on, tuned to a movie station with the sound muted, making me wonder what the last thing Tripp had watched might have been, and if that had had anything to do with him rolling his wheelchair against the window on an angle that pressed the sheer curtain against his face. At that point, his breath acted like glue in pinning the material to his nose and mouth, ultimately suffocating him.

"I've got to admit," Barnes was saying, "I've never seen anything quite like this before."

There were five others squeezed into the room, two uniformed officers from Newburyport and three state police crime-scene techs measuring distances and taking samples of pretty much everything, whether innocuous or not.

"According to the log," Barnes resumed, "a night nurse had given him a sleeping drug just after midnight when he couldn't sleep. She found him this way four hours later on her rounds."

"You think he requested it to facilitate the process, make it harder to change his mind," I presumed.

"Until something suggests otherwise."

Tripp's body was canted forward, so the back of his head was no longer flush against the headrest, which I remembered had been supporting it during my first visit here with George Sutherland instead of Mort in tow. The walls on both sides of the window were bare, leaving him nothing to gaze at while he took his final breaths, other than whatever might've been outside at the time.

"How do you see it, Sheriff Metzger?"

"Well, Mrs. Fletcher," he started, a glint flashing in his eyes, "it looks to me like he drove his chair forward with as much speed as he could muster. You can see the footrests riding the radiator down low. That's what stopped his chair and when it did, it rocked his face forward into the curtain."

"Exactly his plan from where I'm standing," Barnes agreed.

The lack of a comment from the two crime-scene techs working the body and the general area confirmed they were in agreement on that general scenario as well.

"Sorry you wasted a trip, Mrs. Fletcher," Barnes continued, rather smugly. "But not every death is a murder."

"I'm sorry, Captain, but I still have my doubts about this one."

"And why's that?"

"Well, for starters, Mr. Van Dorn phoned me just a few hours before his death. We made an appointment to meet this morning at his insistence, because he had something vital he wanted to share with me—potentially related to his mother's death," I added for effect more than anything. "It seems strange that he would have taken his life under those circumstances."

"As opposed to just changing his mind, you mean."

"The captain has a point, Jessica," Mort chimed in. "It could very well be that the young man decided not to bother with this meeting. Maybe whatever he wanted to discuss pushed him over the edge. So he called for a sleeping pill and staged his own death."

"At first glance, that's almost surely what happened," I agreed. "At the very least, the most logical solution."

"She said 'at first glance,'" Barnes noted to Mort.

"And she said 'for starters' before," Mort added.

"Because, gentlemen," I told them both, "I don't believe Tripp Van Dorn committed suicide. I believe he was murdered."

No one in the room, including Mort and Captain Barnes, argued my point or asked me why. They just went silent, affording me the opportunity to continue.

I looked toward the crime-scene techs. "Did you or anyone else to your knowledge examine or disturb the back of the young man's head?"

The two techs, a man and a woman, looked at each other and then shook their heads.

"No, ma'am," the man said.

"No," the woman followed.

"I'm not sure what you're referring to, Mrs. Fletcher," Barnes said.

He crouched slightly as he moved closer to Tripp Van Dorn's body to better examine the rear of his scalp.

"There's no disturbance in his hair," Barnes resumed. "No marks or depression of any kind suggesting someone had forced him up against the sheer curtain and then pressed his face against it."

"That's exactly the point, Captain," I observed. "There's no depression or mark of any kind, even though there should be."

Mort and Barnes exchanged a glance, Mort's being one of wry understanding, while Barnes had narrowed his gaze upon me.

"What am I missing here?" he asked.

"Nothing, because what we should be seeing isn't there."

I pointed toward the back of Tripp Van Dorn's head, draped in a mane of thick, long hair, careful not to draw close enough to disturb anything with an accidental touch.

"When I was here two days ago, I noticed the young man's head rested flush against this headrest here," I continued, pointing that out as well. "So at the very least, there should be a depression consistent with that mold. The fact that there isn't suggests someone, the killer, smoothed the hair back into place to hide a different depression resulting from his hand forcing Tripp Van Dorn's face against the sheer curtain, which I believe, effectively, was the murder weapon. Captain Barnes, I believe if you have your medical examiner do a thorough examination of the back of the young man's scalp, he'll find bruising consistent with his head being held in place for several moments."

Barnes turned to Mort. "Does she come up with these conclusions a lot?"

"Oh, yes. More than you care to know."

"And do they usually turn out to be well-founded?"

"Almost always."

"So how is it you still have a job?" Barnes shook his head, turning back my way. "I don't suppose you have a notion as to the identity of the killer, Mrs. Fletcher."

"Not yet, Captain. I don't want your job to end up in jeopardy, too."

Good Shepherd Manor had an exterior security camera but none inside, to create a more comfortable, homey feel for its residents and avoid the sense of institutional living. The medical examiner's cursory inspection estimated the time of death to be in approximately a ninety-minute window between midnight and one thirty, the body having been found just after four a.m.

"How'd Good Shepherd know to call you?" I asked Mort, while we lingered outside Tripp Van Dorn's room, pondering our next move.

"Either the state or Newburyport police must have noted your name and Cabot Cove address on the guest sign-in sheet from two days ago. By all indications, you and George Sutherland were the young man's last visitors."

"Save for one," I noted, drawing a grim nod from Mort.

"Anyway, they reached out to me as a matter of course, doing exactly what I would've done in their shoes."

"Meaning they considered me a possible suspect."

"Until I explained the reason for your visit."

"How'd you do that?"

"With the truth, that you were friends with the young man's mother, who'd recently died."

"And you left it there?"

"For now, because there was no point in raising the rest of this yet. I might have still been on the phone if I'd tried to bring them up to date on the entire case."

Mort was right. Between the potential involvement of Charles Clifton in Mimi's death, the duplicitous lawyer Fred Cooper, and these clinical trials the Clifton Clinic was somehow conducting off the books, we had a lot of pieces, but nothing that added up yet. No way the Massachusetts authorities would've been able to make any sense of it all, and Cabot Cove was well out of their jurisdiction anyway.

"I'll bring Captain Barnes up to date when we have something to update him with that's relevant to his case."

"'When,'" I repeated, "as opposed to 'if.'"

"Do you really have any doubts to that effect, Mrs. Fletcher?"

I rolled my eyes. "There you go again . . . Sheriff."

"I like when you call me Sheriff," Mort said, as we made our way back to the lobby. "Reminds me you know who's in charge."

"Well, you did drive here."

"Next time we can fly, so you can drive me."

"I was thinking about giving you a ride on my bicycle."

"Best way to negotiate Cabot Cove traffic this time of year," he noted. "Little did you know that the lack of a driver's license was going to make you a trendsetter."

We reached the bottom of the ornate staircase that climbed through the three levels of Good Shepherd Manor.

"What does it mean that the security camera picked up no visitors coming or going since eight o'clock, around five hours before Tripp Van Dorn was murdered?"

"That his killer was either an employee already inside or someone familiar with the placement of all three cameras."

"Leaving one means of access unmonitored."

"My thoughts exactly, Mrs. Fletcher. What say we take a look?"


There was no sign of forced entry, or any entry at all, on the door in question. It was a fire door to be used only in the event of emergencies and would have triggered an alarm had it been jarred open. That left any number of first-floor windows. Mort fit a pair of plastic gloves over his hands and tried all the ones out of the cameras' reach, finding two unlocked.

He made a note of which ones they were in his magical memo pad. "I'll let Barnes know these should be checked for fingerprints and DNA samples."

"Expect the killer to have left either?"

"You never know."

"But here's something we do know: Chances are he knew this building well, from past visits perhaps, even regular ones."

"Visits to the late Tripp Van Dorn?"

"That's what I'm thinking, Mort, meaning he was likely well acquainted with his killer."

He jotted down another note. "Another job for Barnes. I'll ask him to send us his findings. Anything else?"

"Yes, I'm missing something."

"What?"

"If I knew what it was, I wouldn't be missing it. Something about Tripp's room I can't quite put my finger on . . . But there is something else I *can* put my finger on."

"What's that, Mrs. Fletcher?"

"When he called me last night, he was scared."

"Care to be more specific?"

"Hard to do that when it's a tone, a feeling."

"Instinct, then."

"I suppose so, yes, Mort."

"How exactly did you learn to see and hear things nobody else seems to notice, Jessica?"

"My ancestors came here from Ireland, toting any number of family legends along for the ride. One of those was a string of my great-great-aunts and grandmothers who had what they called 'the Gift,' referring to an intuitive sense."

"You mean like psychics?"

"Something like that." I nodded. "Though the nearest I ever came to that was doing palm readings at the Harrison College Fall Festival for my sorority. Surprised myself how often I got things right without really trying."

"Ever solve any murders in that sorority?"

"Fortunately, I never had the opportunity. But I did use Delta Alpha Chi as the setting for one in a book."

"*The Corpse That Wasn't There*," Mort said casually.

I shook my head. "Another sleepless night?"

"Several of them. I figure since it's usually your fault I'm awake, the least you can do is help me to fall asleep." His expression flattened again. "Getting back to the late Mr. Van Dorn, you didn't push the issue of what was scaring him any further?"

"I saw no reason to, given that I thought I'd be seeing Tripp this morning."

"Well, you saw him, all right," Mort said, and narrowed his gaze on me. "You do that a lot, you know."

"Do what?"

"Refer to victims by their first names. You do that in your books, too."

"So you have been reading me!"

"Like I said, only when I can't sleep," he said.

"It makes feel closer to them," I explained. "Gives me more of a reason to catch their killers."

"Makes sense. And how do you intend to catch this one, Mrs. Fletcher?"

"As far as Tripp's concerned, all this goes back to the car accident in Marblehead that put him in that wheelchair. We're already halfway there, Mort. You up for a drive farther south?"

"Guess that answers my question."

# Chapter Eighteen

"This is where the crash happened," Marblehead chief of police Tom Grimes told us. "I was a patrolman at the time and reviewed the report after you called and can tell you the investigative team determined he lost control of his car, one of those Mialta convertibles, back maybe a quarter mile."

"Miata," Mort corrected. "My wife had one once."

"Well," said Grimes, "I hope she's okay."

Tripp Van Dorn had grown up just a few miles from where we were standing, in a seaside cottage on Goldthwait Road in the tony town of Marblehead, located on the northern shore of Massachusetts. Then and now, it boasted a population of twenty thousand, although, like Cabot Cove, it encountered more than its share of summertime traffic, though Tripp's accident must have occurred sometime in the spring.

Of course, I hadn't met Mimi yet, so I knew their home only

from her description of a sprawling, five-thousand-square-foot home she modestly classified as a "cottage." I'll never know. A holdover, I suppose, from the Gilded Age, when the rich who'd made their original fortunes as industrialists built these massive so-called cottages as testaments to their wealth. Any number of them even today were occupied only in the summer by Boston Brahmins or New York hedge fund managers who'd driven up home prices in Marblehead just as they had in Cabot Cove.

Chief Grimes stood between Mort and me at the corner of Ocean Avenue and Beach Street just short of what locals referred to as the Causeway.

"It was raining that night, so the road was slick," Grimes continued. "Young Mr. Van Dorn took that corner back there way too fast, and by the time his Mialta stopped here, it had rolled an estimated three or four times."

"Was alcohol involved?" Mort asked.

"The victim was in no condition to be Breathalyzed. I seem to recall an elevated level in a blood test, but the former chief didn't press things, since he figured the young man had suffered enough. Van Dorn was medevaced to Massachusetts General Hospital, where they were able to save his life. Not much they could do about the severed spinal cord, though. He lasted more than many in that condition, I suppose. How'd he die again?"

"It's still under investigation, but a probable suicide."

Grimes let his gaze linger on me before moving back to Mort. "So was it the suicide that brought you all the way down here, or the investigation, Sheriff?"

"Combination of both. Mrs. Fletcher here was well acquainted with the young man's mother, who also died recently under mysterious circumstances. Two of us thought the night of the crash might provide some clues."

Grimes scratched at his scalp through his thinning hair. "Well, I made a copy of the report for you. First time I've ever actually seen it myself. The chief then, the man I replaced, Alvin McCandless, was a hands-on guy, known for protecting the interests of our residents."

"I believe Alvin was finishing up his career here just as I was starting out in Cabot Cove," Mort noted. "Could command a room, as I recall."

"Could he ever! Big Al was a character, all right. Old-fashioned cop who knew how to keep a lid on things. He used to tell me, 'Tommy, we're here to look out for people, not bust their chops.' Back when he was a patrolman, Big Al was known for putting kids suspected of DUI in the back of his squad car and putting the fear of God in them before driving them home. Wasn't one of them who didn't stumble through his or her front door in tears, but thanking their lucky stars it had been him who pulled them over. Yup, he was a legend in this town for sure. Hell, he might still be chief if not for . . ."

"For what?" I coaxed, when Grimes's voice tailed off.

"He boxed Golden Gloves, won some trophies, and went pro for a time. But it took its toll and by fifty he was diagnosed with early dementia. Big Al's still alive today—what's left of him anyway—living at one of those memory-care centers for Alzheimer's patients. I visit him whenever I can. Some days he knows me. Most days he doesn't. But his memory of cases resurfaces from time to time with surprising clarity. Doesn't recognize a single family member from one day to the next, including his kids and grandkids, but he can tell you all about some bar brawl he broke up or that riot act he read to some celebrity he caught snorting coke in the front seat of his car, like they happened yesterday. Go figure."

Grimes stopped there and scanned the intersection, as if he expected Alvin McCandless to emerge from his cruiser.

"Anyway, as I recall," he continued, "Big Al took charge of the scene himself and buttoned things up the way he always did when locals were involved. We could never get away with some such today, too many rules and regulations, too much paperwork to fill out. But back then Big Al's word in this town was law. Nobody questioned him because he kept the riffraff out and knew how to have a resident's back. Just about everyone in Marblehead was in his debt at one time or another, but he wasn't the sort to call those debts in. He took me aside one day and said, 'Tommy, you know how you can tell when you're doing a good job? When folks smile at you and call you by your first name.' Yup, Big Al was old-school, all right."

"Anything else you remember from the night of the accident, Chief?"

He scratched at his scalp again, his uniform fitting a little too snugly, the pants looking like they were going to split at the seams. "Well, the chief had me drive the victim's mother to Mass General, once we got word that's where he was being taken. What was her name, Missy or something?"

"Mimi," I elaborated.

"Anyway, she didn't say much to me, nothing really. Rode in the back of my squad, talking on her cell phone much of the time. Couldn't say to who, though it seemed strange under the circumstances."

"Could you hear what she was saying?"

"It wasn't my business to. The same storm that had soaked the roads was plenty loud, and what I could hear didn't really register, except for the fact that she did an awful lot of talking and not much listening. I remember her hanging up just as we reached Mass General. Opened the door and disappeared inside without saying a word to me, even a thank-you. I guess she was in shock. I've heard it can manifest itself with just that kind of detachment. Go figure," he said again.

"Did Chief McCandless ever say anything else about that night?"

"Not a word," Grimes told us. "Like I said, he kept things buttoned up tight. Besides, it was pretty clear-cut. Accident on a rainy night with a single victim, nonfatal. Even the local paper didn't have much to say beyond that. I included the article in that case file I copied for you. Not that there's anything in it I haven't told you already."

"Anyone else from back then still with the department?" I asked him.

"Nope, just me. Everybody else has moved on to greener or more exciting pastures than what Marblehead has to offer. These days I got my share of officers like your sheriff here, looking for a second career after the first one nearly burned them out. They may not have Big Al's chops, but they know there's still a way we do things here likely different from where they came from." Grimes shook his head, scratching at his scalp yet again. "I guess the Van Dorn boy went as far as he could with what the accident had left him. If it was me, I'm thinking it would've happened sooner. You think it was his mother's death that spurred him to do it?"

"That would be a logical assumption."

"What was it that got her?"

"Seizure," Mort said before I could chime in.

"Well," Grimes resumed, "at least you didn't have to worry about murder, in her case."

"Anything?" Mort asked me as I continued scanning the contents of the case file encompassing the night of the accident.

"Nothing that tells us anything more than the chief did."

"Seems like a thorough man."

"I thought you were going to ask him if he was hiring."

"It did cross my mind, Mrs. Fletcher. But I couldn't bear the thought of subjecting my successor to Cabot Cove's murder rate. Maybe we should advertise those numbers to deter more of the influx from moving in. Who wants to get murdered, after all?"

"When it comes to beachfront property, that's just another of the risks you take," I told him.

The contents of the file folder were all boilerplate, from the crime-scene reports and photos to the accident depictions, to the individual incident reports from all public safety personnel—fire, rescue, and police—who had responded to the scene. The rescuers had had to employ the Jaws of Life to get Tripp Van Dorn from the crushed car, only to learn he'd been crushed, too.

We drove past the former Van Dorn home on Goldthwait Road on our way out of town. Marblehead offered a distinctly different atmosphere from Cabot Cove, more upscale, lacking the layers of hardscrabble fishermen who still populated our docks, given our heritage as a working-class village as opposed to a tony Boston suburb. We clung to our roots, holding on with our fingernails against the determined efforts of progress to move us in a different direction. That's what made the invasion of chain stores and trendy shops replacing the old staples of Main Street so disconcerting. There wasn't much left besides the bookstore, the pharmacy, and the hardware store, and I knew locals made a conscious effort to give those as much business as possible to avoid their suffering the same fate as their former neighbors. I think that's what I enjoyed so much about the Friends of the Library, our role not just to support the old-fashioned wonder of books but also to uphold the traditions of our town.

"Who do you suppose Mimi was talking to in that drive to Mass General with Tom Grimes driving his squad car?" I asked, when we were finally on our way back home.

"Haven't got a clue," Mort told me. "Seems strange, though, doesn't it?"

I tried to reconcile that with a woman I'd considered a close friend yet knew so little about.

"As a matter of fact," he continued, "maybe you should think about making Marblehead your second home. I'm sure Chief Grimes would love to have you."

I was about to comment on Mort's suggestion when something struck me like a lightning bolt, something I seemed to recall about the lawyer Fred Cooper's online profile. I traded the case file from Tripp Van Dorn's car accident for my phone and pressed the Internet icon, googling Cooper again to find what I was looking for.

"Mort, turn the car around!" I said, once I was looking at his profile again.

"Huh?"

"We need to go back to Marblehead. I've got some more questions for Chief Grimes."

We found him in his office, seeming a bit perturbed by our sudden return when he greeted us.

"Hope this won't take so long," he said, offering us the two chairs set before his desk. "I need to be somewhere else in an hour."

"It shouldn't," I said. "I just have a few questions."

"*You* have a few questions?"

Grimes looked toward Mort, who could only shrug. "Welcome to my world, Chief."

The Marblehead Police Department was headquartered on Gerry Street in one of the best-looking buildings of its kind I'd ever seen: both modern and functional in design, featuring plenty of windows, and dominated by a curved entrance with checkerboard glass panes running above and alongside the entry doors. The chief's office offered a view of the American flag flapping in the stiff breeze beyond.

"Proceed, Mrs. Fletcher," Grimes said, frowning.

"Did I mention a lawyer named Fred Cooper when we spoke earlier?"

"I don't believe so, no."

"Mr. Cooper was representing Mimi Van Dorn's interests when he was approached by Tripp Van Dorn about possible representation in a complaint against his mother."

Grimes leaned forward. "I don't believe you mentioned that either," he said, turning toward Mort. "Either of you."

"We didn't want to take up any more of your time than was

necessary. The point is, according to an online profile I found, Fred Cooper comes from here—Marblehead."

"I don't think I've heard the name. . . ."

"No families named Cooper?"

"None of the ones I know have anyone named Fred in them."

"Would it be possible to check?"

At first it looked like he might decline my request, but then he settled in behind his computer, tapping away for a few moments, then eyeing the screen before looking across the desk back at me.

"No Fred Cooper anywhere in any town database, and I have access to them all."

"Even going back a few years?"

"How many?"

"I'm not sure. Cooper's profile listed him as thirty-three."

Grimes's eyes widened. "You want me to go back thirty-three years?"

"I was thinking just birth records."

"They're not included in my database."

"School records, then. Are you able to access school records?"

Grimes went back to his keyboard. It took longer to get a result this time.

"Sorry, Mrs. Fletcher, no one by the name of Fred Cooper was enrolled at any of Marblehead's schools for the past twenty-five years."

I looked toward Mort, the apparent inconsistency not seeming to matter as much to him.

"What is it you're after here, Mrs. Fletcher?" Grimes asked me.

"I don't believe in coincidence, Chief."

"Neither did Sherlock Holmes, as I recall. Do you fancy yourself an amateur Sherlock Holmes?"

"More like Arthur Conan Doyle, but that's a bit of a stretch." I leaned forward in my wooden armchair. "Mimi and Tripp Van Dorn, mother and son, died within forty-eight hours of each other, and Fred Cooper was connected to both of them. The fact that his hometown is listed as Marblehead suggests that connection may go back longer than Cooper's tenure in Cabot Cove."

At which point I swung toward Mort. "When did Cooper open his office?"

"Can't say for sure. Let's see. . . . When I took over from Amos as sheriff, there was an accountant upstairs there. Leo Grunwald was his name. I don't remember who came after Grunwald, but Cooper came after them, at least five years ago."

"Maybe more?"

"Maybe, one or two anyway."

"Are we finished here?" Grimes said, rising impatiently behind his desk.

"I'm sorry, Chief," I told him. "I tend to go off on tangents sometimes."

"Really? I hadn't noticed."

I extended my hand across the desk. "Sorry for the intrusion. Thank you for your time."

"You let me know how it all turns out," he said, gaze rotating between Mort and me.

Then it settled just on me, as Grimes shook his head. "I think I'll take Cabot Cove off my vacation list, Sheriff."

"Good idea, Chief."

\* \* \*

Mort had parked his SUV in the sun, so it was scorching hot when we climbed back inside.

"I can't make sense of any of this," he said, firing up the air-conditioning. "Why would someone bother murdering a quadriplegic?"

"He might've been bound to a wheelchair," I said, "but he could still talk."

"Too bad he didn't live long enough to tell you what had him so spooked."

"Whatever it was almost certainly explains why someone would bother murdering him," I said as my cell phone rang, HARRY lighting up on my screen.

"Where are you?" he greeted me.

"Not New York."

"And not Cabot Cove either, which is where I am. When do you plan on getting back? Because I've got some information I want to deliver in person."

# Chapter Nineteen

Harry McGraw was waiting when Mort and I stepped through the door of Mara's Luncheonette four hours later. He rose, looking more rumpled than usual and flashing a deeper scowl.

"Two of you took your sweet time getting back here. You'd think I had nothing better to do."

"Do you?" I asked him.

"No, but that's not the point. And, by the way, this place needs a better variety of pies."

"Did you try the daily special?"

"They were out. Had some of yesterday's special left, but seemed peeved when I asked for tomorrow's instead. Nice to see you again, Mort," Harry said, retaking his chair as Mort took the one across from him, leaving me in the middle.

"You, too, Harry."

"Who's she got you chasing today?"

"Ghosts, in more ways than one."

"Just another day at the office, then."

"Harry," I started, "Mimi Van Dorn's son was murdered last night."

"You think he was murdered, or he was murdered? Never mind—they're the same thing, aren't they? And that's kind of what brought me here, the kid's mother anyway."

"You found something?"

"My friend at the FDA did, after I asked him about the drug that may have killed her."

"Benzipan," I elaborated, having forgotten I'd even asked Harry to see if he could look into it with Arthur Noble. "The cancer drug."

"Well, turns out it's not just a cancer drug, my dear Jessica. According to Noble, Benzipan has also demonstrated—anecdotally, he said—some pretty remarkable antiaging effects."

"How so?"

Harry fished through his jacket pocket and came up with a clump of papers he proceeded to separate and page through in search of the one he was looking for.

"Nope, that's not it."

Another.

"That's not it either."

A few joined the growing pile.

"Where is it? . . . Ah, yup, here we go." He cleared his throat. "According to Noble, Benzipan is something called a TORC1 inhibitor, which is known to affect a crucial cellular pathway that plays a role in the immune system and other biological functions. Well, also according to Noble, it turns out some of the cancer patients taking it exhibited some dramatic reversals of what he called the normal effects of aging. He didn't get specific beyond that, but did mention laboratory studies with mice, rats, geese, or something had showed real promise, as demonstrated in the process that predates the clinical research stage."

"So did the manufacturer apply for a clinical trial?"

There was that scowl again. "You think I'd drive all this way to tell you something obvious? No, I drove all this way because the manufacturer never filed a request to have Benzipan formally tested for its potential antiaging properties. I drove all this way because you told me the autopsy on your friend Missy—"

"Mimi."

"—showed concentrations of the drug in her system, even though she didn't have cancer. Which got me thinking what else might she have been taking it for." He settled back in his chair and interlaced his fingers behind his head. "You can thank me by getting your friends here to get me a piece of tomorrow's special."

"I think you'll have to wait until tomorrow, Harry."

I heard myself say that as if someone else had spoken the words. Seth Hazlitt and I had discussed the likelihood of Mimi Van Dorn suffering from body dysmorphic disorder, explaining her obsession with looking, and acting, younger than her years. Certainly, an antiaging drug with the potential shown by Benzipan would've excited her no end, and it seemed equally certain that she would've done anything, under the circumstances, to get it, including break the financial trust her son, Tripp, had been relying on for the care he'd be receiving for the rest of his life.

I could feel the pieces falling together, but still couldn't grasp the entirety of the picture they revealed. Why would someone murder Tripp Van Dorn? I was still missing something here, missing plenty, which made me think back to those bare walls in Tripp's Good Shepherd Manor room, having no idea why my mind kept showing me that image.

"You know they got this place in Texas, a town called Marble Falls," I heard Harry saying, "where they have Pie Happy Hour every day, two slices for the price of one. Why can't they do that here?"

"What's the difference if they've already run out?" I said, breaking off my train of thought.

"Wishful thinking, I guess," he groused, laying his hands back on the table.

"What's the name of the company that makes Benzipan?"

"LGX Pharmaceuticals," Harry answered.


The same company that made Torimlisib, the drug to be administered to George Sutherland at the Clifton Clinic!

As part of a clinical trial that the FDA had no record of, because according to their records, the Clifton Clinic wasn't conducting any clinical trials or approved to do so.

*Mimi . . .*

Had I even known her? I guess not, guess we shared nothing other than card games and an occasional meal. I considered her a friend, a close one even, and I could never have suspected any of this about her.

"I don't like that look, Mrs. Fletcher," Mort said sternly.

"What look?"

"The one that makes me warn you to stay away from Charles Clifton and the Clifton Clinic."

"Oh, that look . . ."

"I'm serious, Jessica."

"You made your point, Mort."

"Doesn't mean I won't lock you up to prevent you from becoming an accessory to murder."

"And to just whose murder would I be an accessory?"

"Your own."

# Chapter Twenty

"You forget to tell the good sheriff something, my dear?" Harry asked me, after Mort had taken his leave to get, he claimed, some real work done.

"Did I?"

"I saw your face light up when I mentioned LGX Pharmaceuticals, girl."

"Girl?"

"Figure of speech."

"Oh, is that what it is?"

"Don't change the subject, and spill the beans."

"My friend George Sutherland . . ."

"Ah, yes, the chap from Scotland Yard," Harry said, in the worst British accent I'd ever heard.

"He's here being treated for a rare form of cancer."

"Don't tell me: at the Clifton Clinic."

I nodded.

"As part of another clinical trial that doesn't exist."

I nodded again.

"LGX Pharmaceuticals is based in Rhode Island, Jessica," Harry said, checking his watch. "Too late to drive there now. What say I stay overnight and we set out fresh in the morning?"

I stood up and Harry rose stiffly in my wake. "Where to now?"

"I think I'll take a walk, Harry, while you see if Hill House has any rooms available."

"I already checked in. Got the last room. Want to make sure I'm good and rested for our drive to Providence tomorrow."

"You were using Uber last time when I was in New York."

"I rented a car for the occasion," Harry told me. "Good thing I'm getting free miles."

"Hope you wrangled an upgrade."

"Hey, it's your dime."

"Good," I said, "then you can give me a lift to the Clifton Clinic."

Harry scowled at me. "Bad idea, in case I didn't make that clear."

"George Sutherland started treatment today. I just want to see how he's doing."

Harry agreed, on the condition he got to wait for me in the car. My head was swimming, as I was having difficulty keeping hold of all I had learned. I thought I might have been pursuing two separate investigations, but now I believed they were intrinsically connected, with the Clifton Clinic being the key.

"You can't park here," I warned him after he'd parked in a tow zone flush against the entrance.

"What's the worst they can do?"

"Tow you."

"But I'm not leaving the car."

"Tow it with you still inside, then."

"Do that and they'll be facing the wrath of a truly higher power."

"The Almighty?"

"No, Hertz. You don't want to mess with them."

A polite receptionist greeted me inside and looked up George Sutherland's info on her computer. Then she handed me a pass and summoned a uniformed security guard to escort me up to the fourth floor, where George currently was.

One thing for sure was that Charles Clifton had spared no expense in constructing the flagship facility of Clifton Care Partners. All the furnishings were clearly top-of-the-line and state-of-the-art, as upscale as any medical facility I'd ever seen.

I was issued not a physical ID card but an electronic chip containing all the information the receptionist had entered. The chip was fitted inside a black housing I wore dangling from my neck.

The fourth floor contained a slew of what could only be individual treatment rooms or suites in which patients received their drugs amid an assortment of luxury furnishings, which included a flat-screen television and a sitting area constructed to make their friends or family members as comfortable as possible while they endured however long the treatment procedure took. Most of the doors on the hall were open, the closed ones likely indicating that treatment was under way at this time.

The security guard stopped before one of these closed doors and knocked before waving his key card before a colored grid, which flashed from red to green as the door clicked open. He opened it slowly, poking his head in.

"Mr. Sutherland, I have Mrs. Fletcher here to see you."

"Well, send her in," I heard George's voice call.

I entered and closed the door behind me.

"How nice of you to stop by, Jessica," George said to me.

He was seated in a plush leather reclining chair, facing a television tuned to the BBC America, no drugs, IV poles, or anything of the sort anywhere in evidence.

George read my mind. "Came down with a fever. Probably just a touch of the flu or something, and they can't start treatment until I'm back to normal."

"The guard addressed you as 'Mr.' instead of 'Chief Inspector.'"

"Because in America, 'Mr.' is all I am, my dear lady."

"You've solved more than your share of crimes in Cabot Cove, George."

"But we're not in Cabot Cove, are we. Not technically anyway."

"I suppose not."

I'd fully intended to stop in just to check on George's well-being. But now that I was here, and there was really no well-being to check up on, I couldn't help myself.

"Would you mind terribly if I reverted to form for a moment?" I asked him.

He flashed a smile identical to the one that had left me smitten in our first meeting back at author Marjorie Ainsworth's English manor house. "Since when are you not in form, Jessica? I've only known you to have a single mode."

"And right now that mode begs the question, how much do you know about the Clifton Clinic?"

"That it can save my life."

"That's all?"

"It's enough," he said tersely.

"Thanks to a clinical trial for this drug that's already being prescribed to treat several other cancers."

George nodded. "Where are you going with this?"

"According to the Food and Drug Administration, there is no clinical trial—not for Torimlisib or any other, including the one I have strong reason to believe Mimi Van Dorn was receiving."

George regarded me disdainfully. "Now I see what you meant about reverting to form. I guess I should have said I did mind, because I do. I do mind you making me a part of your latest investigation."

"I didn't make you a part of it; you already were. And there's something else I wanted to tell you. Tripp Van Dorn is dead."

"The young man we met the other day, the one in the wheelchair?"

"The very same."

The expression he showed next wasn't unlike Harry Mc-Graw's trademark scowl. "And—don't tell me—you're convinced he was murdered."

"Because he was."

"I don't suppose we can discuss this later."

"I'm worried about you now."

"My fever?"

"Your treatment. If you could postpone it until I can learn more from the FDA . . ."

He smiled thinly, ironically. "In my current condition, I don't believe that's wise."

"I think Mimi Van Dorn's murder may be connected to the trial drug she was receiving here."

"Was she as desperate as I am, Jessica?"

"Entirely different circumstances. And the pharmaceutical company that manufactured the drug she was receiving is the very same one that made the drug you soon will be."

George pushed his recliner farther back. "Would you be terribly disappointed if I told you I can't let myself be bothered with such things right now?"

"There's something wrong with this place," I said, trying not to sound as if I was pleading.

"Perhaps, but there's also something wrong with me."

"There must be other options," I groped.

"I've done the research, my dear lady. There aren't. This is it, all that stands between me and—"

I felt my throat constrict. "Don't say it, George."

"I don't believe I need to."

"You need to trust me."

He rocked his chair all the way forward, leaning close enough to reach out and take my hand. "And you need to trust me."

I had trouble swallowing, finally managing to gulp down some air. His eyes wouldn't let go of mine, like in one of those paintings where no matter where you're standing, the subject seems to be staring at you.

"Perhaps this fever is a blessing," I said finally. "I should have at least until it passes."

"To do what?"

I remained silent.

"Jessica," George started to say, but a series of three beeps followed by a chime stopped him.

I looked toward an LED readout on the wall over his chair, hadn't even noticed before that the recliner must contain some built-in sensors that monitored his vital signs, currently displayed in large red numbers, including his temperature:

It was 98.6.

# Chapter Twenty-one

"Normally when I'm doing research for a book," I said to Jeffrey Archibald late the next morning, "it's not the company's CEO who gives me the guided tour."

"Well, when I told my wife J. B. Fletcher was stopping by for a visit, it was all I could do to stop her from showing you around our facility herself."

"I'd love to meet her, all the same."

Archibald breathed a genuine sigh of relief. "You have no idea how much that means to me, Mrs. Fletcher. You see, I took the liberty of inviting her to stop by my office later, allotting plenty of time for you to get a leg up on that research for your next book, which centers around pharmaceuticals. Have you a chosen a title yet?"

His question made me feel like a fourth grader who'd been caught in a lie, having given no thought at all to what was a complete fabrication in the first place. "I'm thinking," I started, "of *Cold White Death*. Think your wife might like it?"

"Especially if she gets to tell her book-club friends that she heard it from you firsthand."

"Then we'll make sure she feels free to do so, even more when it goes up for sale on Amazon."

Archibald's smile reminded me of a fourth grader's, too. He was somewhere in his late forties, but looked a good decade younger than that. There was nothing about the frequent smile he flashed that looked fake or forced. In short, the kind of person you get to know, and like, in remarkably short order.

"You just got me off the hook for having to cancel our last vacation," Archibald told me, flashing another smile.

"It's a pleasure to be able to return the favor of your seeing me on such short notice."

I'd phoned LGX Pharmaceuticals—in Lincoln, just outside Providence, Rhode Island—from Harry's rental car after leaving George Sutherland. Fortunately, it had been too late in the day to start his treatment, giving me a bit more time to gather the evidence I needed to convince him of what I believed to be the corrupt, and even deadly, dealings of the Clifton Clinic. Of course, my determination was tempered to a large degree by mixed feelings over the single-minded resolve I could never get past. After all, if this drug really was George's only chance at survival, did I want to risk taking that away from him? Would it be worth my looking the other way, for the first time ever, if it meant a man of whom I was fonder than any besides my husband, Frank, got to live beyond the time stamp cancer had left him?

When Harry McGraw and I set out for LGX Pharmaceuticals

early this morning, I honestly hadn't settled on a decision yet. Perhaps I'd learn nothing at their corporate headquarters to further my investigation into what was really going on at the Clifton Clinic, and this would all be moot. I have to say this was the first time I'd ever pursued an investigation in which a good part of me wanted to fail, wanted to have fallen victim to no more than a writer's imagination.

The CEO of LGX checked his watch.

"How are we on time, Mr. Archibald?"

"Fine, and even if we weren't, I couldn't let you leave without giving you a glimpse of the most advanced assembly line anywhere in the industry."

"Right here in Rhode Island?"

"Right here in Rhode Island." Archibald nodded, clearly proud of, and eager to show off, his company's crowning jewel.

That crowning jewel, it turned out, was housed behind thick glass on an assembly line twice the length, and four times the width, of a football field. Automated assembly lines were hardly anything new; car factories had been using robots to perform menial line tasks for decades. The difference here was that LGX Pharmaceuticals had taken that principle several steps further.

Instead of being moored or anchored to a fixed slot, a number of the "bots," as Archibald called them, moved independently about the line, performing quality-control checks. Kind of like giant, man-sized, sophisticated versions of the robotic vacuum cleaners capable of memorizing room layouts and intuitively deciphering how to avoid getting trapped in a corner or against a piece of furniture.

He stopped his narration for us to watch four of the wheeled, eight-foot-tall contraptions rolling about the various stations of the line below that molded, stamped, cut, apportioned, packaged, boxed, and labeled the dozen drugs manufactured at this facility. Exposed cables ran from their narrow torsos up to their steel shoulders, looking like muscular, rubbery sinews. Their legs were combined into a single base, and their arms were capable of full articulation to the point, Archibald claimed, they could retrieve a single pill that had spilled off the line with their pincers without crushing it. The robots whisked about, stopping at every juncture where a red light garnered their attention to signal something awry. We watched as they removed the snares, snarls, and clogs of cardboard or stuck foil wrapping, moving on to reboot dispensing systems that had shut themselves down to avoid overheating.

"I can't help noticing, Mr. Archibald," I noted, unable to keep my vow to not become confrontational until I absolutely had to, "that something seems to be missing down there on your assembly line."

"People," he conceded.

"It does occur to me that robots can't lobby to join a union, don't complain about working conditions, and never barter over overtime. They also require no medical benefits." I did my best to look amiable when I resumed. "You seem committed to removing people from the equation here, Mr. Archibald."

"Believe it or not, Mrs. Fletcher, I lost sleep over that notion. Would you like to know how I got it back?"

"Very much."

Archibald turned his gaze toward the line, our reflections captured side by side in the glass, looking almost translucent.

"It would seem on the surface to be a measure to reduce our costs, thereby increasing our profits."

"Isn't that what this is?"

"Not when you consider that saving so much money and time in the manufacturing process has allowed us to hire that many more salesmen, R & D techs, and scientists, not to mention increase our research budget fivefold. I'd venture to say that the jobs we've lost down there on the line have been replaced in even greater numbers by employees we've been able to place in equally vital areas, to the delight of our workforce as well as our shareholders and investors."

"What about the men and women who used to stand at those stations? What happened to them?"

"We retrained and retasked as many as we could. But I'm not going to lie to you, Mrs. Fletcher—we did have to let quite a few go, and I'm sure the generous severance packages we provided were small consolation."

"I appreciate your honesty."

"The simple, undeniable, and at times regrettable thing about business is that all companies, in the pharmaceutical industry and beyond, operate based on the principle of the zero-sum game."

"Somebody wins and somebody loses," I elaborated.

"In this case, far more winners than losers across the board, not to downplay the reality of those who came out on the wrong end. Still, numbers don't lie, and since we've replaced three hundred workers with a pile of diodes, microchips, rubber, and steel, not only has our productivity increased, but our safety record has also improved."

"Of course, since there aren't any humans about to get injured anymore."

"I was speaking more of contamination and the potential risk of a dangerous drug reaching drugstore shelves. On their best days, human workers can't even begin to replicate the pace and efficiency of machines. And machines don't carry germs, infections, or environmental toxins capable of ruining entire manufacturing lots."

Something changed in Jeffrey Archibald's expression. It seemed he'd tired of either the tour or defending his actions. Both, most likely.

"Let's adjourn to my office, Mrs. Fletcher, so I can make sure you leave here with all the information you need."


Archibald's office, on the top floor of the facility's administrative section, looked as if it had been designed by machines, instead of populated by them. All steel and glass with nary a piece of wood anywhere in evidence. It was open and sparsely furnished—it seemed to focus on an entire wall of windows, which overlooked a small pond, currently featuring a large family of ducks swimming about. I had to admit it was indeed a pleasant view, though not one worth giving up all notion of traditional furnishings, in my mind.

"Please, Mrs. Fletcher," Archibald said, offering me one of two matching chairs that looked salvaged off a decommissioned NASA space shuttle.

I sat down, both chairs angled to take advantage, you guessed it, of that peaceful pond view beyond the wall of glass.

"Now that I've bored you with the technology behind the

drug business," he started, "what is it you really came here to learn?"

I fished a notebook from my bag, honestly intending to make notes, since I didn't trust my normally reliable recall for a subject with which I was so unfamiliar. "*Cold White Death* deals quite a bit with clinical trials."

I hesitated there. If my statement had rattled Jeffrey Archibald, he wasn't showing it in the least. His relaxed expression hadn't changed at all.

"I was wondering if you could share some of the high- or lowlights from your experience with them."

"Well, let's start with the fact that more than nine of every ten drugs that even make it as far as the clinical research phase fail in human testing and thus never reach market. Not many baseball players, I'd venture to say, would have much career security if they batted only a hundred."

"True enough."

"It's remarkably frustrating, because you begin development of any drug with only the highest expectations in mind. You know what I say the most in describing what it's like to work in this industry? That you need to have a pair of both rose-colored and dark glasses. Rose-colored to see the miracle you believe you're creating and dark to hide the tears when the miracle fails."

"An apt way to put it, I suppose," I said.

"The challenges posed by the clinical-research phase make this business a study in rejection and failure." Jeff Archibald leaned back casually in his chair. "But you're not here to listen to me ramble on and on."

"I'm here for insight into your industry in general and the

whole business of clinical trials in particular. For instance, in the book, in *Cold White Death*, I focus a bit on what happens when a hospital is conducting trials no one even knows exists, including the FDA. Might such a thing be possible?"

Archibald didn't look bothered at all by my question. "You're talking about rogue studies. And they do happen from time to time, very rarely, usually when a company like LGX gains distribution rights for a drug, say, manufactured in Sweden or France. A rogue study might be commissioned in advance of entering into an agreement, to at least confirm the drug's efficacy before making a major marketplace commitment to it. I can't say it's something I support or would entertain myself, Mrs. Fletcher, but it does happen."

I thought of Mimi Van Dorn dissolving the trust dedicated to her son's care, how Seth Hazlitt suggested the reason behind her doing so might be her body dysmorphic disorder.

"What about paid studies, Mr. Archibald?"

That got a slight rise out of him, kind of like a shock to his spine. "You mean, as in a potential subject buying their way into a trial? It's virtually impossible, given the breadth of the oversight involved."

"With a standard trial, sure," I elaborated. "But what if the trial in question was one of those rogue studies you mentioned?"

"I can tell you it happens more than anyone realizes. Take for-profit stem cell clinics, for example, that are known to charge patients to get experimental 'treatments' that have not been proven to be safe or effective. But it doesn't stop here, Mrs. Fletcher. Also pertaining to stem cell clinical trials, the FDA occasionally permits the institutions involved in the research to charge patients, especially if an approved drug is being tested for a not-yet-approved use. It's kind of a gray area."

"Murky, at best," I agreed.

"You'd be surprised to learn just how often the FDA grants permission to charge patients for trials involving more than just experimental therapies like stem cells. And that, of course, raises its share of ethical questions. Should someone, even if that someone is an academic clinical researcher, be able to charge a patient a large access fee to be in a clinical trial in which that patient will be subject to an experimental therapy that could ultimately prove to be unsafe and ineffective? The general term for this is 'pay-to-participate' trials, and they're becoming more and more common as drugs are being made available, especially for terminally ill patients, on an increasingly open basis without the safeguards and oversight that used to be the norm. What do these patients have to lose, right? The problem is the industry, as a whole, stands to lose plenty, because those kinds of lax practices tend to filter down to more established clinical research. In for a penny, in for a pound, as they say. Because of that, the National Institutes of Health has begun to clamp down on that practice."

The sun streaming through the glass was in my eyes now, and I shifted in the chair to find an angle that might block it. "What if the FDA wasn't in a position to grant permission for one of these pay-to-participate studies?"

"I don't think I understand your question."

"That is, if the hospital in my book was dispensing unapproved drugs to patients willing to pay for them under the auspices of a clinical trial."

"Well, they'd have to get the drugs in question from the pharmaceutical concern that manufactured them."

"That's what I was thinking—in which case, the manufacturer and the hospital would have to be in league with each other."

"You mean, like a conspiracy?"

"Does such a thing happen, Mr. Archibald?" I asked him, holding a hand up to shield my eyes from the sun's glare, so I might be able to better follow his reaction and body language.

"Only in the minds of writers, Mrs. Fletcher."

"But such a thing wouldn't be possible without the knowledge and participation of the drug company in question."

"Theoretically." Archibald smiled, but it didn't look as engaging or sincere as the previous ones he'd flashed. "In your book, that Big Pharma company's corrupt CEO could have been forced into the game, because he's being blackmailed, or maybe to save his failing companies."

"Ah, a desperate man, then."

"A staple of the mystery genre, I'd imagine."

"Desperation is indeed, Mr. Archibald. But it wouldn't have to be the CEO, right? It could be another high-level executive, somebody with the power and access to make the drugs in question effectively disappear. The perpetrator might then split some percentage of the profits with the hospital conducting the study. Such a practice could be quite lucrative, I imagine."

Archibald nodded his agreement. "Do the math, Mrs. Fletcher. If there were a hundred people in this paid study, just multiply the access fee by a hundred. In the case of someone desperate to reap what the drug might be able to give them, that could amount to a very significant sum."

"Stretching into the six figures, I imagine, even seven."

"Again, do the math."

I did, in my head. A hundred thousand dollars times a hundred patients would be ten million dollars for one study alone.

I thought of Mimi Van Dorn's broken trust.

I thought of the desperate plight that had brought George Sutherland to the Clifton Clinic. How much would people of limited means like Jean O'Neil be willing to pay to extend their lives, however modestly? I imagine savings would be drained, bank accounts emptied. A monstrous practice, but one that would have no problem finding willing participants, if handled properly and discreetly.

The way Charles Clifton would be handling it, in other words. Reflecting on his part in this reminded me that this clinic was envisioned as the flagship of a nationwide chain.

*Do the math. . . .*

I tried. Several ongoing rogue trials at each facility, involving dozens of patients on a fee basis to gain access and acceptance, a fee potentially of the order requiring that a trust be broken or maybe a house be sold. It was difficult to even calculate the potential profits to be split between the hospital and the manufacturer slash supplier.

"How close do your books come to real-life scenarios like this?" Archibald asked me.

The sun must've dipped behind part of the steel framing supporting the wall of windows, allowing me to meet his stare, which had gone cold and distant. "It's all about justice," I told him. "Stopping a villain who's already claimed at least one victim before he can claim any others."

Archibald managed a smile. "Are we talking about Jessica Fletcher or J. B. Fletcher?"

I met his gaze, unable to glean the message behind it. "To tell you the truth, sometimes I don't know myself."

"Well, Mrs. Fletcher, here's something *I* know. You might have a negative opinion about paid clinical trials, but what do you call it when an insurance company fails to provide a desperately needed drug because the cost is deemed too exorbitant?"

"Unfair."

Archibald nodded. "Indeed. That leaves the patient with the choice to either accept a far cheaper drug, certainly not to be nearly as effective, or to pay for the superior drug out of pocket. Then consider all that treatment would be subject to the patient's ridiculously high deductible and eighty percent of hospital costs. You really see a lot of difference between that scenario and paying to receive a drug that might be the only thing that can save a person's life?"

"You mean, besides the fact that one's legal and the other plainly isn't?"

Archibald was about to respond when the double doors to his office opened and a woman entered, grinning from ear to ear.

"I'm sorry to intrude, but I just couldn't help myself."

She made a beeline toward me, and I realized this must be Jeffrey Archibald's wife.

We both rose.

"I was just helping Mrs. Fletcher with her next book."

Her jaw practically dropped. "No? Really?"

"Tell Allison the title, Mrs. Fletcher."

"*Cold White Death.*"

"I love it!" She started to reach into a tote bag she'd slung over her shoulder. "I hope you don't mind I brought a few books for you to sign."

"It would be my pleasure," I told Allison Archibald.

"Make that one out to my husband."

"Sure thing." I met Archibald's gaze as I started scrawling with my trusty Sharpie. "For Jeff," I recited, "who made my next book possible."

# Chapter Twenty-two

I spotted Harry McGraw standing outside his rental car when I finally emerged from LGX Pharmaceuticals.

"You took your sweet time in there," he groused. "Good thing the meter's running."

"Keep it running. There's another stop we need to make."

"I do have a life, you know."

"Really?"

"No, but don't rub it in. Your chariot awaits, my lady. Where to next?

"A memory-care facility where Big Al McCandless currently resides."

"Who's Big Al McCandless?"

"Former police chief of Marblehead, Massachusetts."

"Do I want to know why you need to see him?"

"I'm not sure myself yet. Just a feeling."

"Ah, one of those . . ."

"It's called Briarcliff Gardens and it's in Johnston, Rhode Island, pretty close to where we are now. That's what made me think of it. You okay with extending your chauffeur's duties long enough for me to pay a visit?"

"So long as you don't leave me there," Harry said, climbing back behind the wheel.

I couldn't get out of my mind what Tom Grimes, Alvin Mc-Candless's successor as police chief in Marblehead, had said about driving Mimi Van Dorn to Massachusetts General Hospital in the wake of her son's car accident. How she'd been on her cell phone practically the whole time, speaking to someone in too hushed a tone for him to discern even her end of the conversation. And though all the revelations of the past few days had made me wonder how well I actually knew Mimi, such behavior didn't seem even remotely possible for a mother confronted with the tragedy that her son might never walk again.

Grimes may not have been in a position back then to know any of the other particulars about that night, but Big Al certainly was, although it might test the limits of his beleaguered recall.

"Learn anything helpful in there?" Harry asked me as we reached the on-ramp for Route 146, heading from Lincoln to Johnston, Rhode Island.

"I'm not sure."

"What happened to yes or no?"

"LGX's CEO is a tough guy to read."

"Even for you?"

"I think he knew more than he was saying, even though I can't pin down what makes me feel that way."

"Maybe because everybody knows more than they say."

I looked across the seat at Harry. "I don't think the Clifton Clinic could be carrying out rogue clinical trials with drugs manufactured by LGX without him, or somebody else high up in the company, knowing."

"And what's that *say*?"

I reached inside my bag for my cell phone. "That George Sutherland needs to know exactly what he's dealing with here."

But George's phone went straight to voice mail, and it would now be evening before I got back to Cabot Cove to check on him in person. If my suspicions were correct, Mimi Van Dorn had liquidated her trust to pay for an experimental antiaging drug that was part of an off-the-books study. And since LGX also manufactured the drug George would be receiving in another of those potentially illegal studies, it stood to reason that he, too, had paid for his place.

Franklin Roosevelt once said, "When you reach the end of your rope, tie a knot and hang on." In a predicament like George's and even Mimi's, though, sometimes you keep slipping to the point that you're willing to grasp for any modicum of hope, no matter how slight. Their situations were entirely different, of course, but Mimi's condition would've rendered her equally desperate for a drug that could impact how she looked in the mirror.

All that made sense, to some degree anyway. I couldn't find the sense, though, in the murder of Tripp Van Dorn, to the point where I began to question my own conclusions. I was basing my suspicions solely on the back of his hair having been smoothed into place, to cover the slight bruise I was certain a closer examination would reveal. If that was all there was, though, maybe my power of observation had deceived me and Tripp's hair had lost the depression through entirely mundane means, like memory foam.

"Oh my," I said just loud enough for Harry to pay attention.

"Oh my, *what*?"

"Tripp Van Dorn."

"The crippled kid?"

"It was missing."

"What was missing?"

"The family picture. It was on the wall when I came to see him, but was nowhere in evidence when he was found dead."

Harry started to change lanes, until a big truck already there honked its horn and chased him back. "So the kid was killed because of this missing picture?"

"More likely, the killer took it with him for reasons I can't see yet."

"You sure can pick 'em, Jessica," Harry said, shaking his head.

"People?"

"Cases."

"I've come to the conclusion that they pick me."

"And if I was any kind of friend, I wouldn't be driving you to see Alvin McCandless. I think you're driving yourself crazy with all this."

"All writers are a little crazy, Harry."

"But this is a lot crazy."

*       *       *

Big Al McCandless was still big. Just ask anyone who tried to change the channel on the flat-screen television in the Briarfield Gardens lounge when he was watching an old cop show on one of those nostalgia stations.

"Can I ask you a few questions, Chief McCandless?" I said, taking the chair next to his, while Harry hovered back in the doorway.

He seemed to perk up at being referred to that way. "Not yet. Bad guys to catch. Can't you see?"

And he returned his attention to the screen, where I thought I recognized an episode of the classic *Untouchables* playing.

"Do you remember catching bad guys, Chief?"

"I can't remember because it hasn't happened yet. Never does until the end of the episode." He gave me a longer look. "Are you my wife?"

"No, Chief."

"Do I have a wife?"

"I believe you do."

I realized a commercial was playing, explaining Big Al re-focusing his attention on me, looking suddenly wary. "If you're not my wife, who are you?"

"My name is Jessica Fletcher."

"Are we friends?"

"We've never met before."

"Then why are you here, Ms. Ness?" he asked, confusing me for the Eliot Ness character on the TV show he was watching.

"I wanted to ask you about a tragic car accident that happened while you were still chief of police."

"Chief of police for what?"

"The town of Marblehead."

Big Al shook his head, starting to refocus his attention on the flat-screen, as if knowing the commercial was going to end. "Nope, I worked in Chicago," he said, pointing at the screen. "See, there. Windy City, they call it, home of the Bears and Cubs."

"Do you remember Tripp Van Dorn, Chief?"

"Did he play for the Bears?"

"No."

"The Cubs?"

I shook my head.

"Then I don't know him."

"He was in a car accident."

"You mentioned that before."

"Back when you were chief."

"In Chicago." Big Al nodded.

*The Untouchables* had come back on. I still claimed his attention but needed to make every moment count.

"It was a rainy night. Slick roads. The accident happened around the intersection of Beach and Ocean. His car flipped several times and Tripp suffered a broken neck that paralyzed him from the neck down. Maybe you remember his mother."

"Whose mother?"

"Tripp Van Dorn's. Her name was Mimi."

"What kind of name is that? What's yours, by the way?"

"Jessica."

"Jessica what?"

"Jessica Fletcher."

"Never heard of her. We done now? My show will be coming

back on, Miss Ness," Big Al said, apparently not registering it was already back on.

"You don't remember anything about the accident?"

"What accident?"

"The one from ten years ago when you were chief of police."

He waved me off. "Oh, that." Big Al pressed a finger against his lips and made a *shhhhhhhhhhh* sound, his tone suddenly so hushed I could barely hear his voice. "Can you keep a secret?"

"Yes, I can."

He looked back at the television without continuing.

"Chief?"

He turned back toward me.

"You were going to tell me a secret."

"Then it wouldn't be secret anymore, would it?"

"What were you going to tell me?"

"That it wasn't him."

"Wasn't who?"

"Him, that's who. You know."

"I really don't."

"Ness, Eliot Ness! It wasn't him. He never even lived in Marblehead!"

Big Al was starting to get agitated, explaining why one of the nurses had made a point to mention that the other residents here didn't enjoy watching television with him. An orderly standing off to the side started to advance until I signaled him to stop.

"Can I tell you a secret, Big Al?"

He grinned from ear to ear. "I love secrets!"

Then he placed a finger over his mouth and made the *shhh* sound again.

"Is it about the Van Dorns?" he asked me, perhaps indicating a rare moment of lucidity.

"Yes."

"Mimi's kid was a pain, a troublemaker. Spoiled rotten."

"We were talking about the car accident."

"Were we?"

"You were going to tell me what you remember from that night."

Alvin McCandless continued staring at the television screen but was no longer following Eliot Ness or any of the other action, somewhere else entirely, his expression utterly blank.

"It was raining," he said finally.

"What else?"

"Bad accident. Very bad. Not much left of the car. Hard to believe anyone could've survived, thought he'd be dead for sure when we pulled him out."

I shuddered, trying to picture what Tripp Van Dorn must've looked like when the paramedics finally extracted him from the crushed vehicle.

"Didn't even recognize him," Big Al elaborated.

"Perfectly understandable, Chief."

He seemed to like being called that, at least for the moment. Then he started to rise, having forgotten all about *The Untouchables*.

"I should get over to the station."

I gently grasped his wrist. "You were telling me about Tripp Van Dorn's accident."

He sank back into his chair. "Bad mistake on my part. Didn't see the harm at the time."

"Harm in what?"

"That Mimi," he reflected, "she was something. You're not going to tell people in town about us, are you?"

"I told you, Chief, all this is our secret."

"Because my wife . . . You know."

"I do."

"I'd do it differently if I had it to do again. You make mistakes. People get hurt. But people had already been hurt. Didn't see the harm. Was it a bad thing I did?"

I lowered my voice and patted his arm. "It's our secret, Chief."

"You won't tell anyone?"

"Not a soul."

"Because it's too late now. Damage has already been done. Two lives ruined. Can't ruin them twice."

And in that instant Alvin McCandless's attention returned to *The Untouchables*, as if I'd never been there at all.

"What I miss?" he asked me.


"Looks like you finally met your match, my dear girl," Harry said, as we headed down the hall of Briarcliff Gardens back toward the lobby. "Just remember I charge for the hours that are a waste of time, too."

"That wasn't a waste of time at all, Harry."

"What, did I miss something?"

"You weren't listening to everything Big Al said."

"Because it was gibberish."

"Most, but not all."

"Care to enlighten me on what you're talking about?"

We reached the front of the building and passed outside from the air-conditioning into the stifling August heat.

"Not yet, Harry. We've got one more stop to make first."

"Where?"

"Mass General."

# Chapter Twenty-three

I tried George Sutherland five more times on the ride from Rhode Island to Massachusetts General Hospital, the stately assemblage of different styles of buildings perched on the banks of the Charles River in Boston. Each time my call went straight to voice mail, and I kept my phone clutched in my hand to make sure I'd feel the vibration when he finally called back.

My meeting with Jeffrey Archibald, CEO of LGX Pharmaceuticals, had further convinced me that Charles Clifton was up to no good with either his clinic outside Cabot Cove or all the others Clifton Care Partners was on the verge of building. I had no idea how deep either Archibald's or LGX's complicity went, but the connection was clear, and the money involved in getting desperate patients to pony up for their spots in these so-called clinical trials was utterly staggering.

If nothing else, the fate of Mimi Van Dorn had revealed how they dealt with patients who might otherwise do them harm.

*Mimi Van Dorn . . .*

I'd had no idea what I was going to learn about her, and particularly Tripp's accident that rainy night a decade earlier, from former Marblehead police chief Big Al McCandless. What I believed he'd told me, though, was beyond anything I'd expected.

He'd spoken in a totally nonsensical manner in keeping with his deteriorating mental state. But hints about that night ten years ago made perfect sense—that is, if I'd heard his words right.

*That Mimi, she was something. You're not going to tell people in town about us, are you?*

Suggesting they were having an affair, not an especially pertinent fact in this case, except that it revealed the great lengths Big Al would have gone to for Mimi, particularly where her son was concerned.

*I'd do it differently if I had it to do again. You make mistakes. People get hurt. But people had already been hurt. Didn't see the harm. Was it a bad thing I did?*

If my suspicions were correct, McCandless had indeed gone well beyond the call of duty in following the instructions of a woman with whom he was having an affair. I thought back to what Marblehead's current police chief, Tom Grimes, had told me about driving Mimi Van Dorn to Mass General that night, how she'd talked on her cell phone in a hushed tone virtually the whole way. Might she have been talking to Big Al, plotting this "bad thing," which had already been set into motion?

*Because it's too late now. Damage has already been done. Two lives ruined. Can't ruin them twice.*

I knew what Harry McGraw had heard from the doorway, but I didn't believe it was what Alvin McCandless had said at all. His words held an entirely different meaning to someone listening for their content amid the jumble of his mind. Not unlike learning a different language. And the one spoken by Big Al suggested that somehow the murders of Mimi and Tripp Van Dorn went all the way back to the night of the accident.

I watched Harry check the rearview mirror for the fifth time in the past minute.

"What's wrong?" I asked him.

"Nothing. Maybe I'm just a careful driver."

"You think we're being followed."

"When you owe your ex-wives as many back alimony payments as I do, you always feel like you're being followed."

"I had the same feeling."

"Why didn't you say something?" Harry said, checking the mirror yet again.

"Because you'd tell me I was crazy."

"Then I guess we're both crazy, because there's no tail I've been able to spot."

His statement failed to assuage my fears, and I angled my frame so I could somewhat follow the traffic behind us in the side-view mirror.

I thought I felt my phone start to vibrate, about to ring. I jerked it to my ear, ready to say hello, but the screen remained dark, no incoming call from George Sutherland at all. So I brought up FAVORITES and called Seth Hazlitt.

"Sorry to be bothering you in the middle of the day, Seth," I greeted.

"You must have me confused for a doctor who has patients to see."

"You still have plenty of patients."

"Not as many as I used to. And how would you know anyway? Been talking to Clara?"

Clara was Seth's longtime receptionist. "If I was, what would she have told me?"

"That she's getting her résumé together."

"She's seventy-five, Seth."

"It's a long résumé, ayuh."

"Can you check on George?" I asked him, without further small talk. "I've been trying to reach him all day without success."

"Want me to pick you up and we can head over to the Clifton Clinic together?"

"I'm in Rhode Island."

"What are you doing there, Jess?"

"Heading to Mass General at the moment."

"Tell Harry I said hi."

"How'd you know he was with me?"

"Because I'm not and Mort isn't, which leaves Harry. Must be his lucky day."

"I'll tell him to play the lottery."

"I'll check on George straightaway. You have new reason to suspect he may be in danger?"

"I might. It's a long story."

"Is it ever a short one?"

"I need you to help me make sense of it, Seth."

"How?"

"Can you pull Mimi Van Dorn's autopsy report?"

"What am I looking for?"

"I'll tell you as soon as I get back home."

I ended the call and looked across the seat of the rental car toward Harry.

"How good are you at getting hospitals to release medical reports?"

"I've had my moments."

"You're going to need another when we get to Mass General."

According to its Web site, Mass General's primary Boston-based location boasts more than 1,000 beds and admits about 50,000 patients each year. The surgical staff performs more than 34,000 operations yearly, and the obstetrics department delivers more than 3,800 babies. The trauma center where Tripp Van Dorn had been brought by helicopter after his crippling accident was the oldest and largest American College of Surgeons–verified Level One center in New England, evaluating and treating more than 2,600 trauma patients per year.

"Not interested in anything like that," Harry said, cutting me off in the midst of my showing off my knowledge of all things Mass General. "And how do you know so much about this place, anyway?"

"Guess."

"You used it in a book?"

"Researched it for a book, but never used it."

"Waste of time, then." He nodded.

"Apparently not."

"Okay, smarty-pants, where's billing located? Because that's where we need to go."

I was going to enjoy this, in spite of everything. "Fourth floor of the Jean Yawkey building under the auspices of something called Partners HealthCare."

"Tell you what, why don't you try your luck getting what you want out of them while I wait in the car?"

"And how would you feel if I came back with Tripp Van Dorn's medical file?"

Harry shot a quick glance my way from behind the wheel. "Tell you what, you can tag along just so you at least feel useful."

There was no lobby security station to check in at inside the sleek, modern Jean Yawkey building, so Harry and I simply rode the elevator to the offices of Partners HealthCare on the fourth floor.

"Why billing, Harry?" I asked him as we stepped into the cab, alone once the door slid closed.

"Watch and learn, smarty-pants."

"I'd rather listen first."

He smirked instead of scowled. "You'll see. How's it feel to be following my lead for a change?"

I saw him fish a badge and ID from the ever-present Go Kit he brought with him wherever he went.

"Just in case," Harry said. "And with you 'just in case' seems to happen all the time."

Harry hung a lanyard holding the cased badge around his neck, just as the cab door slid back open on the fourth floor. I said nothing as he approached a long reception counter.

"May I help you?" a smiling young woman in standard, as opposed to medical, dress asked, approaching us.

Harry stuck his badge out toward her, then flashed an ID. "Yes, I'm Cale Yarborough from the Department of Health and Human Services, and this is my assistant, Agnes Beasley. Unfortunately, I'm afraid your department has hit the lottery today."

"I'm afraid I don't under—"

"Let me explain, Ms. . . ."

"Chase, Vicky Chase."

"Let me explain, Vicky. As I'm sure you're aware, HHS regularly conducts random audits of different health-care providers going back ten years, and would you believe our system flagged one of yours from ten years ago. Could you direct me to whoever can access the records in question?"

"Well, Partners HealthCare didn't even exist back then."

"But once you did, you'd be legally required to maintain all records for ten years and transfer all archives to digital form. This particular flag came in just under the deadline. Your lucky day again, I suppose."

Vicky Chase's expression flashed the concern of an underling afraid she was about to get blamed for something. "Medical-billing archives are located down this hall, last door on the right. Should I tell them you're coming?"

Harry actually smiled. "Good idea, Ms. Chase. Just don't mention I can order a forensic audit of this entire department if need be. Don't want to worry them, now, do we?"

A woman named Frances Drummond was waiting expectantly behind a waist-high counter when we entered the offices of the Billing Archives Department. In the old days, such records reservoirs would have rows and rows of color-coded patient file folders stored alphabetically in shelving that stretched from floor to ceiling, so high a ladder would be required to access them all. Today, not a single paper record or file was in evidence. Just Frances and two more workers facing the adjacent walls, clacking away at their keyboards and showing Harry and me, Cale Yarborough and Agnes Beasley, no interest at all.

"Mr. Yarborough," Drummond greeted, as routinely as she could manage, "how can Billing Archives be of service to HHS?"

Harry flashed his badge again, more to show off for me, I think. "It's the darndest thing, Frances, but we've encountered what we believe must be a glitch in the system. See, a routine audit of this hospital's records by our computers turned up what appears to be a rather large billing discrepancy."

"Do you have a case file for me?" she said, sidestepping closer to the computer resting atop the counter.

"No, Frances—that's why we feel it may be a glitch, and they dispatched Mrs. Beasley and me to investigate further in person. I'm truly sorry for the intrusion and for the government wasting two perfectly good tickets on Amtrak to send us up here. It's just policy. Nothing personal, you understand, given the stellar record Partners HealthCare maintains with HHS."

"How about a name and date of admission?"

Harry tapped the counter dramatically. "Now, that I do have," he said, smiling.

I think he'd smiled more in the past five minutes than I'd seen him do in the past five years.

"The name is Tripp Van Dorn."

Harry pretended to consult a memo pad, which was almost the same as Mort's, except for the fact that the pages were all blank save for a single date, before he responded with the date I'd provided him. I watched Frances Drummond enter a few commands, wait, and then enter a few more. From where I was standing, I could see her monitor springing to life, filled from edge to edge with something.

"He was admitted after being transported via medevac." Her eyes, widening, froze on the screen. "Oh, I see what you mean."

"You were able to bring up the records?"

"Nearly a hundred pages of them," Drummond said, turning her monitor toward Harry. "Does this figure match the one flagged in your audit?"

Harry whistled while squinting to better regard the bill for Tripp Van Dorn's treatment, which stretched into the seven figures. "It does. Boy, oh, boy, right?"

Drummond turned the monitor back around. "I think I can explain the discrepancy your system caught. Normally, convalescent and rehabilitative care is separated from the general bill. But in this case, for some reason, they were lumped together."

"Yes." Harry nodded. "That makes sense. It would explain pretty much everything. Guess the machines did their job this time."

"Thankfully."

"Think you'd be able to print that file out for us, Ms. Drummond?"

Her expression tightened, looking like that of a student who'd just gotten a bad test grade handed back to her. "Actually, Mr. Yarborough, we don't use paper anymore. A cost-saving measure. I'm sure you understand."

"Of course I do. That was just a little test we're required to perform. You'd be shocked at the paper expense many hospital billing systems continue to maintain. Talk about waste, right?"

Drummond looked visibly relieved. "Indeed, sir, indeed. I can e-mail the records to you if you wish."

Harry stiffened a bit, having no Department of Health and Human Services e-mail address he could provide. "Well, I was actually thinking that, well . . ."

I fished a thumb drive I always carried from my bag. "We prefer portable storage drives these days," I explained, handing it over. "Because of the concern over viruses and our security software not letting certain attachments through."

"Very wise." Frances Drummond nodded, taking the drive. "It'll be just a few minutes."


Harry's trademark scowl returned as soon as we were back in the elevator.

"Had to one-up me, didn't you?"

"I didn't know it was a competition."

He smirked again, something I could get used to. "I was pretty good in there. Admit it."

"You were terrific. You really should raise your fees, Harry."

"How would you know? You never pay your bills anyway."

"Because you never send me any."

"Always hiding behind the technicalities, aren't you, Jessica?"

While my faith in Harry's detective prowess didn't really need any further reinforcement, the truth was I seldom got to see him in action. I'd ask him to do something, and almost invariably, he got it done. Out of sight, out of mind, right? But today I'd witnessed firsthand the kind of magic he did that normally flew under even my radar. Along with George Sutherland, Harry was probably the best detective I'd ever worked with.

*George . . .*

I realized it had been well over an hour since I'd last tried him, and pulled out my phone as soon as we were headed back to the adjoining parking garage.

"Damn," Harry said, pulling the ticket from his pocket.

"What's wrong?"

"I forgot to ask them if they validate. Could have saved you twelve bucks."

"Add it to my bill," I said.

I was about to press George's number again when an incoming call came in from Seth Hazlitt.

"I'm at the Clifton Clinic, Jess. Where are you?"

"Mass General. I'll explain everything when I get home. Tell me about George."

"Just come straight here once you're back. I'll be waiting."

"That's four hours from now, Seth."

"I know," he said flatly. "Like I said, I'll be waiting. Oh, and Mort gave me a message to relay."

"Pray tell."

"Autopsy report came back on Tripp Van Dorn. You were right about that bruise on the back of his head. Under closer examination, it was there plain as day. So consider your suspicions confirmed, Jess. The young man was murdered."

# Chapter Twenty-four

True to his word, Seth was waiting outside the Clifton Clinic when Harry McGraw and I pulled up. My thoughts were coming so feverishly, and my heart was pounding so hard, that as I climbed out of Harry's rental, I thought the sound of the surf pounding the rocks below was coming from inside my own head.

As Seth approached us, I couldn't help but consider how the sheer face and precarious grade of the bluffs on which the clinic had been constructed formed an apt metaphor for the past four days, starting with Mimi Van Dorn's collapse at the library. I was just trying to hold on for dear life when we met Seth halfway to the clinic entrance.

"I've got nothing new to tell you," he reported. "All they've said is that George Sutherland is no longer a patient and they have no idea of his whereabouts."

"Did you try Hill House?"

"No sign of him there either, but he hasn't checked out."

"Meaning he's disappeared," Harry concluded.

"Or somebody made him disappear," I said, holding my gaze on the wide facade of the building, which narrowed to conform with the general shape of the bluffs. "You call Mort?"

"I figured it best I wait on that for you to get here."

I pushed a hand into my bag. "I'll call him."

I was trying to recall the last time Mort had used his siren, but he pulled off the road that had been built to accommodate access to the clinic with the heavy *whop-whop-whop* splitting the air and flashing lights piercing the darkness. He pulled right up to the no-parking zone directly in front of the entrance and practically leaped down from the driver's seat.

"I'm guessing you had another eventful day," he said to me, after exchanging a nod with Harry.

"It's not over yet, Mort."

"Well, Mrs. Fletcher," he said, reverting to calling me that yet again, "let's see what we can see."

The Clifton Clinic was required to remain open and accessible twenty-four hours a day, even though it lacked an emergency room. I wasn't sure why exactly the law required that and didn't much care at this point, as I fell into step alongside Seth, trailing Mort through the sliding glass doors into the lobby, which was bright and airy even at this hour. Harry McGraw brought up the rear.

"Sheriff Metzger to see Dr. Clifton," Mort announced upon reaching the front desk.

"I'll let him know you're here, Sheriff, but he's seeing patients at present."

"Please tell him to come down, unless he'd prefer we go up. His choice, ma'am."

"I understand."

"Make sure your boss does as well."

The receptionist picked up her phone, dialed two numbers, and spoke too softly for me to hear before cupping her hand over the receiver mic.

"Dr. Clifton would like to know what this is about."

"His missing patient," Mort snapped in response, before I could chime in.

I still wanted to say something to ease the helplessness I was feeling, but remained silent, since I was well aware that nothing I could say at this point was going to make things any better.

The lobby was so quiet at this hour that we could hear the elevator descending through the walls. We were all watching when the cab slid open and Charles Clifton emerged. He was wearing a white lab coat for the first time in my presence, his usual stoic demeanor noticeably flustered as he approached us.

"What can I do for you, Sheriff?" he asked Mort, his eyes inventorying the rest of us.

"Just hoping you can clear something up for us."

"I'd be happy to do that for you, but I'd like to keep this private if you don't mind."

"I don't mind at all, Doctor," Mort told him, "so long as you want me to consider this a formal investigation, as opposed to a nice friendly chat. Your choice."

Clifton nodded grudgingly. "If this is about George Sutherland, I really can't help you."

"Is he or isn't he your patient?" Mort asked.

"He was. He is no longer. He had a change of heart this morning when we were about to start treatment."

"This happened in person."

"It did," Clifton affirmed, trying very hard not to look in my direction.

Seth, meanwhile, was glaring at him so intensely that I was glad there was nothing he could use as a weapon anywhere nearby.

"Here at the clinic?" Mort resumed.

Clifton nodded. "We thought it best he spend the night so we could monitor whatever infection had led to his fever. That way he'd be ready to start treatment as early as this morning."

"This would be treatment with a drug manufactured by LGX Pharmaceuticals," I interjected, unable to hold back any longer. "The same company that manufactured the antiaging drug you prescribed for Mimi Van Dorn—both as part of clinical trials. Do I have that all right, Doctor?"

Clifton looked surprised that I knew so much, no longer able to ignore me. "Mrs. Fletcher, this clinic's dealings with such trials are strictly confidential, and as such, I'm not at liberty to discuss them. I'm sure Dr. Hazlitt here can explain the law to you, if need be."

"No, I understand the law, Doctor, just as I understand clinical trials can only proceed legally under the approval and supervision of the Food and Drug Administration. So when you say 'confidential,' it appears you mean keeping your trials a secret from the FDA as well."

"Mrs. Fletcher, I don't expect you to be an expert on the procedures involving clinical trials, in which—"

"I'm not," I interrupted, "which is why I consulted with one at the FDA itself to explain how things work. So perhaps what you should be explaining is how you're enrolling patients like Mimi Van Dorn and George Sutherland in clinical trials that, for all intents and purposes, don't exist."

"She's got a point, Doctor," Mort noted.

Clifton swung his way. "Are you in the habit, Sheriff, of letting civilians participate in your investigations, even run them, by all appearances?"

The question didn't rattle Mort at all. "We decided not to call this an investigation, remember? That was your choice, Doctor, and that means this conversation falls under the category of a nice friendly chat between neighbors. And you and your clinic are our neighbors, no matter how much you might want to pretend otherwise. So if you'd prefer not to answer Mrs. Fletcher's questions, that's fine; I'll just pose the same ones to you myself down at the station."

I stared at Clifton when he turned back toward me. "Well, Doctor?"

"Was there a question somewhere in those accusations you hurled at me?"

"How about you answer this one: How much did you charge Mimi Van Dorn to receive that antiaging drug you claim was part of a clinical trial?"

"Even if that were the case, the clinic would be breaking no law on the books anywhere at present, as I'm sure Jeffrey Archibald would've told you himself."

"Let me try another question: What's your relationship with LGX Pharmaceuticals?"

"I wouldn't have to answer that question, even if a professional had raised it, because of medical privilege."

"How about another question, then?" I persisted. "How much does LGX have invested in this clinic, or Clifton Care Partners as a whole?"

"That's two questions, Mrs. Fletcher."

"So it is, and you know what they add up to? A pretty interesting scheme. Clifton Care Partners opens a bunch of these high-end, private clinics in order to enlist far more patients in pay-to-participate clinical trials."

"That's an absurd accusation. I have no idea what you're talking about, and whatever relationship I maintain with LGX is about the drugs we test on their behalf and nothing more."

"Really? Because that doesn't jibe with the fact that you obviously spoke with the company's CEO, Jeffrey Archibald, earlier today," I told him. "Otherwise, how could you know he'd told me anything? I certainly didn't mention it."

Clifton swallowed hard. I'd caught him and he knew it. But that meant nothing if it didn't help me learn the fate of George Sutherland.

Mort stepped forward between us. "When was the last time you saw George Sutherland, Doctor?"

Clifton fingered his chin, nearly losing the tip in his deep cleft. "That would have been this morning when I informed him we couldn't start his treatment until absolutely certain he wasn't still suffering from the infection that caused his fever yesterday. He seemed disappointed and very perturbed. Practically stormed out of his treatment room."

"At which point he left the premises."

"As far as I know, yes."

"And you haven't seen him since."

"No, Sheriff, I have not."

Harry McGraw cleared his throat. "Now, that's funny," he said, holding his cell phone up for us all to see a flashing dot on a grid map. "Because I just plugged his number into this locator app and, strangest thing, apparently he's still in the building."

"And who are you?" Clifton demanded. "Don't tell me: another friend of Mrs. Fletcher's."

"Her private investigator, exactly. Want a card?"

"I don't think I'll be retaining your services anytime soon."

"I've got too much work as it is, and I don't have a business card to give you anyway."

"Dr. Clifton," Mort said, as if it was his turn again, "why don't you show us Mr. Sutherland's treatment room."

Upstairs, the private treatment room where I'd seen George last night, and Clifton claimed to have seen him this morning, was exactly the same as it had been yesterday, except no George.

I fished the phone from my bag again and touched GEORGE on my Favorites page. No phone rang, as I'd expected, but I heard the buzzing sound of a phone left on vibrate, and sure enough, Mort scooped George's phone out from beneath a throw pillow on a love seat, finished in the same leather upholstery as the recliner in which George had been sitting when I'd last seen him.

"Well," I said, "guess that explains why George hasn't re-turned any of my calls."

There was another explanation, though, one I dreaded beyond all measure.

Back at Hill House, I asked the front desk to fetch the hotel manager and part owner, Seamus McGilray, for me. He ap-peared from his back office moments later in his ever-present bow tie, as prim and proper as always.

"I trust there are no issues with your suite, Mrs. Fletcher," he said, his English accented with just a touch of his native Ireland.

"Not at all, Seamus. But a friend of mine recently checked in who's slipped out of touch. I'm afraid we need to check his room."

*Very* afraid, I might have said.

McGilray didn't need to hear anything further. He made sure the key card providing universal access to all the rooms was clipped to his belt, and he led me down the hall and up a short flight of stairs toward George's room on the first floor.

Fortunately, he wasn't inside, given the condition we would've likely found him in if he had been.

"Well, that's a relief anyway," Seamus said.

Whatever relief I felt was tempered, though, by one obvious reality: George Sutherland was still missing.

I returned to my room and plugged the thumb drive with Tripp Van Dorn's medical file from Mass General into my computer. I intended to give it a more thorough check later, but for starters, I was just after one small bit of information to allay my suspicions about what I couldn't quite grasp here.

I found it on the second page of his voluminous file, just a simple notation that shouldn't have surprised me at all, but still did.

Because it changed everything.

# Chapter Twenty-five

I was seated in that nest of brand-new office furniture, waiting, when Fred Cooper stepped through the door at nine o'clock sharp.

"Your assistant said you had an opening," I said, rising.

"For clients and potential clients only, Mrs. Fletcher," Cooper said, clearly irked by my presence.

"This is about a potential client, Mr. Cooper, just not me."

"Who, then?"

"You, of course."

"Why don't we talk in my office?"

Cooper closed the door behind him. I'd come alone, unless you counted Harry waiting downstairs in his car, because I didn't think I had anything to fear from Fred Cooper during a workday with the assistant he shared with another lawyer just steps away. Then again, I could be wrong, of course.

I sat down in the same chair I'd occupied in my first visit to this office. "I've come by some new information I thought you might be interested in hearing, Mr. Cooper."

"And how could you possibly think that?"

"Well, because you showed such an interest in Mimi and Tripp Van Dorn. Representing the mother and then dangling the son about for a time when he wanted to hire you, without ever telling him about your conflict of interest. You never did adequately explain that to me."

"But it's not what brought you here today."

"Not at all. I actually just misspoke when I referred to Mimi and Tripp Van Dorn as mother and son. That's why I'm here," I said, getting to the point about what Tripp's medical records from Mass General had revealed, "because, you see, Tripp Van Dorn wasn't Mimi's son at all."

I'd needed that file for one primary reason: to learn Tripp's blood type, which was AB. Mimi's blood type, according to her hospital records, was O and, as I proceeded to explain to Fred Cooper, a mother with that blood type cannot bear a child with Tripp's.

"There's a simple explanation for that, Mrs. Fletcher," Cooper said, trying to pretend that revelation hadn't rattled him. "Tripp was adopted."

"Not according to state and county records in Massachusetts. See, I know this private eye who's an absolute whiz at turning over rocks. When he looked into turning over that one, there was nothing beneath it. But he did sneak a peek at Tripp Van Dorn's original birth certificate. His father is listed as John Jessup. Care to guess who was listed as his mother?"

Cooper visibly stiffened behind his desk. "I'm not at liberty to say any more."

"Citing attorney-client privilege again, right? Even though your client is no longer with us. But I do understand your not wanting to implicate Mimi in some baby-snatching scheme. At least we know you couldn't have been party to her crimes, since you'd barely been born yourself. Of course, there are the issues to contend with regarding the commission or covering up of a crime. I've never totally understood that term, but I understand enough to know what we're looking at here is likely a textbook example."

I waited for Fred Cooper to say something, then resumed when he didn't.

"I wonder if breaking the trust that was paying for Tripp's treatment was made any easier by the fact that he wasn't her flesh and blood. And I also have to wonder how this might have been connected to his murder."

"Which hasn't been confirmed, Mrs. Fletcher. It's still listed as a suicide."

"Not for long," I corrected, thinking of the bruise the medical examiner had found on the back of Tripp's head, confirming my theory as to how he'd been killed. "His killer was good, almost perfect. But, like all *almost* perfect killers, he made one mistake."

Cooper rocked forward in his new desk chair. "Anything else I can do for you, Mrs. Fletcher?"

"I was hoping you could tell me who Tripp Van Dorn was.

I mean his true identity. Because I'm thinking his real parents have a right to know the truth, as doubly sad and tragic as that is."

He shook his head, obviously not getting the point of that at all. "This isn't a book. You can't make everybody happy in the end."

"That doesn't mean I can't try."

Cooper came around his oversized desk, pulling one of those fancy titanium business cards from a holder near the edge. "This is where the real police can find me."

I rose, able to look him right in the eye even in flat shoes.

"Please don't come here anymore, Mrs. Fletcher, unless you'd like to retain my services."

I dropped the card into my bag. "I'll keep that in mind."


Harry McGraw was still waiting patiently when I exited the building.

"You look like you've been in a scrape," he noted.

"Close enough."

"Worth the damage inflicted?"

"No. I don't know what I was expecting to get out of Fred Cooper, but whatever it was never emerged. There's something . . . well, *off* about Cooper, about this whole case."

"You mean, besides the multiple murders?"

"Yes, Harry. I think I'm too close to this thing. The answer I'm looking for is right in front of me, but I can't see it."

"You mean like that feeling somebody was following us yesterday?"

"You're sure there wasn't, right? You're not just trying to make me feel better?"

That scowl came with a nod this time. "I'm almost sure there wasn't, and I'm not just trying to make you feel better. Don't forget, Jessica, I'm a trained investigator."

"It's just that, well . . ."

"What?"

"I could have sworn an old Jeep Cherokee drove past us after we pulled into Mass General."

"Didn't you say something about an old Cherokee nearly running Mimi down?"

I nodded. "I think you're getting my point."

"I also need to get out of town." Harry moved around to the driver's side of his rental. "And get this car back to the city before I have to pay for a whole week."

But Harry wasn't able to leave as quickly as he thought he'd be able to, because standing beside a BMW when we pulled into Hill House's cramped parking lot was Jeffrey Archibald, CEO of LGX Pharmaceuticals.

"May I have a word with you, Mrs. Fletcher?"

I joined him by his BMW, leaving Harry out of earshot but close enough to make me feel safe in Archibald's presence.

"In search of another signed book for your wife?" I asked, approaching him.

He forced a smile. "No, but she hasn't stopped talking about meeting you." Archibald's expression tightened. "I heard about your, er, visit with Dr. Clifton."

"From Dr. Clifton, no doubt."

"You've got this all wrong, Mrs. Fletcher, particularly about LGX Pharmaceuticals' association with Charles Clifton and Clifton Care Partners. You're aware, of course, of the prohibitive costs associated with bringing a drug to market."

"I know very few of them ever turn a real profit. I know about so-called orphan drugs used to treat rare afflictions."

"I believe we're on the same page," he said, not bothering to disguise the bad pun. "I'm not going to deny the truth you've uncovered behind my association with Charles Clifton."

"You mean that the two of you have concocted fake clinical trials to influence vulnerable people to give up everything they have to participate in them?"

"The alternative for your friend Mr. Sutherland could be far worse than that. The trial he signed up for, until you must've made him change his mind, was the only chance he had. That drug showed great promise in treating his particular form of cancer, but there wasn't enough anecdotal evidence to petition the FDA for a trial."

"So you leapfrogged the process by faking your own trial. Tell me, what did you and Clifton charge George Sutherland? Was it as much or more than you bilked out of Mimi Van Dorn?"

Archibald glanced toward his gleaming black sedan, as if he wanted very much to be inside it driving away from Cabot Cove. "Nobody twisted their arms in either case."

I took a step closer to him. "Mr. Archibald, I understand the point you're making about George Sutherland and even the more general one about drugs like the one he'd come all the way to Cabot Cove to get. But Mimi Van Dorn didn't have cancer. She had a psychological disorder you preyed on to the point she liquidated a trust that was providing for her quadriplegic son's care."

Archibald nodded. "Have you spoken to your nephew Grady recently, Mrs. Fletcher?" he asked, getting to the basis for his driving all the way up here.

"Choose your next words very carefully," I warned him.

"Don't get the wrong idea. I didn't mean that as a threat, nothing like that. I only thought you should know he's had some . . . employment issues at his accounting firm. Not easy finding a comparable position these days, which I'm sure is a source of anxiety for him, since he has a young son to provide for."

"Did you arrange these employment issues, Mr. Archibald? Is that what you're telling me?"

"Not at all."

"Because a more suspicious and jaded woman might see that as a threat."

"Quite the opposite. If you'd have let me finish, I was going to say we have a top-level opening in our accounting department that would suit him perfectly. He'd have to relocate to Rhode Island, but I don't imagine that would be too much of a bother. And he'd be closer to you to boot."

"I see. And this would be in return for my backing off the case involving you and Dr. Clifton. Is that it?"

"There is no such case."

The moment froze between us, my own thinking trapped between being repulsed by his involving my nephew in this and concerned over Grady's current plight, my emotions as jumbled as my thoughts.

That's when I heard a *pop*, followed by *pop, pop*.

The windshield of Archibald's BMW had exploded and one of his side mirrors had broken off. I twisted instinctively toward the expected origin of the shots to spot a male figure at the edge of the woods rimming the rear of Hill House, one eye pressed against a rifle sight.

And that's when something hit me with enough force to knock me off my feet and steal my breath.

# Chapter Twenty-six

I looked up to find Archibald over me, having tackled me to the ground.

"Are you all right?"

"Fine, yes," I managed, huffing.

*Had Jeffrey Archibald just saved my life?*

I recovered enough of my bearings to perch myself against his BMW and peer over the hood, just as the figure I'd glimpsed disappeared into the woods.

"Harry!" I cried out.

He'd already lit out into motion, but got only halfway to the woods. I swiftly caught up with him, leaving Archibald behind.

Harry had his hands on his knees and was heaving for breath.

"Wouldn't happen to have a gun, would you?"

"I haven't carried since the nineties," he managed, between gasps.

"I'm going after him, Harry."

He flailed a hand outward, trying to grab hold of me, but it flopped back down having not even come close. I was in motion by then, running as fast as I could into the woods on the trail of the rifle-wielding man. I'd been a jogger for years, enjoying nothing better than following Cabot Cove's beloved coastline as my favored route. That, along with my daily bike rides around town, except in the winter months, had kept me in good shape for years, a practice I'd renewed thanks to the Hill House basement gym, open only to guests. I wasn't all that fast but boasted decent stamina, again thanks to those workouts, and I knew these woods well enough to follow the trail blindfolded.

*Had the shooter been firing at me or Archibald?*

Given the angle of the shots and the shooter's positioning, it must've been Archibald. That made no sense I could find, even if trying to chase down the gunman hadn't stolen all other thinking from me. I thought I detected his pounding steps no longer that far ahead of me, but it could have been the pounding in my own head instead as I heaved for breath myself.

Another sound greeted me, and I realized it was the sound of cars heading down a back road at the rear of the woods, still known almost exclusively to locals as one of the last well-kept secrets of Cabot Cove. A bit out of the way but nonetheless utilized to get around when the traffic was at its worst during the summer.

I thought I'd caught another glimpse of the figure when the woods thinned briefly, close enough to note the rifle slung from his shoulder bouncing behind him. By the time I reached the road, though, he was gone.

\*    \*    \*

I was retracing my path back through the woods when I found Harry McGraw in the very same position I'd left him in back at Hill House: doubled over with hands on his knees.

"You know how much I charge when gunshots are involved?" he managed, the words emerging in stops and starts. "Did you at least get a look at him?"

I shook my head. "Never got that close."

"A good thing maybe," Harry said, finally straightening himself up. "I already called nine-one-one."

Just then, I heard the first sounds of sirens screaming toward the area.

"When are you going to stop playing one of your characters, Jessica? The danger's real out there, in case you haven't noticed."

I thought of Mimi and Tripp Van Dorn. "Tell me something I don't know, Harry."


Mort's SUV squealed to a halt on the street fronting Hill House just behind two Cabot Cove cruisers that had beaten him there.

"Don't make me say it, Jessica," Mort said, storming toward me and having dropped the "Mrs. Fletcher" again.

I realized Jeffrey Archibald's damaged BMW was nowhere to be found. "It wasn't me he was after—it was Archibald."

Mort's eyes widened. "The drug guy from Rhode Island? He was here?"

"The shooter was gunning for him," I said, nodding. "I'm sure of it."

"Sure, Mrs. Fletcher, given that you're such an expert on gunfights."

Well, that didn't last.

Meanwhile, two of Mort's deputies were canvassing the area around where Archibald's BMW had been parked. Two more trotted toward the woods to look for expended shells and any other evidence that might help lead to the shooter's identity. Not that I was holding out much hope as far as that was concerned.

"What did Archibald want from you?"

"To keep me quiet, with a combination of an apology and an explanation," I said, stopping short of adding what he'd told me about Grady losing his job.

"Any chance it'll work?"

"What do you think?"

His expression looked more like Harry's. "Right, why'd I bother to ask? I'm putting an officer on guard duty."

"I told you, Mort, the shooter wasn't going after me."

"It's not the shooter I'm worried about, Jessica. The officer's instructions will be to protect you from yourself."

"Speaking of which, I paid another visit to our friend Fred Cooper."

"Oh no . . ."

"Don't worry. I had Harry to watch my back."

Mort glanced toward Harry, who was currently leaning against his car still trying to get all of his breath back.

"Right, that's comforting." He looked back at me. "Can you make any sense of all this?"

"I thought I was getting closer," I told him. "Now I'm not so sure anymore."

"That's not so comforting."

"Whatever's going on didn't start a week ago, Mort. It started long before that, even before the car accident that put Tripp Van Dorn in a wheelchair."

"We back to that again?"

I nodded. "Because it's the key, at least one of them. The mystery that explains everything we're facing."

"This isn't one of your books, Jessica."

"That's the same thing Harry told me."

Mort shot another glance Harry's way. "Then I take it back."

"No sign of George Sutherland, I assume."

Mort shook his head. "It's like he's vanished into thin air."

"He'd never do something like that, not without saying a word to me. And his belongings are still in his room here at the hotel."

"You think it was Clifton, don't you?"

"There's another possibility."

"I'm all ears."

"Not yet, Mort. It's probably wishful thinking on my part, not even worth raising yet."

Before he could argue that point, Mort's phone rang and he turned away from me to answer it. I could see fresh concern form over his features as he paced through the course of the brief, terse call, which ended with him turning back to me still clutching his phone.

"Turns out some guy with a rifle just took a potshot at Charles Clifton climbing into his car outside the clinic."

I did a rough estimate on the passage of time, concluding it jibed pretty well with the same shooter being responsible.

"But this time," Mort continued, "we caught him before he

could run off. He's in custody now. Care to join me down at the station?"

"Think I'll be getting back to the big city, if nobody has a problem with that," Harry McGraw told us.

"Thanks, Harry," I said, giving him a light hug.

He flashed that scowl in response, jowls dropping lower than usual. "Don't thank me. Pay me."

"Send me a bill."

"I'm behind on my paperwork."

"How far?"

"I'm finishing out my box of carbon paper."

"How about I just give you a blank check so you can fill in the amount?"

"There isn't room for enough zeros." He looked toward Mort. "Keep an eye on her, Mort. She's bound to do something else stupid before the day's out."

"I'll do my best, Harry."

Harry's expression tightened. "You watch yourself and call me if you need me. Can't wait to hear how this one turns out."

"Neither can I," I told him.

"You had somebody watching Charles Clifton," I said to Mort in the drive over to the sheriff's station.

"Those keen powers of observation tell you that?"

I shrugged. "How else could you have had officers already on-site when the gunman took a shot at Clifton, too?"

"You told me he and Jeffrey Archibald were joined at the

hip. I figured it was a logical move and sent a squad car to the Clifton Clinic as soon as I got word Archibald was the likely target."

"You're pretty good at this stuff, aren't you?"

"I know this writer who keeps me on my toes."

"Got an ID on the suspect?" I asked Mort.

"I do indeed, Mrs. Fletcher. But it's better if you see for yourself."

# Chapter Twenty-seven

The single dedicated interview room in the Cabot Cove Sheriff's Department headquarters was a windowless, converted supply closet in the back, longer than it was wide, so the table had to be placed lengthwise instead of horizontally, which made for an awkward squeeze on those occasions when suspects or witnesses needed to be interviewed. The building itself was located in one of the last truly rustic sections of town, halfway between Main Street and the coast, rimmed by woods that were an extension of the same forest grounds that made up the back of Hill House. I've taken any number of walks in those woods and spot something new every time I stroll there.

The department's interview room, understandably, didn't feature two-way mirrors with blackout glass, and the recording equipment still made use of old VHS tapes. I seem to remember that the money for a new system had been allocated in the last

budget, but Mort must've needed it for something more important. Beyond that, given the strains the summer season placed
on the department space-wise, keeping the interview room
tasked for that purpose was a feat unto itself.

"Now that we're here, care to give me a hint as to who the
suspect is?" I asked Mort, when he was about to open the door
accessing the former supply closet.

"His name is John Jessup. Ring any bells?"

"Tripp Van Dorn's father?"

"Ding-ding!"


I'd never met John Jessup and had glimpsed only a single picture of him, in the company of Mimi and Tripp as a toddler,
after it slipped out of a box I was hauling out to the trash for
Mimi when she was still getting settled in her Cabot Cove
home.

As soon as Mort opened the door to the interview room, I
was struck by the drastic and dramatic change in the appearance of the man seated at the table under a patrolman's watch-
ful eye. I studied John Jessup closer when the patrolman took
his leave. He'd been a hedge fund manager, successful enough
to build Mimi her life in Marblehead. Trim and proper, with a
big smile and a head of thick black hair.

That was before he discovered drugs, cocaine foremost
among them, which destroyed his life and either ate all his
money or emboldened the bad decision making that contrib-
uted to his financial collapse. There'd been some violent
episodes in the end that had resulted in arrest and prosecution,
which ended with probation on the condition he have no

further contact with either his wife or his young son, who'd been named as the victims of his increasingly violent, drug-fueled behavior. I recalled Mimi telling me John had disappeared and never come back. She went as far as to claim she had no idea where he was and believed he might have been dead.

The John Jessup of today had lighter, thinning hair and had gained a lot of weight. His ruddy complexion lined with sun-wrought furrows and lines suggested a man who worked outside, while his calloused hands and chipped nails with grime-coated beds made me think he might be a carpenter or landscaper. The gleaming smile he'd flashed in the few family photos I'd glimpsed had been replaced by the yellow-brown teeth of a habitual smoker, and the scent of stale cigarette smoke lifted from his work clothes as I drew closer.

"We've never met, Mr. Jessup," I said, extending my hand after Mort had introduced himself. "But I was a good friend of your wife's."

He took my hand in cursory fashion, still wearing handcuffs, trying to size me up while questioning my presence in the room.

"Is that why you're here, because you were a friend of Mimi?"

"Mrs. Fletcher assists us in our investigations from time to time," Mort explained, leaving it there. "This is one of those times."

Jessup didn't press the matter further, eyeing me closer. "You were at the hotel, standing near that son of a B Archibald."

"You could have shot me instead."

"I couldn't even hit him. Guess my aim is a bit rusty."

"I find it interesting," I said, taking the chair opposite his at the table squeezed into the renovated supply closet, "that you took potshots at the two men the sheriff and I believe are somehow implicated in your wife's death."

"Ex-wife," Jessup corrected. "Guess I won't be going to her funeral now, my son's either."

"You've got no one to blame for that but yourself," Mort chimed in.

"Just wish I had better aim. Won some trophies for marksmanship in my day."

Mort pretended to be impressed. "You don't say."

"How about you, Sheriff? You pretty good with a gun?"

"I try not to be."

"I'm curious as to how you learned of the potential involvement of Jeffrey Archibald and Charles Clifton in your wife's death, Mr. Jessup," I told him.

"You know the whole business they preach in Alcoholics Anonymous about making peace with your past?"

"I do."

"Well, I've made peace with the bunch of years that were pretty much a black hole in mine, Mrs. Fletcher, with one glaring exception: my wife and son. Losing that chance almost sent me back to the bottle and worse."

"So you opted for a rifle instead," I concluded.

He flirted with a smile. "I'd rather be a guest of the state than a prisoner of the drugs and booze again. And a part of me figured if I couldn't make it up to Mimi and Tripp while they were alive, I had to do the best I could with the little I had left."

"When was the last time you saw your son?" Mort asked him.

"The day I left Marblehead for the last time, Sheriff. I wrote him out of my life because I wasn't man enough to have a son. I blew it and figured it was best for him to never see me again."

"Even after the accident?" I wondered.

"I didn't even know about that for a long, long time. I only recently moved back to the area after stretches in both Colorado and Oregon, with a few places sprinkled in between. I found a lot of solace in not laying down roots, Mrs. Fletcher. That hadn't worked for me the first time I tried it. It was only last year, ten months ago, I came back and settled in Appleton."

The town where I'd first met my husband, Frank, I reflected, and where we'd lived before moving to Cabot Cove.

"To be close to Mimi, I presume."

Jessup nodded. "But I was never able to work up the courage to see her again, to ask for her forgiveness. I thought I could when I moved back." His expression sank and he looked down at the Formica surface of the table. "Then I found out what happened to Tripp. That set me back to square one, close to doing even worse. I almost moved away again, but ended up sticking it out and actually came to Cabot Cove the day of that lady's funeral."

*Jean O'Neil,* I almost told him.

"I saw Mimi outside after it ended. Sat in my Jeep looking right at her, hand on the door. But I couldn't open it, couldn't move. I looked at her, saw my past, and knew I wasn't ready and screeched out of there as fast as I could."

And then it hit me: John Jessup had been driving the old Jeep missing its front license plate that had almost run Mimi down!

"You weren't trying to kill her at all, were you?"

"I hit the gas pedal instead of the brake. Because of you."

"Me?"

"I saw you talking to her, Mrs. Fletcher, and truth be told, I knew who you were right away. When you spend as much time alone as I have, you make friends with a lot of books. I don't fancy mysteries much, but I recognized you from your book covers at the library. You've built quite a reputation."

"Hasn't she ever?" Mort added.

"So after Mimi died, and then Tripp, I started doing some nosing around town, getting the lay of the land."

I held Jessup's stare. "You followed me, didn't you?" I asked him, recalling that strange feeling I'd articulated to Harry Mc-Graw when we'd driven down to Rhode Island to see Jeffrey Archibald at the headquarters of LGX Pharmaceuticals. "You followed me to Rhode Island, then back to Cabot Cove. You must have glimpsed that confrontation I had the other night with Charles Clifton, before I called Mort."

Jessup nodded. "I saw enough to put things together for myself. I didn't care what happened to me. Like I said, I just wanted to make up for the fact that I'd never had the guts to make amends with my wife and son. Kept telling myself there would be more time and then bought that rifle when it turned out there wasn't going to be any more."

I could sense his genuine heartache and self-loathing. John Jessup had traveled across the country to flee his past, only to find that the past is a state of mind, not a place. And that realization had brought him back to Mimi for what would likely have been a strained, fruitless meeting. But at least Jessup could rest easier that he'd made the effort at an apology, if not a reconciliation. How ironic that in finding himself unable to approach Mimi, he'd almost run her over in the process of tearing off, and now he was bent on bringing those responsible for her death to justice.

He'd been relying on me to effectively point them out to him and had ultimately painted crosshairs on Jeffrey Archibald and Charles Clifton as a result. His desperation had led him to form assumptions that might just as easily have been mistaken. William Faulkner said, upon receiving the Nobel Prize, that all stories are about the human heart at war with itself. I think what he was getting at was encapsulated in the lives and fates of men like John Jessup. Figures who go from hopeless to tragic with little in the middle.

"Can we talk about Tripp?" I asked him.

Jessup swallowed hard, then nodded. "Probably be a short conversation, Mrs. Fletcher. I don't know a thing about him."

"This pertains to something else, specifically some oddities that have turned up in the course of this investigation."

"Oddities," he repeated. "You mean, besides me?"

I didn't want to prolong this any more than I had to, but needed to ascertain how exactly it was that Tripp and his mother didn't share the same blood type. "He was adopted, wasn't he?"

"Who?"

"Your son, Tripp."

"Adopted?"

"Was he the result of an affair you had with another woman?" I asked John Jessup, fitting together the pieces wrought by my imagination. "Did Mimi agree to raise him as her own?"

"I have no idea what you're talking about, Mrs. Fletcher."

"Mr. Jessup, Tripp might have been your son, but he wasn't Mimi's. I know that for a fact."

"Well, you're wrong. I might've been a lousy husband in those days, married more to money and coming home only when I had to. But I made it a point to be around when Tripp was born."

I tried to make sense of what I was hearing, reconcile it with what I knew to be the case. I fought to rein in my imagination as I continued, sticking to what I knew to be true.

"Then how can you explain how your ex-wife couldn't be your son's mother?"

"I can't, because she *was* Tripp's mother," Jessup insisted. "I was in the delivery room when he was born, Mrs. Fletcher. Believe me when I tell you he's Mimi's son, too."

Which made no sense, of course, none at all.

"Mort," I said after he'd closed the interview room door behind us, "I need you to rush a DNA test on something. And first thing tomorrow, we're going for a drive."

"Where?"

"Back to Rhode Island to visit Big Al McCandless. After a stop at Cabot Cove Hospital."

"What for?"

"To look at some more of those security tapes."

# Chapter Twenty-eight

B ig Al was seated in the very chair where I'd left him, the
lounge at Briarcliff Gardens empty save for him again as
well.

"Remember me, Chief?" I asked him.

"Nope," he said, without regarding me. "My show's on. Talk
to me later."

*Hawaii Five-0* was playing on the flat-screen this time, the
original version starring Jack Lord. The show had just started
and McCandless was humming along with the classic theme
song. Then the screen cut to a commercial, giving me three
minutes or so to get his attention.

"I was here the other day," I said, positioned to make sure
he could see me.

His eyes flashed recognition. "Oh yeah, I remember now.
You sold me Girl Scout cookies."

"I stopped in to see if you wanted to order any more boxes."

"Just the mint ones. I love the mint ones."

"How many boxes?"

Big Al's expression blanked for a moment. "How many did I get last time?"

"Six."

"Then I'll take six again! Six!"

"Done. While I'm here, could I ask you a few questions?"

He peered around me to make sure the commercial was still playing. "Six boxes," he repeated. "Six."

"Do you remember Mimi Van Dorn, Chief?"

"Does she like Girl Scout cookies?"

"Only the mint ones."

"Explains why we got along so well." He lowered his still strong voice, as Mort drew near enough to listen in. "You're not going to tell anyone about us, are you?"

"Wouldn't think of it."

Big Al seemed to notice Mort for the first time, eyes bulging as he thrust a finger forward. "Who's he? You didn't tell him about Mimi and me, did you?"

"This is Mort Metzger, Chief. He's sheriff of the town where I live in Maine."

"I like Maine."

"So do I."

"And I like sheriffs. Sounds better than 'police chief.' I wish they'd called me sheriff."

Mort had positioned himself next to me to further block the flat-screen's picture, hoping Alvin McCandless would forget he'd been watching it for a few more minutes.

"We were talking about Mimi," I prompted.

"We were?"

I nodded. "Remember the last time you saw her?"

Big Al seemed to think for a moment before beaming with certainty. "Yesterday! I saw her yesterday!"

"Did the two of you talk about Tripp?"

"Who's that?"

"Her son."

"She had a son?"

"He was in that terrible car wreck, remember?"

He didn't think for as long this time. "No, I don't remember."

"You did a favor for Mimi that night. Do you remember what it was?"

"I'd do it differently if I had it to do again. You make mistakes. People get hurt. But people had already been hurt. Didn't see the harm."

That was virtually the same thing he'd said the other day, as if he'd committed it to memory. More likely, he'd lived with what he'd done that night for so long that this particular memory clung to his consciousness like few others were able to. Embedded into his very psyche because of what he'd done in the wake of the accident that had turned Tripp Van Dorn into a quadriplegic.

"Two lives were ruined that night," I said, recalling something else McCandless had told me. "Weren't they, Chief?"

"I can't see the television."

"Were two lives ruined that night?" I repeated.

"I can't see the television." His eyes found Mort again, seeming to relish the sight of his uniform. "You're a policeman."

"A sheriff."

"I used to be a policeman."

"You were a chief," Mort told him.

"I was?"

"In Marblehead, Massachusetts," I picked up. "Do you remember Marblehead?"

Big Al's gaze darted between Mort and me, as if trying to decipher who we were again.

"Of course I do," he said suddenly.

Mort's turn. "Do you remember that rainy night the accident took place?"

"I called her myself."

My turn now. "Mimi?"

"Had to tell her what had happened. She told me what I should do."

"About Tripp?"

"Who's Tripp?"

"Mimi's son. He was driving the car, Chief."

Big Al seemed to have forgotten all about *Hawaii Five-0*. "She told me what to do."

"You had a long conversation with her on the phone," I prompted next, thinking back to what Tom Grimes had told me about driving Mimi Van Dorn to Mass General, the fact that she'd been talking to someone on her cell phone almost the whole time. "Do you remember what she told you to do?"

"No."

"Do you remember anything, anything at all about what she talked about?"

"We had to protect him," he said, looking more between us than toward either Mort or myself.

"Tripp?"

"I don't remember."

"You had to protect Mimi's son."

He finally regarded me again. "I just said that, didn't I? Damage has already been done. Two lives ruined. Can't ruin them twice."

Something else he'd said the last time, almost verbatim. I didn't want to risk him losing his train of thought again by hesitating, so I resumed immediately.

"What two lives, Chief? You mean, Tripp and Mimi?"

"Who's Tripp?"

"Her son. Mimi was his mother."

"No."

I thought I might be on to something, the very issue I'd come back here with Mort in tow to probe. "Mimi *wasn't* Tripp's mother?"

"Everyone has a mother, Girl Scout lady."

"Yes, Chief, they do."

"And the answer's no."

But I didn't know which question he was belatedly answering. "It wasn't Tripp and Mimi's lives that were ruined?"

"No."

"Whose lives were ruined, then?" I asked, stealing a glance at Mort, who stood there like a statue, with his Cabot Cove sheriff's uniform, for Alvin McCandless to see.

"Tripp and . . ."

"Tripp and who, Chief?"

His eyes sought me out, pleading and desperate. Big Al looked as if he might be about to cry.

"Are you mad at me for what I did?"

"Not at all."

"I just wanted to help. That was my job—to help." His eyes

found Mort, focusing on his uniform. "That's what we're supposed to do, isn't it, Sheriff?"

"It sure is, Chief."

"What was it you did?" I asked, again hoping to hold Big Al to this train of thought.

"What Mimi told me. She'd figured it all out. I couldn't argue with her. It was a good thing we were doing, not a bad thing. I believed that." His gaze jerked back to Mort. "You would have done the same thing, wouldn't you?"

"For sure. Any good lawman would."

Big Al smiled serenely. "Lawman . . . I was a lawman. . . ."

"You still are, Chief," Mort told him. "It's something you never stop being just because you stop wearing the uniform. You know why?" He tapped his head. "Because being a lawman's up here."

"I helped them. I did what I had to do."

I looked toward Mort, yielding the floor to him.

"Helped who?" he asked Big Al.

"Tripp Van Dorn and . . ."

"And who, Chief?"

"Tripp Van Dorn and . . . the other one."

"His mother?"

"Not his mother—the other one. Hey, my show's on."

"Who's the other one?" Mort asked him.

"You're standing in the way! Get out of the way!"

"You helped Tripp and who else? What was his name?"

"Da-da-da-da-da," he started in, mimicking the *Hawaii Five-0* theme song.

"Who was the other person you helped that night after the accident, Chief?"

Big Al looked up at Mort, and I was certain he was finally ready to answer the question.

"Book 'em, Danno," he said instead.

"McGarrett would have done the same thing you did that night," I tried.

"He liked helping people, too."

"Yes, he did."

"Lives shouldn't be ruined. It was the right thing to do and the wrong thing to do."

"Of course."

"I couldn't say no to Mimi."

"No, you couldn't."

"You won't tell on me, will you? People in Marblehead have been known to talk, you know."

"Yes, I do," I said, knowing the same thing was true about Cabot Cove.

"When do I get my cookies? Remember, Thin Mints."

"Six boxes."

Big Al stiffened, looking suddenly out of sorts. "Where did I put my checkbook? Have you seen my checkbook?"

He started sweeping his eyes about in search of something he hadn't laid eyes on in years.

"Don't you remember, Chief?" I chimed in quickly. "They're free. Buy six and get six free."

"Buy six and get six free! Buy six and get six free! Buy six and get six free!"

"And you already bought six, so these next six are free."

"Oh, that's good, that's very good."

Then he went back to humming the *Hawaii Five-0* theme song, as Mort and I finally moved out of his way.

\*     \*     \*

"Well, that was helpful," Mort said, sarcasm lacing his voice, as we emerged from Briarcliff Gardens.

"You weren't listening," I told him. "Alvin McCandless gave us everything we needed in there."

"Everything we needed?" Mort stopped and shook his head, eyeing me the same way he'd been eyeing Big Al. "Maybe I should check to see if this place has any rooms available. . . ."

"I'm serious."

"So am I. I think you're finally cracking up. I think all this is finally getting to you, Jessica."

"That's 'Mrs. Fletcher' to you, Sheriff."

"Did you treat Amos Tupper this way?"

"Do you know how many times you've asked me that over the years?"

"Then I guess one more won't matter."

Mort moved in front of me and ground to a halt when we were still halfway to his SUV, roasting in the Rhode Island sun, which had me longing for the pleasant sea breeze for which Cabot Cove was known. "Did you actually say McCandless gave us what we needed?"

"Yes."

"Well, I didn't hear it."

"I guess you don't speak his language as well as I do, Mort."

"Care to enlighten me?"

"Not until we get the results of the DNA test back for proof positive," I told him. "But I already know who killed Tripp Van Dorn. And I know who killed Mimi, too."

# Chapter Twenty-nine

Mort dropped me at Hill House nearly five hours later, after slogging through interminable summer traffic on every road we found ourselves on. Cabot Cove was in the midst of a beautiful sunset he wasn't about to let me enjoy.

"Notice how quiet I was during the drive."

"I thought you were mad I didn't explain my theory on who I believe killed Tripp and Mimi Van Dorn."

"No, ma'am. I was quiet because I didn't want to pester you. I know you'll tell me when you're ready."

I nodded, waiting to see if Mort had anything further to say and then continuing when he didn't. "Not like you to show so much patience when murder is involved."

"I thought I'd make an exception in this case, Mrs. Fletcher."

"Not going to let that go, are you?"

"I like changing things up once in a while."

I eyed him closer. "So what do you want in return?"

"Just one thing," Mort said, getting to the point. "Stay away from the Clifton Clinic until we get all this sorted out."

"By 'sorted out,' do you mean an arrest warrant for Charles Clifton?"

"Don't jump the gun here. This is a matter better handled by the Maine attorney general's office."

"Since when do you refer murder to the attorney general?"

"I was talking about all these shenanigans he's pulling with clinical trials."

"I was talking about Mimi Van Dorn's murder."

"So I gathered," Mort told me. "Do I need to put a cruiser on this place to make sure you stay put?"

"I doubt you can spare the manpower."

"Watch me."


I knocked on the door to the room George Sutherland had yet to check out of, a part of me fully expecting him to open it with a hearty smile and a sensible explanation as to where he'd been for two days now. But my rapping went unanswered, which didn't stop me from pressing my ear against the door, in the hope of detecting some sign George was actually inside.

Thanks to that imagination of mine again.

The suite I was occupying at Hill House—while my beloved home on Candlewood Lane was being rebuilt following that fire—overlooked the wooded rear of the property, instead of the front. But a return to the lobby a few minutes later revealed a Cabot Cove squad car was indeed parked on the street beyond the hotel.

Of course, I had no intention of letting its presence deter my next move. George Sutherland's disappearance, and his ultimate fate, might very well lie squarely in the hands of Charles Clifton and Jeffrey Archibald. There was no other rational explanation for what had become of him. Truth be told, I'd come to fear that sharing my suspicions and trepidations about George's trust in the Clifton Clinic may have had ended up placing him in more jeopardy instead of less. I always told myself that, one of these days, I'd learn to leave well enough alone, but so far, anyway, that day hadn't come.

I returned to my suite and switched on the television, tuned perpetually to CNN. I hoped to be able to find some way to talk myself out of what I intended to do next, some rationale to dissuade me from doing something I was already committed to in my mind. I can't say exactly where this penchant originated. No single event in my past jumped out. I'd never suffered the kind of injustice that might explain my obsession with seeing justice done. It was, instead, likely the point where my fictional and actual selves melded into one; instead of writing a role, I was playing one. I didn't consider myself a crusader, but found it impossible not to act in the wake of someone close to me being harmed.

And there were few closer than George Sutherland. Why had it taken so long between visits? Why had I thought of him so infrequently since our last meeting? I think you reach a certain age in life when you're more afraid of being together than alone. The fact that George and I were separated by so much distance meant the times that brought us together were treated as special occasions. The end of each visit inevitably came with the melancholy sense that it was over, mixed with the sense of relief we were going our separate ways, secure in the knowledge we'd be coming together again.

But not so much now.

When I insert myself into an investigation, it's almost always out of no more than an obsession to see justice done. That sounds like a cliché until someone loses their life at the hands of another, often throwing numerous other lives into turmoil. Murder is many things, but at its heart it almost invariably comes down to one:

Evil.

Evil is what lies at the heart of almost all murders. Evil is the ultimate bully, making us feel weak and helpless in its face. I had dabbled in writing before my husband Frank's death, but I didn't actually start my first book until the days following his funeral, I thought both to honor his longtime advice to go after my dream and to distract from my grief. Now I realize that I turned to writing to create a world that was mine to control, where I'd no longer feel weak and helpless as I did with Frank's illness and ultimate passing. Trying to do the same in real life, I suppose, was just a natural progression.

But this was different.

This was about George. Sure, it was about Mimi and Tripp Van Dorn, too, but there was no one I was serving by uncovering their killers. I fully believed George was still alive, and on the chance he wasn't, the evil behind his murder could be laid on the desks of two men: Charles Clifton and Jeffrey Archibald.

And that was exactly what I intended to do, starting with a phone call.

\*     \*     \*

"Sheriff Metzger's not in the building, Mrs. Fletcher," the night duty officer at the sheriff's department told me. "Would you like to leave a message?"

I breathed a sigh of relief, glad I'd be spared explaining what was essentially a Hail Mary pass to Mort. "No, I just had a quick question about something we're working on. Might Deputy Andy be available?"

"Let me check."

"What can I do for you, Mrs. Fletcher?" Deputy Andy greeted me moments later.

"I just have a quick question I don't want to bother the sheriff with."

"Happy to help, if I can."

"Oh, I'm sure you can. See, the question's about parking tickets. . . ."

I kept my bike in a storage shed that contained, among other things, the old chaise lounges for the pool Hill House had covered over to make room for the hotel's expansion years ago, which had proved very handy when Cabot Cove turned trendy.

I'd purchased something called a town bike, put out by a company called Pashley, after my older Schwinn was destroyed in a riding accident. A front slot fitted for an old-fashioned wicker basket was what had first attracted me to it in the store, my interest also stoked by some of the very qualities that turned others away. First of all, it was heavy and came standard with an abuse-proof frame that promised to last a long time and

even withstand any further encounters I might have with ne-
farious pickup trucks. The salesman explained about the challenges its internal gear hub drivetrain posed for climbing hills,
but since coastal Cabot Cove boasted virtually no hills to speak
of, I took the Pashley out for a spin and fell in love with it instantly. Its heft had an old-fashioned feel and sense to it. Not
the choice to make if you intended to be racing around, but
since I didn't, I'd purchased it on the spot.

It was a beautiful night for a bike ride, and I would have
normally worn a reflective vest to go along with the reflective
spinners, but tonight I wanted to avoid getting any attention—
and especially to avoid being detected by the patrolman Mort
Metzger had assigned to watch over Hill House.

The night was better than beautiful to be on the road in the
open air; it was perfect. As always, I pedaled slowly, taking my
time, aware of the considerable distance from here to the Cabot
Cove bluffs where I'd find my quarry. And, true to that fact, my
jaunt to and through the center of town itself was covered in
comfortable fashion, the breeze in my face and the summer
daytime traffic having finally ebbed. Many in Cabot Cove will
tell you their favorite day of the year is Labor Day, because
that's the time we get our streets back.

I hadn't been riding as much as I normally do, with the
summer heat to contend with during the day and mosquitoes
at night, and I was feeling the effects of that when the Clifton
Clinic bluffs came into view after I'd passed through the center
of town. One thing I'd learned living on the coast was the difficulty in judging distances with no frame of reference between
here and there. In this case, the bluffs looked only a stone's
throw away, but another mile covered on the two-lane coastal

road that followed the town's contours seemed to bring me no closer.

By the time my bike's tires finally touched the narrow stone-paved road that led across the rocky bluffs to the clinic itself, I was questioning the wisdom of not simply walking down the street from Hill House and bringing the Uber app up on my phone. I guess I needed the time to figure out what I was going to say to Charles Clifton when I showed up unannounced, even though I knew all my preparations would be thrown out the window once I sat down before him. I couldn't dictate my books; I had to type them. Similarly, I needed to be seated in front of somebody before I could actually form what I wanted to say to him or her.

Cruising through the clinic's parking lot, though, drew me past a BMW 6-series coupe with a recently repaired windshield but still missing the passenger side mirror, meaning Jeffrey Archibald was on the premises as well.

An unexpected bonus.

Charles Clifton didn't seem at all surprised by my arrival, coming to meet me in the lobby after being alerted to my presence by the same receptionist who'd been on duty the other night.

"You came alone, Mrs. Fletcher," he said, peering over my shoulder and perhaps spotting my bike perched against a stanchion outside the entrance. "I must say I'm a bit surprised, given how your last visit went."

"Maybe that's precisely why I came alone this time."

"Not a social visit, I presume."

"Not at all, Doctor. But I do have some advice for you."

"What's that?"

"You need a bike rack."


"Flames without heat," I said to Clifton, after he'd offered me a chair set before a desk in his spacious book-lined office, which would have made for a nice Victorian sitting room, right down to the ornamental gas fire glowing in the hearth built into the far wall. "Why do I think if I stuck my hand into them, I'd still get burned?"

"Appearances can be deceiving, Mrs. Fletcher."

"Not in this case, I expect, Doctor. I think you're everything your appearance suggests: shallow, superficial, and supercilious. You should feel free to invite Mr. Archibald to join us, by the way."

"What makes you think he's here?"

"Seeing his car in the parking lot was kind of a giveaway."

Clifton nodded. "He warned me to expect you, Mrs. Fletcher."

"Warned or told?"

"He said you were a difficult person to bring to your senses."

"I guess he was dismayed when I rejected a lifetime supply of aspirin in exchange for letting all this go."

"That's not what I heard."

"Actually, it was two lifetimes," I said. "The fact is, Dr. Clifton, Mr. Archibald crossed a line with me."

"Something you seem very comfortable doing yourself."

"But this line was about family, when he mentioned my nephew Grady. That's a *red* line for me."

"As I suspect threatening his livelihood was to Mr. Archibald."

"You mean because he's engaged in illegal activities, in which you're complicit, too? I must say it's a brilliant scheme. Too bad Mimi Van Dorn had to go and ruin it. But I guess you couldn't let her risk exposing the fact that she was being treated under a fake clinical trial with a drug she had to pay exorbitantly for. I put the amount at mid–six figures. Would that be about right, Doctor?"

"Does it really matter, Mrs. Fletcher?" he asked with a sigh, looking impatient and almost bored.

"You mean the actual figure or Mimi's life? The one thing I don't understand is why you still provided her with the drug in spite of the warnings about its effects on those suffering from either type one or type two diabetes." I studied his expression, saw enough to realize something I should have already. "You didn't know, did you? You either never checked the potential side effects or brushed them aside and paid them no heed."

"Mimi Van Dorn signed a waiver, as all my patients do."

"You mean the patients you deceive and steal from, Doctor."

I expected Clifton to bristle at that, but he didn't. "So what brings you here on your own tonight, Mrs. Fletcher, if not to make trouble?"

"To make a deal."

# Chapter Thirty

"I know you killed Mimi Van Dorn."

Clifton bristled visibly at that, remaining silent to see what I'd say next.

"You had help, Doctor," I continued, "but you're still a direct party to her murder."

"You've read too many of your own books, Mrs. Fletcher. Not everyone you don't like is the boogeyman."

"In my experience, there's no one boogeyman—there are thousands. Many of them dressed in the best costume of all, that of respectability and success. Boogeymen like that believe their power shields and emboldens their deeds. I read and write about them because it helps me deal with the fact that they're out there, living right next door or around the corner. Just like you and this clinic, where you're supposed to be helping people instead of killing them."

"Last I checked, Mimi Van Dorn didn't die here."

"But this is where she was killed, because it's where you gave her this potentially groundbreaking antiaging drug supplied to you by LGX Pharmaceuticals." Something occurred to me in that moment I hadn't considered yet. "Tell me, Doctor, if one of these drugs you're conducting fake trials for hits, how much might you and Jeffrey Archibald stand to make? Ten million dollars, fifty million, a hundred? Even more? I guess it might be capitalism at its best, if you weren't endangering the lives of so many like Mimi Van Dorn."

I waited for Clifton to comment, but instead he sat smugly in his desk chair, his pasty face caught in the glow of the fake flames coming from the equally fake hearth.

"And how much richer might the two of you get once all those other Clifton Care Partners clinics open? A friend of mine is having a forensic audit conducted to reveal the names of your investors. I suspect Jeffrey Archibald will be at the top of that list."

"Which proves nothing," Clifton said, finally finding his voice. "Particularly my complicity in Mimi Van Dorn's death."

"Maybe not, but it does suggest motive. All that money you stood to make jeopardized by a patient—subject actually—suffering devastating side effects in public view. You couldn't risk Mimi awaking from that coma and coming clean about the clinical trial she'd paid you a fortune to be a part of. So she had to die, which explains your presence at the hospital."

"Except I left the hospital at least an hour before the code was called. I suspect the security footage of the lobby and doctors' parking lot will confirm that."

"This would be the footage from the day of her death?"

"What else would it be, Mrs. Fletcher?"

"The day before, like the footage from the ICU, which had been tampered with."

"And that makes me a suspect?"

"It does indeed, Doctor, because you're the one who tampered with it."

Again, Clifton showed no response, remaining smug and stoic, which was plenty of response in itself.

"You seem partial to three-piece suits," I noted. "Glen plaid being your favorite."

"Is that a crime, too, Mrs. Fletcher?"

"Only as far as fashion goes. You might recall, though, when I saw you in the ICU hall after you returned upon learning of Mimi's death, I noted the tears in your pants, even with the knees. You told me you'd slipped on the pavement someplace and scraped them up."

"Because it's the truth."

"No, it's not," I told him, reaching into my bag and handing a folded sheet of paper across the desk. "Take a look."

I watched Clifton straighten the page out to reveal a still shot of him entering Cabot Cove Hospital, lifted from a lobby security camera.

"What is this?"

"It was taken a few minutes before you paid that fateful early morning visit to Mimi Van Dorn. It was your knees I was most interested in."

"My knees?"

I handed another picture across his desk. "You can see them better in this version." Clifton didn't unfold the printed photo this time, but I continued anyway. "No tears in your suit, Doctor, which means you were lying about that fall, because you tore your trousers after you entered the hospital and not before."

He remained stiff and silent behind his desk.

"You entered Mimi's room on the pretext of wanting to check in on her. But what you really wanted was to access the crawl space through the hatchway in the closet. Turns out that crawl space runs directly to the video-monitoring station, which was empty at the time. I imagine you reached it without incident, besides those tears in your pants, and proceeded to change the security loop for the ICU camera to the day before for the next several hours. Something you could've been quite adept at, given that your clinic boasts an almost identical security system."

"Interesting," Clifton noted, summoning all the bravado he could. "You can't prove any of this, but it does make for a great story. More interesting, I suspect, than the ones you make up."

"Reality always is, Doctor. What I couldn't figure out for the life of me was what you were trying to hide. What was it that would've been visible for all to see if you hadn't swapped that day's loop for the previous day's?"

I made him wait for what I was going to say next.

"The arrival of Jeffrey Archibald," I said finally. "He waited until the nurses' station was empty before entering Mimi's room. That's when he pulled the cord of the machine out just enough to cut the power, while still making it appear like an accident, an explanation everyone would have otherwise accepted."

"Unless it really was an accident, Mrs. Fletcher. And now

you, and that vivid imagination of yours, are making the rest up."

"But here's something I didn't make up: Jeffrey Archibald's BMW."

"What about it?"

"The car was parked on a street just beyond the hospital right around the time of Mimi Van Dorn's death."

Clifton nodded dismissively. "Don't tell me—it was caught on a traffic camera that must've been installed that very day, since Cabot Cove doesn't boast any traffic cameras."

"No, Doctor, it wasn't a traffic camera; it was a parking ticket."

"The sheriff's department has been issuing them all day and night to deal with the clutter of cars packing our streets without parking permits," I told him, reveling in his blank expression. "It helps Sheriff Metzger fund the extra deputies he needs for the summer months. And in this case, a patrolman issued the ticket perhaps at the very moment the car's owner was pulling the plug on Mimi Van Dorn's ventilator."

Charles Clifton looked like a man coming to grips with the fact that his GPS app had gotten him lost, nothing he could do to easily dismiss the information Deputy Andy had provided in response to my query.

"Just because his car was here," he groped, "doesn't mean Archibald was driving it."

"Reasonable doubt, in other words."

"You take issue with that, Mrs. Fletcher?"

"Not at all. It's why I came here."

"To make a deal, you said," he recalled.

"You're right, Doctor, I probably don't have enough proof or hard evidence to get Sheriff Metzger to arrest you. But my mere trying would, at the very least, draw attention to what's really going on here, including your deal with the devil in Jeffrey Archibald."

"He mentioned his wife was a big fan of yours."

"Not quite enough for me to let him get off scot-free on this. I can't put him in jail for the rest of his life, but I might be able to ruin the two of you for just about that long. Unless . . ." I finished dramatically, letting my voice trail off.

"Unless what?" Clifton asked, taking the bait.

"You give me George Sutherland."

"What makes you think I have him?"

"He's gone, and he was last seen here, on these premises."

"*I* last saw him here, too."

"He's also a chief inspector of Scotland Yard, and thus a threat if he latched on to what you're really up to in this place."

"You mean, all the things you planted in his mind? Did it ever occur to you, Mrs. Fletcher, that you are very likely responsible for his turning away from the only treatment that can save his life? That kind of responsibility is a hard burden to bear."

"Coming from someone as expert in the matter as you, Doctor, I suppose I should take that to heart."

"You think I kidnapped George Sutherland. You think I'm holding him here against his will when a far more rational explanation is that he threw himself off these cliffs to the rocky waters below. But you don't want to face that possibility, because it would mean you were responsible for his death. So you concocted this ridiculous story to blame me for whatever happened to him."

"Don't forget Jeffrey Archibald."

"That would be hard to do," a voice rang out from behind me, "given that I'm standing right here."

# Chapter Thirty-one

"Then you heard my proposal," I said, turning toward him in my chair.

"Dr. Clifton is telling the truth, Mrs. Fletcher. George Sutherland isn't here. And whatever fate he suffered came from his own volition."

"And you know that because—let me guess—the good doctor assured you it was true. I wonder if you might be reacting differently if he admitted the truth."

"Assuming this hidden truth reveals itself, or if we were in a position to turn Sutherland over to you, what guarantees do we have you wouldn't continue this investigation of your anyway?"

"Because you think you've covered every base, a couple of would-be geniuses who believe they committed the perfect crime. And that might well have been true if it hadn't been for that parking ticket, Mr. Archibald."

"I'm glad I decided not to buy a place up here."

"Speaking on behalf of all of Cabot Cove, so are we." I rotated my gaze between the two of them. "What I really don't understand is, why take the risk involved with murdering Mimi when she was likely never going to wake up anyway? Killing her made necessary the autopsy that revealed your drug to be the cause of her seizure. Sure, it would have come out eventually anyway, thanks to the anomaly that came up in the tox screen. But your actions basically assured we'd find out about that potential antiaging miracle you must have sold her some bill of goods on. Unless . . . " I continued when Clifton and Archibald exchanged an uneasy glance. "Unless you were more worried about the possibility Mimi was going to wake up, afraid of something she'd say that was worth killing her over."

"You knew the woman better than we did," Archibald proclaimed, drawing a caustic glare from Clifton. "So why don't you just tell us, make it up as you go along just like you did all the rest of this?"

"Blackmail," I realized. "You actually knew Mimi even better than I did, didn't you? You knew she'd spent just about every dollar she had left on this treatment. I think she figured out what the two of you were really up to, which would've made great fodder to bring you down . . . unless you paid her off, of course."

And then it hit me, something that hadn't even entered my mind until that very moment. "Oh my . . . How could I not have seen it?"

My eyes darted between the two men as their stares locked knowingly.

"That seizure she suffered in the library was supposed to kill Mimi. The two of you murdered her twice."

I focused my gaze on Clifton. "I blamed you for giving her a drug you knew might kill her. Except you did it on purpose, the last dosage anyway. You gave her enough of that drug to produce exactly the effect on her nervous system that you expected it to. And when that only resulted in putting her in a coma, from which she could conceivably awake with quite a story to tell, you came back and finished the job."

Jeffrey Archibald started clapping. "I can see why my wife's such a fan. You really can tell a story, Mrs. Fletcher. I suspect you might call this one *Murder in Red*—red for blood."

"Nice title."

"I look forward to you inscribing a copy of that one for me, too."

"Well, they do have libraries in prison, Mr. Archibald."

He shook his head. "It's really true, isn't it, what they say about you?"

"What's that?"

"That you've got a sixth sense for murder."

"I like that title, too," I told him.

"But you won't be needing it, because you're never going to get the chance to write another book."

I remained in my chair. "So you're planning on making me disappear, too?"

"We didn't make George Sutherland disappear," Dr. Clifton insisted, repeating the claim yet again.

"You, on the other hand . . ." Archibald started, leaving it there.

"You think nobody knows I'm here?"

I'd aimed my question at Clifton, who cast a sidelong glance toward Archibald instead of responding. That glance suggested subservience, one man looking for direction from another.

"I had it all wrong, didn't it?" I realized, moving my gaze between the two of them, before letting it rest again on Clifton. "I thought you were the one driving this, Doctor, what with your plan to expand Clifton Care Partners all over the country."

"Don't forget the world, Mrs. Fletcher." Archibald smirked, virtually confirming my suspicions.

"Of course," I said, my thoughts forming into words, "it all started with you, with seeking a way to exploit LGX Pharmaceuticals' considerable collection of drug patents to make yourself a fortune. All you needed was a patsy, a doctor whose ambitions mirrored your own. And you found your front man in Dr. Clifton. Tell me," I continued, addressing both of them, "have I got it right now?"

Clifton sat stoic and still behind his desk, leaving the floor to Archibald, which further confirmed my suspicions.

"You did us a great favor by riding your bike here," Archibald said. "A moonless night, all those rocks on the bluffs, anyone could lose their way and end up in the waters below."

I felt the steady creep of fear swallow the determination and resolve that had gotten me this far. I began to suspect that I'd been wrong in one crucial assumption, something my presence here should have invoked that had not yet proved the case. Still, I did my best to hold fast.

"A biking accident?" I tried, aiming my words at Archibald. "Really?"

But it was Clifton who answered me. "There'll be doubts, suspicions, but nothing that can possibly lead anywhere, especially on the part of that two-bit cop you call a sheriff."

"Mort did twenty years with the NYPD, Doctor. Maybe you've heard of them."

"All the same," interjected Archibald, "there'll be nothing to investigate, because it's going to look like an accident. And, from what I hear about these waters, your body may not even wash up until next summer."

I weighed my options, found none. My life now depended on a ridiculous assumption I'd led myself to believe was the truth, based on a cryptic clue that could've been explained several other ways.

I heard the door to Clifton's office open and close, turned my head round just enough to see two big men who might as well have been twins from their black outfits, close-cropped haircuts, and steely demeanor. They had private military written all over them. Professionals, as opposed to thugs. I guess Clifton and Archibald were pulling out all the stops to ensure nothing impeded the continued building of clinics all over the country. Patients be damned, they were going to expand their plan of fake clinical trials that were pay-to-participate, to reap hundreds of millions in profit.

I felt the two men, the Almost Twins, approaching my chair, their grasps when they took me by either arm feeling like steel vises.

"It looks like the legendary Jessica Fletcher has finally met her match." Archibald smirked, as the Almost Twins led me past him toward the door. "Looks like I'm going to have to put that book you signed for my wife away for safekeeping, since it's going to be the last one you'll ever sign."

"We'll see about that," I managed, lamely.

"Still putting on a brave face," noted Archibald. "If I didn't know better, Charles, I'd say the little lady here still has a trick up her sleeve."

"This little lady," I said to him, starting to realize I didn't have that trick or anything else up my sleeve, that what I'd come here expecting to happen had been wishful thinking all along, "is an inch taller than you."

Archibald grinned, his teeth so blindingly white, it looked like he gargled with Clorox. "It was nice meeting you, Mrs. Fletcher. Thanks for signing my wife's book."

The Almost Twins pulled me the rest of the way from the room, looking like androids from some science fiction movie. Their expressions didn't move; their hair didn't move. Their motions seemed more programmed than planned. I'd dealt with other men like this in my time, though hardly under this kind of dire threat from them. They could kill a person and give it no more thought than swatting a fly or stepping on a cockroach. The secret to their success was to dehumanize their victims, regard them as no more vital than that fly or roach, to be swatted or stepped on. Go about their business of tossing me and my bike over the side of the bluffs and then report back for further duty.

*George, where are you?*

The Almost Twin on the right swung toward me, and for a

moment I thought I must have said that out loud. But I hadn't. And the Almost Twin hadn't actually been looking at me so much as something we'd left behind in our wake heading to the elevator.

And that's when all the lights went off.

# Chapter Thirty-two

The emergency lights snapping on cast long shadows, while barely breaking the darkness that was thickest right where we were standing in the hallway. The Almost Twins tightened their grasps upon me, but then let them slacken enough to whip out their pistols.

I heard a crash and the emergency light behind us went dark. A figure whirled past me, and I thought for a moment it must be one of the Almost Twins. But that made no sense, since they were still on either side of me.

Until they weren't.

I heard grunts, groans, felt dark shapes whipsawing about me. One frame slammed, or was thrown, into me, rattling me to the very core. I staggered but kept my feet, my right shoulder feeling like someone had ripped it from the socket. It went numb, my fingers tingling, as the blur of struggling shapes continued to unfold before me.

Thuds now. Then the hall was alive with a burst of one muzzle flash and then another, the shots absurdly loud in the confined space, pushing air through my ears and the smell of cordite and burned sulfur into my nose.

A shape emerged from the whirling maelstrom, a hand stretching out toward me like a tentacle.

"This way, Jessica!" George Sutherland said into my ear, tugging me toward the stairwell on our right and crashing through the door.

"I knew it!" I yelled out, fighting to keep George's pace down the stairs.

"Whatever 'it' is, dear lady, I'm sure you did."

We spun onto the next flight.

"Every time I called you the other day," I resumed, holding on to the railing as we dipped and darted down the stairs, "your phone went straight to voice mail. But it rang, at least vibrated, when I dialed it inside your treatment room. Because you set us up. You vanished because you wanted to."

"And had to, thanks to you."

"Me?"

We turned onto the final stairwell that would take us to the first floor.

George spoke between sucking in big breaths. "I knew you'd figure out my little ruse, if left to your paces. I should've known better than to keep you in the dark, should have told you the truth from the start."

"Which is?"

We burst outside into the torrid heat of the night through an emergency exit door at the bottom of the stairs.

"I'm not sick, Jessica."

I felt George tugging me on, away from the clinic, following the general contours of the rock-made causeway that was the one road on and off the bluffs.

"Unlike a countryman of mine who came to the Clifton Clinic for treatment and never made it home."

"Treatment, as in a clinical trial?"

"*Supposed* clinical trial," he elaborated.

"Just like you're suffering from a supposed disease."

"Perfect cover, once we learned Clifton was conducting another of his clinical trials for a drug meant to treat it."

"Manufactured by LGX Pharmaceuticals."

"I didn't get that far in my investigation."

"Good thing I did, then . . . So, that bit with the phone . . . You wanted me to know you weren't really missing at all."

"But I didn't expect you to come here and bait the killers I was trying to catch."

I somehow managed a smile. "Then I guess you don't know me as well as you think you do."

And that's when gunshots began to pop behind us, muzzle flashes that looked like fireflies lighting up the night.

George tugged me harder, steering us for the bluffs. "Our only chance for escape, dear lady."

"The rocks?"

"I've never known you to be scared of anything."

"Because you've never known me to be scaling a rock face of these bluffs." I looked at him through the darkness, as our feet toyed with the sharply angled edge. "Who are you, George Sutherland?"

"Somebody else entirely before I joined Scotland Yard, dear Jessica. Same name, different rank. With the British Special Air Service."

"The SAS? Now I'm really impressed."

George shifted to help lower me onto the bluffs, as more gunshots coughed up chips of stone around us. "I should have told you."

"I'd never have let you go through with it if you had."

"You're making my case for me. And, by all accounts, from what I overhead you saying in Clifton's office, you've busted the case wide open."

"We always did make a great team, George," I said, and continued with him to the edge of the plateau atop the bluffs.

Those famed bluffs looked forbidding from a distance. From this close, when I contemplated trying to traverse them, they were downright terrifying. Rock climbing was something I'd never sampled for one of my books, but I imagined this was as close as it got to that. The sharply ridged face appeared to be formed by craggy rock formations. But there seemed to be an equal amount of crushed stone that felt like gravel beneath my feet, as I began my descent, every muscle in my body seeming to tighten in protest.

George had lowered himself even with me. We'd never discussed his background in the British military's elite SAS unit, but I shouldn't have been surprised. My husband, Frank, had been in the air force, so in a lighter moment I might have considered myself attracted to men in uniform.

We continued an uneasy, zigzagging descent, until George laid a hand on my back to press me tighter against the face of the bluffs. I could hear muffled voices maybe thirty feet above cutting through the wind and the mist the humid conditions were whipping in off the sea. Waves of it rolled past us, making me feel like I was high enough in the sky to be hiding in a cloud.

But I wasn't. I was pressed against the steep side of a bluff, precariously balanced on a narrow ledge that was shedding layers of gravel-like stone along the natural downward slope.

The muffled voices drifted off, and George gave me a tug. I thought it was a signal it was safe to move again, but it was also a means of directing me to follow in his steps. I imagined that, with his newly revealed military background, he was no stranger to such terrain, and thought training on something like the cliffs of Dover would've made perfect preparation for what we were facing tonight.

For the first time since we began our descent, I registered the crashing of the sea against the rocks beneath us, a reminder of the fate awaiting us should we fall. I felt a flutter in my stomach and was glad the night kept me from seeing what was beneath me or judging the meager amount of progress we'd made so far.

George made sure I could follow the placement of his hands, and I stayed as close to him as I dared, fearful a slip might leave me reaching out instinctively and risk toppling both of us to our deaths. Flashlight beams swept over us from above now, a pair of bright beams slicing through the mist. Each time they crossed, I followed George's lead and pressed as close to the face of the bluffs as I could.

I remembered once learning, while doing research for a book, that eyes glowed as big as baseballs when struck by a flashlight in the darkness, and resolved not to look up no matter what. Once the beams moved on, George started leading the way on again, only to freeze when fresh gunshots spit flecks of rock into the air, stinging my skin. I could feel warm blotches where those flecks left their pinprick marks.

I felt George stiffen as he tried to determine our next move. I thought how much he must've craved his pistol, which he was prohibited from carrying overseas and had only begun carrying back in England over the course of the last few years. Even that had been a source of frustration for him at times, and now, having learned the depth of his military background, I could understand why.

"We need to try going straight down," he whispered to me, "at least until we're below that ledge."

"What ledge?"

"Take my hand."

"What?"

"So I can help lower you."

I felt every muscle in my body seize up at once in protest. "I don't think I can do it, George."

He nodded. I was close enough to see the grim bent of his expression, as he gazed upward to contemplate our chances of climbing back up instead.

"No," I said, realizing the utter foolishness and desperation of such a move, "I can do this."

I stole a quick glance downward, the mist parting enough to reveal the ledge to which George had been referring. It looked as straight as a scaffolding platform strung to a building and about as big to boot. Get beneath that and our descent would be far better shielded. But I couldn't spot any rocky extensions for our feet, much less decent holds for our hands.

Instead of side by side, to reach the ledge we'd have to descend more in single file. I felt George squeeze my arm reassuringly and start to ease himself downward. I studied the way his hands never seemed to lose touch with the rocky face; he dragged them against it instead of lifting his hands off and putting them back in a different place. And I mimicked his actions as best I could, the moisture from the mist seeming to make my hands cling better to the rocks, which glowed wet from a combination of the wave spray and that mist.

I'd probably covered about six feet through the biting mist and the swirling flashlight beams that struggled to find us the farther we drew from ground level. I'd found a strange rhythm to my movements that helped release the tension in my legs, arms, and torso. Then I reached out and down to the right for a craggy extension that must not have been there, because the next thing I knew, I was sliding, flesh and clothes alike stung by the friction.

Still gathering speed, I slid past George and he flung a hand out and latched on to my wrist just in time. I reminded myself to breathe, could feel my heart hammering against my rib cage. I wanted to scream, the grip of terror so palpable it actually felt like someone was tightening a belt around my entire being. The sea air stung my eyes, some stray, breeze-blown hair catching beneath the lids. Nothing I could do other than try to blink my eyes clear, as the thickening mist washed over us.

I realized my feet were still flailing about and managed to kick one into the soft, stony gravel for a hold and then repeated the process with the other. This wasn't what I pictured rock climbing to be like at all, the bluffs softening more the closer we drew to the sea. Though my feet were now secure, George's grasp on my arm remained the only thing keeping me from falling.

A flashlight beam froze on us and then moved on. I would have breathed a sigh of relief if my breath hadn't deserted me once more. And before I could find it, a fresh hail of bullets rained down on us. Hard to tell whether the Almost Twins had a fix on our position or if they were firing randomly, as desperate in a different sense as we were.

I realized the sweep of the flashlight beams and the echoing clatter of gunfire were coming at the same time now. I thought that Archibald and Clifton must've joined the battle, could only hope the receptionist manning the lobby's main desk might have already called 911, unlikely given who it was that signed her checks.

My free hand groped across the face of the bluffs, seeking a spot I could latch on to as I'd found for my feet. I managed to claw inside a soft patch and dig my hand home, but a bullet impacting just inches above it left me jerking the hand back into the air.

I looked up at George and saw the strain of exertion on his gritty expression. My arm, though, was slowly sliding from his grasp, caught in the crisscrossing sweep of two flashlight beams before a fresh volley of pistol fire separated me from George.

I slid down the face, kicking and flailing for something to grab, dislodging a thick spill of what felt like a mix of coal and shale, which showered me when I came to a crashing halt upon the ledge George had pointed out earlier. Safe for the moment, but the moment didn't last long, since I was now exposed to both the light and the bullets. Fresh fire spit rock and stone in all directions, chips of it feeling like ground glass shredding skin wherever it struck. I'd turned my ankle upon impact, but seemed otherwise intact.

I couldn't see George above me and then spotted him off to my right, lowering himself beneath the ledge and gesturing for me to follow. The next flurry of bullets did the trick where that gesture had come up short. Careful to put as little weight on my ankle as possible, I slid to the side of the ledge and followed George's gaze to the holds he'd uncovered.

I think I'd slipped into a kind of shock, the whole scene feeling surreal, more dream than reality. I finally worked my way off the ledge, save for a single leg, my injured one, which buckled when I tried to move it. Again George saved me from a fall and then pressed my frame close to his and tight against the rock face to avoid the next spray of gunfire.

He'd somehow managed to wrap an arm around my waist to guide and steer me, an impossible task because we were side-stepping to get below the ledge, where we'd be covered from the fire of the Almost Twins.

Beneath the ledge, the grade steepened into a straight drop to the rocky waters below—no margin for error, since a single slip would mean a plunge to our deaths. We weren't going anywhere. I could see the resignation on George's face and imagined mine had taken on an even more desperate and terrified bent. We'd managed to find foot- and handholds beneath the ledge, but our feet and hands kept slipping out when the soft rock we'd dug into continued to loosen and spill past us. We couldn't do this forever, and dawn was still too far off to bring any hope either. Sooner or later, I'd lose my grasp, and George would follow me in a plunge when he tried to save me. I had never thought I'd find something to fear more than being shot at.

I heard a distant wail, thinking, *If only the siren sound was closer.* But then it was, closer and louder. I glimpsed the glow of flashing lights off in the distance, the sirens indicating the imminent arrival of the Cabot Cove Sheriff's Department on the scene.

Those sirens were still screaming when I heard the fresh clack of gunfire coming from above, no longer aimed at George and me. That fire was returned in kind by a shattering barrage, which gave way to nothing at all, until it was broken by the voice of Mort Metzger.

"Jessica! Jessica!"

"Down here, Mort!" I yelled back up at him. "We're down here!"

"Hold on, you hear me? Fire department on its way!"

And, true to his word, a fresh howl of sirens split the night air, our rescue just moments away.

A pair of Cabot Cove firefighters rappelled down the face of the bluffs with ropes fastened through carabiners. They'd each towed spare gear along for the ride, which they proceeded to wrap around both George and me before guiding us upward under the pull of more firefighters and Mort's deputies from above.

For some inexplicable reason, I think I was more scared through that process than at any other point of the ordeal, certain the rope was going to give way at the last and send me falling to my death. But it didn't, and I crested the surface to find a breathless Mort Metzger, still with gloves donned, glaring at me.

"Don't make me say it, Jessica, don't make me say it," he snapped, waving a reproaching finger in my direction.

"That's 'Mrs. Fletcher' to you, Mort."

I looked around to see both Charles Clifton and Jeffrey Archibald under arrest and under the careful eye of Mort's deputies. Paramedics, meanwhile, were tending to the Almost Twins.

"Those were trained operators," I told Mort. "Your men should be proud."

"Those trained operators ran out of bullets. That sort of helped." Mort's glare returned. "Remember I warned you I was going to place you under arrest for recklessly endangering yourself?"

"Yes."

He made a show of snapping the handcuffs from his belt. "Stick out your hands."

"I'm too tired."

"Well, I'm not going to give you the results of that DNA test you asked me to rush, until you're suitably restrained."

I managed a smile. "Sounds like we've got another murderer to arrest."

"I believe we do, Mrs. Fletcher."

# Chapter Thirty-three

"You again?" Fred Cooper said, only halfway through the door as he flashed me a closer look, noting the pinprick-like wounds caused by the spray of chipped stone into my face the night before. "Looks like you got into a tussle with a rosebush, Mrs. Fletcher."

"Just a bad case of the chicken pox, Mr. Cooper, and I brought some more friends with me this time."

He closed the door to reveal Mort and two deputies standing against the wall, then jerked his gaze back to me. "You never give up, do you?"

"Not until the last page is written, just like a book, Mr. Cooper. Or should I say Mr. Van Dorn?"

"Tripp Van Dorn," I continued, my eyes never leaving his.

I'd remained seated to avoid putting weight on my injured

ankle. Paramedics had immobilized it outside the Clifton Clinic before spiriting me off in the rescue squad car to Cabot Cove Hospital for a precautionary X-ray. Seth Hazlitt met me there and confirmed there was no break. Then he secured me a pair of crutches and a walking boot.

"Not that I expect you to use them, ayuh," he groused.

I'd opted for the boot this morning, unable to get the hang of using the cumbersome crutches. I'd been up most of the night watching old movies and keeping ice on the ankle, which felt better when I awoke in a chair just past dawn.

The man Cabot Cove knew as Fred Cooper, meanwhile, hadn't said a word since I'd called him by his rightful name.

"The young man in the wheelchair, the man you killed," I resumed, instead of waiting any longer, "he was in the car with you the night of the accident. He was the one crushed and broken when it rolled over, while you were thrown free. How am I doing so far?"

Fred Cooper, born Tripp Van Dorn, still remained silent, so I went on.

"You must have managed to walk off, either in panic or shock. And when your mother got to the scene, she saw someone else being hauled away on a stretcher. I imagine she put the pieces together pretty fast, probably even before you approached her. The real victim was hurt so badly, the first responders likely couldn't tell who he was or didn't even care. All they cared about was keeping him alive, and that's where the trip to Mass General came in, since nobody would know the difference between Tripp Van Dorn and somebody else.

"Your mother planned the whole thing on her ride to the hospital, on the phone with Big Al for much of the time. Since they were having an affair, I'm sure he was more than willing to go along with the charade and even abet it. The ruse never would've worked otherwise. The medical and insurance information was yours, not the real victim's. He effectively became you. What was it, Tripp, were you drunk behind the wheel? Were you and Mimi afraid of you spending a big chunk of your life in jail?"

"He didn't have any insurance."

I remember Alvin McCandless said it had been the right thing to do, and to a point I suppose it had been, but only to that point. "Who was he, Tripp?"

The man Cabot Cove knew as Fred Cooper tried to smile but failed, his expression suddenly reflective. "It's been ten years now, ever since the night of the accident, that anybody's called me that. Even my mother disciplined herself to call me Fred."

"What I just said about her concocting the whole scheme— that's true, isn't it?"

Cooper nodded slowly, just once. "She was trying to do the right thing, Mrs. Fletcher."

"The right thing would've been for you to have owned up to what you had done, not engage in this cover-up."

"And face jail? My mother wouldn't have that, not if it meant ruining the Van Dorn name."

"Speaking of names, who was the man who became Tripp Van Dorn?"

"A friend from college who wasn't even from around Marblehead. He always hung out with us for holidays because he'd lost his own family in a boating accident a few years before."

That spurred a memory, something I'd lost in my second visit to Good Shepherd Manor, after the fake Tripp Van Dorn's murder. "That picture on the wall, the one you removed after you killed him—it was of his family, not yours."

"That's why I removed it," the real Tripp said, not bothering to deny it.

"So what happened when your friend woke up in Mass General?"

"My mother was sitting by his bedside, playing the dutiful parent. She explained his options to him, promised to make sure he was taken care of financially. Tell the truth and he'd end up indigent, with no way of paying for the kind of quality care he was going to need for the rest of his life. As you know, Mimi Van Dorn could be a most persuasive woman."

"And I'm sure she made herself out to be a saint," I reckoned. "Convinced the young man she was doing this for him, looking out for his best interests, that he really didn't have a choice. Quite a story she must have concocted."

This time, Cooper's nod was stronger. "With me cast as the villain. I was pretty much out of the picture by then, in law school, thanks to the real Fred Cooper's academic record and college transcript. And our ruse worked for ten years, longer than anyone expected the guy to live. We provided for all of his needs, until my mother's obsession with staying young swallowed up the trust. When a third payment in a row was missed to Good Shepherd, and he was faced with being moved to a state facility, the man the world knew as Tripp Van Dorn threatened to expose the whole ruse."

"I'm surprised you didn't keep up the charade yourself instead of buying new office furniture."

A look that reminded me of his mother's after she'd beaten me at a game of cards crossed his face. "Killing him was easier."

It was clear now why Mimi had never mentioned she had a son. I'd thought it was because she didn't want it to tarnish her image of a hard-charging socialite, when the truth must have been that she didn't want anyone asking questions. To all intents and purposes, Tripp Van Dorn had died in that car accident a decade ago, Fred Cooper born in his place.

"How'd you figure it out?" he asked, his face flat with resignation.

I think I liked him more now, with his guard down and showing no airs. "Started with something Alvin McCandless said about two lives being ruined, not one. At first, I thought he meant you and your mother. Then I started to realize he was talking about a second person in the car. A second person who couldn't possibly be Mimi's son because of his blood type. But it was you who provided the final clue, Tripp, when you handed me your business card the other day."

"DNA," he realized. "You must have tested it against my mother's."

"Your father's actually, John Jessup," I said, not bothering to elaborate further. "When it came back a match, all the remaining pieces fell into place."

"It was my mother's fault," Tripp said in more of a hiss.

"She had to have that antiaging drug, didn't she, no matter the cost? Of course, it didn't matter to her that breaking the trust would hurt her son . . . because he really wasn't her son at all. And Mimi wasn't your client, as I originally thought; she was your mother, which must've been what brought you to Cabot Cove in the first place. You kill fake Tripp and there's no one left who can hurt you, who knows the truth. Too bad you left that bruise on the back of his head. Otherwise his death would've gone down as a suicide and we probably wouldn't be having this conversation. You knew that building like the back of your hand from visiting the fake you regularly. I'm guessing during one of those visits you even unlocked the window through which you gained entry the day you killed him."

"Rory Tait," the real Tripp Van Dorn said softly.

"Who?"

"My friend's name."

"The one you murdered at Good Shepherd, ten years after the accident paralyzed him," I elaborated. "You tried to talk your mother out of breaking the trust, didn't you, Tripp? You knew what would happen if she did that in order to get into that fake clinical trial."

"She never gave me the chance," Tripp admitted. "By the time I found out, it was too late. The money was gone."

"And once Rory Tait, who'd effectively become you at Good Shepherd Manor, found out . . ."

I let the rest of the sentence dangle in the air.

Cooper left it there, unsure about going on himself, until he stole a glance at Mort and then back at me. "Who killed her, Mrs. Fletcher?"

"They're in custody, too, Tripp."

"It was Charles Clifton, wasn't it?"

I looked at Mort, who nodded. "He had an associate as well," I confirmed. "It's a long story."

"With an unhappy ending."

"For most."

"There's an exception?"

I pushed myself up to my feet as Mort bent Tripp Van Dorn's hands behind his back. "You know, I believe there is."

\*    \*    \*

"Well, my dear lady, I guess this is so long," George Sutherland said, sliding up to me with luggage deposited at his feet.

"I'm glad you said that instead of good-bye," I told him, tightening my grip on the front porch railing outside Hill House. "I hate the word 'good-bye.'"

He grasped my shoulders and eased me around to face him. "With us, it's never good-bye. You should have figured that out by now."

"It was almost good-bye the other night on the bluffs."

"Speaking of which, I was quite impressed with your skills."

"Which skills would those be?"

"The ones that kept you from falling to your death, of course."

"You kept me from falling to my death, George."

He shook his head, grinning again. "You'd still have me believe that you confronted Clifton and Archibald just to flush me out?"

"Which wouldn't have been necessary if you'd told me the truth of what you were up to beforehand."

"I was under strict orders."

"So you were hoping to slip in and out of Cabot Cove without me knowing?"

George held my gaze. "I thought I might surprise you once my job was done, dear lady."

"Well, you certainly did that."

He let go of my arms, our gazes dipping to his luggage.

"You can't stay any longer?"

George's smile suddenly looked forced. "I've had enough

excitement to last me quite a while, and I've lengthened my stay in your wonderful town as long as I could. But the Yard wants me back in the office tomorrow."

"I'll write you a note," I offered. "Should I address it to your boss or the queen?"

"Well, you've met the queen, but not my boss."

"We need to plan a get-together not connected to murder," I suggested.

"Then what, pray tell, would we have to talk about?"

"We could rehash this case for starters. For instance, how exactly did Scotland Yard get wise to what was happening at the Clifton Clinic?"

"Two Londoners died there, both under mysterious circumstances, one of whom was a friend of mine, as I mentioned before. The Yard chose me to do the dirty work for any number of reasons, mostly my familiarity with the area and my age."

I nodded. "Since we're getting up there in age, it makes sense that we'd need some new drug available only in clinical trials. But how did you fake your illness?"

George didn't answer my question right away. "Cabot Cove Hospital kindly substituted the fake test results I brought with me for the real ones, making it appear I was as sick and desperate as advertised."

"Cooperation agreement," I mused. "Hmmmmmmm, why is it I get the feeling you're not the only one who deceived me? You never intended to start treatment, of course. I'm guessing you faked the fever as a stall tactic. Do you have an app for that, too?"

A playful look flashed across his face. "By that time, I was suffering from something far more perilous than a deadly disease."

"What's that?"

"You, dear lady. Our association had been noted by too many, raising Clifton's suspicions that something was wrong about my presence."

"So I was right about the cell phone! It was a signal to me you were alive, wasn't it?"

"Indeed it was. Can you believe I was afraid you might not catch it?"

"No, I can't."

"And I owe you more than a bit of thanks, Jessica. The Yard had no knowledge of LGX Pharmaceuticals' role in all this or the exact nature of the conspiracy between Clifton and Jeffrey Archibald. I'm sorry to have deceived you, but I'm sure you understand."

I moved in and hugged him tightly as the cab that would be taking him to the airport pulled up on the street. "Rain check?"

"Rain check."

I kissed him lightly. "Promise?"

"Promise."


The sudden closing of the Clifton Clinic brought many patients back to Seth Hazlitt, both young and old. So many that, to manage the flow, Seth was keeping office hours into the evening. He even spoke of bringing on a young associate for the first time in all the years I'd known him.

But he made time to join us at Mara's Luncheonette two weeks later to finish the celebration for Jean O'Neil, whose reception at the library had been postponed after Mimi's seizure.

I entered still limping but having shed the boot after only a single week. I also no longer looked as if I'd gone a few rounds with a rosebush or had come down with chicken pox.

We had commandeered the whole coffee shop for the occasion, and because of Cabot Cove's deep affection for our long-time librarian, the turnout was strong. I moved toward a table currently manned by Mort, Seth, and Harry McGraw, who'd made the trip from New York even though he'd never even met Jean O'Neil.

"Hey, it's a free meal, right?" he said after I'd mentioned the celebration to him in passing and ended up inviting him out of guilt.

Only to the extent that the Friends of the Library organization was footing the bill up to a certain point. I had agreed to cover anything in excess of that to allow anyone who'd attended the library reception to come to this one as well.

I reached the table and stowed a shopping bag I'd lugged along with me on an empty chair next to the one I'd taken.

Seth Hazlitt looked up from his plate, impressed. "Getting around better and better every day, Jess."

Harry McGraw didn't look up at all from his overstuffed plate, courtesy of the buffet line. "You should get yourself something to eat. After all, you're paying for it."

"Don't forget the Friends, Harry."

"I don't have any, save for the people at this table."

I looked at the empty chair where I'd stowed my shopping bag and thought of George Sutherland, who would've been occupying it if he'd been able to remain in Cabot Cove for a bit longer.

"Anything you forgot to tell me regarding the investigation, Mort?" I said across the table.

"Just tidying up some loose ends, the kind of stuff you never have to worry about in your books."

"From where I sit, you and George Sutherland teaming up against me doesn't really qualify as a loose end, does it?"

"He told you?"

"I didn't leave him much choice."

"Well, Scotland Yard didn't leave me much of one either. I was under strict orders not to say a word to you about the truth behind George's presence in Cabot Cove. Apparently, your exploits are as well-known as your books over there."

"Should I take that as a compliment?"

"I'm sorry, Jessica, truly sorry, for keeping you in the dark."

"You can make it up by doing me a favor."

"Anything. Just name it."

"I've got a loose end of my own," I said, tapping the shopping bag alongside me.

Mort narrowed his gaze. "What's in the bag, Mrs. Fletcher?"

"Six boxes of Girl Scout cookies for Big Al McCandless," I told him. "And I know you won't mind giving me a ride so we can deliver them in person."